ISBN: 978-0-646-81644-9

PROLOGUE

MENA SAT ON the soft green grass, shaded by the old oak tree against which she rested. The long skirt of her sky-blue, satin party dress—now ruined—billowed out around her. A smile danced across her face as she stroked the cat in her lap, listening to the sounds of her parents' party drifting with the breeze. The melodic tunes of the string quartet mingled with the steady flow of conversation. Friends and family had travelled far and wide to see the grandest house in the province. Completed at last—an architectural marvel, her father called it. Many of the guests were residents from local towns, and most of them Mena had never seen or heard of before.

Raising her hand, she pressed her thumb to her finger, marvelling at the stickiness of the blood. She found it fascinating how it changed from warm and fluid to thick and cool in such little time.

"Here you are," her father said. "We've been looking all over for you. Everyone's asking after you. That nanny of yours…" He stopped when he realised what she was doing.

Mena grinned up at him. "Hello, Papa. Kitty and I are having our own party. The grown-ups were boring." She wiped a stray piece of her ebony hair off her forehead with the back of a hand, leaving a streak of blood in its wake.

"No. Not again…" Her father's voice trembled with anger. Mena could see the weight of the sadness in his eyes, but she felt nothing for it. He stepped forward and grabbed his daughter by the wrist, yanking her to her feet.

Mena gasped when the dead cat tumbled from her lap. "Kitty!" she cried. Her father stormed off, pulling her along behind him.

"Wait, Papa. I want my kitty!" she wailed, hot tears spilling down her cheeks. In her distress, it took her a while to realise they weren't headed back to the house. Instead, her father led her toward the woods behind their estate. "Papa? Where are we going?"

"Somewhere I should have taken you sooner."

Confused by the unsuspected turn, Mena soon forgot her tears — and her Kitty — and hurried along after him. Her tiny feet scurried across the grass as she struggled to keep up.

They slowed when they entered the woods so her father could better navigate his way through the trees. He paused here and there, as though unsure of his bearings. Mena took the time to marvel at her surroundings. Her parents had always forbidden her to enter the woods, but now, she knew it was the perfect place to play with her animals.

Her father came to an abrupt stop, causing Mena to run into the back of his legs. When he didn't move, she peeked around him to find a wall of rock before them. She blinked at it with wide eyes; it rose quite high — at least twice as high as her Papa—before curving at the top. It made her think of a giant, sleeping monster hibernating in the woods. Moss and plants spread out across the stone in patches of damp greenery, and a small stream trickled down the front. She wondered where the water came from; it hadn't rained in weeks. As she followed the water downwards, she noticed a narrow opening in the rocks.

"Papa, is it a cave?" she exclaimed, looking up at him. He stared straight ahead, unmoving for so long, Mena was unsure if he'd heard her. Only when she tugged on his hand did he give a small nod.

"I do love you, Mena." His voice trembled, and he released her hand. She ignored his sentiment and dashed toward the cave.

Without hesitation, she got down on her knees and poked her head into the darkness. When her father gave no further protest, she took it as permission to explore and scurried into the cave.

The darkness enveloped her. Mena wondered what kind of animals she would find inside. Then something shoved her from behind, her hand slipped forward, and she lost her balance. Before she could call out, she was falling.

Falling…

Falling…

CHAPTER ONE

CAMILLE LEROUX STARED out the window of their hired car and stifled a yawn. After over twenty-four hours of travelling, they were almost there—their new home. Her father drove them down the main street of Woodville, and Camille scanned the different shop names, catching glimpses of signs and storefront windows through the numerous trees lining both sides of the street. She could see enough to determine there wasn't a single franchise on the whole street—no Zarraffas Coffee, no Dymocks Books, none of her favourite clothing stores.

Leaning back against her seat, Camille sighed and caught another of her father's intermittent glances through the rear-view mirror. She tried to keep her expression neutral, to hide her disappointment and sadness. Her parents were excited by the move and had welcomed the opportunity to pack up their lives and travel halfway across the world. Unlike her parents, Camille was less than thrilled. As far as she could tell, Woodville, England was a far cry from her beloved city of Melbourne, Australia. She loved the hustle and bustle of the city, the busyness and the people everywhere at all hours of the day and night. The city never slept. In comparison, Woodville looked as though it were still waking up. To add insult to injury, her friends back home were living it up on their spring school holidays. They'd be gearing up for their last school term before summer holidays spent on the beach under the hot Aussie sun, the smell of salt and sunscreen in the air, while they pondered their upcoming senior year. Camille on the other hand, had been shipped off to one of the coldest towns in England, forced to finish year eleven early and with no holidays to speak of before starting her senior year in September at a new school. The whole concept of the school year starting that late was completely foreign to her, only adding another layer of anxiety that she wouldn't fit in.

Biting her lower lip, she did her best to quash the tears before they could become anything more than a painful sting in her eyes. She knew she was judging their new town harshly, but they hadn't reached their new home yet, and already, she was homesick for the old one. While her mother had pointed out it was the age of social media and keeping in touch had never been easier, Camille knew it wouldn't be the same; the time difference felt enormous. She closed her eyes, suddenly feeling exhausted. But it didn't help her empty her mind; instead, thoughts of having to start at a new high school—in her senior year—bombarded her. Knowing the answer before she'd even asked, Camille had tried to convince her parents to let her stay behind to finish school—or even to let her skip senior year altogether. Of course, they would have none of it. The fact of the matter was, an estate was left to her father—on the condition that he live in it.

Camille turned back to the window and yawned, longing to stretch her limbs. "Is it much farther?"

"Shouldn't think so," her father answered as he veered the car slightly off the main street and onto a narrow side road. He shot a dubious glance at his GPS.

About thirty metres in, tall trees now lined the road on either side, their barren branches reaching up out, waving in a macabre welcome. The road inclined, and Camille leaned forward for a better view through the windscreen. Then their new home appeared up ahead at the top of the small rise.

"Holy shit…"

"Language," her mother warned.

"Sorry, Mum, but this place is crazy huge."

Her mother ignored her, and her father chuckled. "Pretty impressive, isn't it? Welcome to our new home. LeRoux Manor."

They drove the rest of the way in silence, mostly because Camille was speechless now. In front of the manor stood an enormous round fountain with a statue of a woman standing in the middle, tipping an empty jug. Camille imagined how it must have looked when it worked, and a smile crept over her face. The only thing ruining her view was the over-sized delivery truck awaiting their arrival.

"I'm guessing a quick nap is out of the question?" Camille asked as her Father pulled the car to a stop beside the fountain.

"Not if you're planning on napping on an actual bed. Yours is still in the truck, remember?"

"I'm not fussy. I'm pretty sure I could fall asleep on the floor right now."

"It's just the long travel and the jetlag, honey," her mother said. "But we do need to try to stay awake to help our bodies get used to the time difference. We'll be so busy unpacking; the day will fly by."

Camille rolled her eyes, opened the door, and got out of the car. Staring up at the house towering before her, she twirled her long auburn hair around her fingers and squinted. With a fuzzy view of the manor, she tried to imagine what it had looked like in its prime. But she knew the state of the house was a far cry from its glory days. The building rose four stories high, topped by a dark, ornate roof of black slate. The roof rose and fell in numerous peaks and spires, complete with a weathervane. Camille strained to work out what shape the weathervane took, but it was too high. Small windows across the top floor made her think there must have been an attic space, and she felt both intrigued and unnerved by the concept. Detailed stonework made up the manor's façade, but it was dark and discoloured with age and decades of grime. A sweeping semi-circle porch fanned out from the front of the house, supporting four majestic columns rising to the height of the first two stories before ending below a full-length balcony. The enormous double front doors of intricately carved wood had seen better days.

Camille thought about all the people who had stepped through those doors since the manor was first built, and an icy chill ran down her back. That was odd, but she quickly shook it off and continued her inspection. The windows were beautiful arches, designed to capture as much light as possible, if it weren't for the thick drapes closed behind every one of them. The building looked like something straight out of a vintage horror movie, and she half expected to see Bella Lugosi peering out from behind the drapes. Camille couldn't believe they'd be living here permanently; it left their two-bedroom apartment in the city for dead.

"How old did you say this place was?" she asked her father as he crunched along the gravel path behind her.

He struggled to see around the boxes stacked in his arms. "Oh, I think it's at least a hundred and fifty years old. Perhaps more. You know, you could help out with the boxes and save the history lesson for when everything's unpacked."

Camille gave her father a wry smile and turned toward the truck. There, she grabbed a box and scuffed her sneakers along the path. Still unimpressed by the move to a new town and soon a new school—like any teenager would be—she still knew she had to at least give it a shot. Now that she'd seen the manor in person, she could see why her parents had been so eager to move. Their excitement, though, had just been fuel for the heated argument the night they'd made the announcement.

Camille had arrived home from school later than usual, and found her parents waiting for her in the loungeroom. The fact that they were both home before her was enough to raise alarm bells as she slowly took her backpack off and lowered it to the floor, not taking her eyes off them. They sat close together, her father's arm around her mother's shoulders, her mother's hand resting on her father's leg. This in itself wasn't unusual — it was the look on their faces that made Camille approach the adjacent lounge chair with caution. Her father appeared solemn, yet there was something akin to a twinkle in his eye and her mother bit her lip as she flicked sideways glances as her father, her free hand fidgeting against the seat cushion beside her. Her father all but rushed through the announcement of the death of her Great Uncle Charles — Camille hardly had the chance to register her own detached reaction to the news before rushed on. As the only living adult relative, the LeRoux estate was now theirs. Her father paused and her parents looked at her expectantly as she failed to make the connection. Her mother squeezed her father's leg and he continued — they planned to move across to the other side of the world and embark on a renovation of the aged mansion.

Camille had not shared an ounce of their enthusiasm, and still didn't.

Her mother smiled as they passed each other on the porch. "Have you had a look to see which bedroom you want yet?"

Camille shook her head. It hadn't occurred to her there would be a choice after living in a two-bedroom apartment. "How many are there?"

"Twelve. Not counting the master — which is ours!" her mother called back, already down the steps and heading back to the truck.

With a new enthusiasm for the house, Camille set the box down and out of the way, then dashed up the enormous, sweeping staircase, taking them two at a time. At the top of the stairs, she could either go straight or continue up the staircase to her left or her right. With a grin, she dashed up the staircase to her left. It led to a wide hallway with doors along one side. She took her time, strolling from one room to the next, trying to get a feel for them.

It didn't take long before she started to feel a little uneasy, almost like déjà vu. But that wasn't possible. She tried to shake it off and focused on the rooms before her. They were all grand, furnished with large beds boasting ornate headboards and posts. Most rooms had either large, three-way mirrors, or large, elaborate-looking dressing tables — though the mirrors, like everything else, needed a good cleaning and dusting. Camille could see herself set up in any of them, yet as she entered the last one, her mouth fell open at the sight.

Compared to the other rooms, this one was all but empty. To her right stood a grand four-poster bed, devoid of a mattress or curtains. Camille only saw this as an opportunity to make it her own. The only other piece of furniture was an oddly large wardrobe on the other side of the room. It was as wide as the king-sized bed and higher than she could reach. It was made of the darkest wood, so dark it was almost black, with gold-filigreed handles on the double doors. She walked toward it and opened those doors, surprised to find that it could either open normally or fold back like French doors to expose the wardrobe in full. While it looked like an independent piece of furniture, it appeared to be fixed firmly to the wall.

Camille firmly closed the wardrobe doors and continued her inspection of the room. The wooden floors were bare, while the walls were decorated with an ornate wallpaper barely discernible through so much dust. She moved to the wall beside the wardrobe and with the sleeve of her jumper wiped a patch of dust and dirt away to reveal a deep green with large silvery swirls. As she stepped back, she wondered how the pattern would look once the walls were clean. Turning to the wall opposite the doorway, she saw two magnificent arched windows, side by side, rising majestically toward the ceiling, each with a generous window seat nestled at their base. A length of wrought iron ran up the centre of each window before peeling off in opposite directions to form two decorative swirls. Two panes of glass completed the arch above, and at the base of the window where the seat met the glass, ran two rows of individual squares of coloured glass framed by the wrought iron.

Camille hurried toward them and pressed her face to the glass, her hands curved around her eyes to darken the glare. The overgrown estate grounds stretched out before her. The rear of the estate was bordered by a dense forest of towering trees. This was far better than her previous bedroom view of the buildings across the road. This was it. Her new room. Just beside her, she heard a faint sigh, as though someone had been holding their breath and finally exhaled. She spun around; her eyes wide in anticipation of whoever had snuck up on her. But there was no one there.

A loud creak—almost more like a crack—made her jump, and she scanned the room for its source. Frowning, she noticed one of the wardrobe doors was ajar, though she was certain she'd closed them both. It was old, she told herself, and the hinges must be worn. Even still, Camille stepped toward the wardrobe and felt a sudden breathlessness, unsure why she was suddenly so anxious.

"Is it a coincidence you've chosen the room farthest from the rest of the house?" her father asked from the doorway.

"Dad! You scared me!"

"What are you talking about?"

"I heard a noise…"

"Honey, this is an old place. You're bound to hear a lot of noises you're not used to. Eventually, you won't notice them at all. Old houses like this shift and settle, that's all."

Camille gave her father an embarrassed smile, feeling a little silly for being so jumpy. It was just a house, after all.

"Come on, then. Still plenty more boxes in the truck."

Camille gave another quick glance around the room, then followed her father. In her new bedroom, the wardrobe door creaked open a little farther.

THE FULL MOON sat like an enormous floodlight in the sky, and even the grime covering the windows couldn't prevent its light from straining into the room, bathing everything in an ethereal glow. Camille marvelled at the ghostly pallor it gave her skin as she sat in the window seat. The height of the moon in the sky told her it was late, yet she still felt too wired to try to go to sleep. She'd thought she would crash at the first opportunity, but there was just too much to take in — too much to look at and explore.

She found the silence a little unnerving, too — stifling, like a heavy blanket wrapped around her in the summer. It made every creak and groan of the house seem all the louder, startling her every time, and she missed the background noise of endless traffic and a bustling population. In the thralls of the night, she slightly regretted choosing a room so far from her parents. Hugging her knees to her chest, she peered back down at the grounds below her.

A red pane of glass beside her knee seemed clearer than the rest, and she leaned forward for a better look through it. Wiping the dust away, she was surprised she could see outside as clearly as if this were a brand-new pane. A light wind stirred the trees at the edge of the woods, and Camille followed its path toward the manor, sweeping through the overgrown grass and sending a shudder through the shrubbery.

Camille gasped, pressing her hands against the window as she angled for a better look. A woman stood out in the gardens, looking up at the manor. The wind picked up, making the black skirts of the woman's dress billow around her. Camille struggled to swallow as she and the woman stared at each other, her throat suddenly feeling like sandpaper. The high black neck of the woman's dress topped with a white, lace collar was outdone in severity only by the woman's strikingly white hair piled atop her head in a tight bun. Despite the hair, the woman didn't look that old—unless the moonlight played tricks on Camille's eyes. This stranger stood with a rare poise, her hands clasped in front of her, as though she were posing for a portrait. The red hue of the glass in Camille's window gave made her seem all the more menacing. There was no mistaking the intensity of her gaze. She knew Camille was there.

Unable to look away, Camille started to feel as though the room was slowly spinning around her. Thick clouds drifted across the moon, bringing an icy shudder through the girl's neck and back. She strained to see the woman in the sudden darkness cast over the grounds, but the moon's previous brightness had all but blinded her. By the time the clouds parted enough to let the moonlight spread across the grounds again, the woman was gone.

CHAPTER TWO

Y OU LOOK TIRED, sweetheart," her mother commented as Camille entered the kitchen.

"I didn't sleep well. First night in a new house and all that." Camille hesitated for a moment, unsure whether to share what she'd seen. "Mum, there's no one else staying here at the manor, is there?"

"Well, the McAllister's were due back sometime last night, but other than them, it's just us."

"The McAllister's?"

"Didn't your father tell you?" Her mother wiped her hands on a tea towel. "They're siblings. Miss McAllister is the housekeeper, and her brother is the groundsman. According to your father, their family has served the LeRoux's before this manor was even built."

Camille raised her eyebrows and glanced around; clearly, the housekeeper and groundsman hadn't done much to improve the state of the manor.

Her mother shrugged. "I know. I think it's more in spirit than in practise these days. They're both well into their seventies. They've lived and worked here all their lives, so it's more their home than ours. It would have been wrong to ask them to leave. Besides, it'll probably come in handy to have someone around who knows the ins and outs of this place. It's going to take some getting used to."

"Tell me about it. I got lost just trying to find my way to the kitchen." Camille grabbed an apple from the fruit bowl and bit into it, enjoying the crisp crunch. Smiling, she told herself it must have been Miss McAllister she'd seen out on the grounds last night. Sure, she was creepy, but Camille felt much better knowing who she was. "I think I'm going to explore a little," she announced, giving her mother a quick kiss on the cheek.

"Don't get lost," her mother half joked.

Camille held up her phone. "Don't worry, Mum. This thing never leaves my side. If I go missing, you can always do that 'find my phone' thing." With the apple still in hand, she left the kitchen and pondered where to start.

Her gaze climbed the elegant staircase. She hadn't really paid that much attention to it the day before, other than to curse the repeated trips up and down them. She made a mental note to ask her parents if they'd consider installing a lift as part of their renovations. The staircase had to be wider than their car was long, the stairs covered in a faded, worn blue carpet that had likely been a pretty shade once. The ornate, wooden balustrades lining either side of the staircase were thoroughly covered in dust. It didn't take much imagination to see how the place would have looked when the house was new.

Camille placed her hand on the wood, drawn to it. An image flooded her mind, like a memory — of shiny shoes and little legs running down the staircase, barely avoiding tripping up on the long skirts of a dress; a gleeful squeal as a child ignored the call of an authoritative voice, calling from above for her to stop running in the house.

Camille pulled her hand back, overcome with the same sensation of déjà vu.

"Old homes like this hold a lot of memories, Miss. Secrets, too."

Camille jumped and turned to find a woman standing there in the entryway. Her face was heavily wrinkled with time and unspoken burdens, making her appear much older than she likely was. The women wiped her hand on her apron and extended a hand.

"Pleased to make your acquaintance, Miss. I'm Miss McAllister, and I care for the house. Well, as best I can, these days."

Camille reached out to shake Miss McAllister's hand, which trembled in her grasp. The woman held their grip for so long, it started to make Camille uncomfortable; it forced her to stare right back at the woman. There was something about her eyes — a watery, sky-blue that might once have been the colour of the ocean in her younger years. They drew Camille in, sparking something like recognition. Miss McAllister squeezed her hand lightly, breaking the spell, and Camille cleared her throat. "Nice to meet you. I was just about to take a look around the manor."

"Very good, Miss. Be careful, mind. The house isn't as young as it once was. Neither of us are. Most rooms have remained untouched for a great many years. Master Charles was happy for us to tend only to the small part of the manor in which he lived. He never ventured beyond his wing."

Camille's hand was finally released, and she gave a small nod before turning to head up the stairs. "It was nice to meet you." Struck by a sudden realisation, she stopped, almost fumbling over the next step. But when she turned around, but Miss McAllister was already gone.

She was definitely not the woman from the garden.

DESPITE THE UNEASE settling over her like a cloak, Camille decided to start at the very top of the house — the attic. It made sense to start there and work her way down while also hopefully ridding herself of her anxiety around the preconceived notion of what a stereotypical attic would look like. Especially as her bedroom nestled directly below a portion of it.

It took some exploring before she finally found the entrance. What she'd initially mistaken for a narrow linen closet door in one of the upstairs hallways, actually concealed the slim staircase leading up into the attic. She pulled the lightbulb string dangling before her — gently, for fear it would snap in its brittle state. The dusty globe clicked on and cast a dim yellow glow. The wooden stairs creaked and groaned in protest as she ascended. It was a rather steep climb, and combined with the narrowness of the space, Camille started to feel a little claustrophobic.

Then, with a pop, the light went out. Groaning at the inconvenience, she braced herself against the walls and forced herself to take deep breaths. She would make it all the way up those stairs. She'd never had an issue with dark, confined spaces before—not that she could recall, anyway.

At the top of the stairs, a channel of muted light swept toward her from the two small, arched windows on the attic's far wall. Camille looked around the large, open space, peering at the random shapes looming around her. Everything was draped in heavy, dust-laden sheets.

She carefully weaved her way toward one of the windows and wiped her sleeve across the glass, hoping to let in more light. But now her cardigan was just as dirty as the window. She took it off and tied it around her waist.

With her hands cupped around her eyes, Camille pressed against the glass to peer out through the window as best she could. Directly below her, the sweeping driveway curved around behind the LeRoux Manor fountain before straightening outside the front of the house. Then it branched off toward either the large garage or back through the trees toward the road.

Her father stood at the fountain, talking to an older gentleman she assumed was the groundskeeper, Mr McAllister. Even from the lofty height of the attic, Camille could tell Mr McAllister was agitated; he jerked his hands toward her father, at the two men standing in front of a handyman van, then back at her father again. Clearly, the family plans to restore the manor to its former glory were not very popular. Turning away from the window, Camille blinked and tried to focus again in the attic's dim light.

Then she saw a face peering at her through the draped sheets. Camille gasped, tripped over a box behind her, and fell heavily to the floor. Sitting up, she groaned and gingerly rubbed her wrist, searching the room for that face again. She squinted through the darkness, her heart thundering in her chest.

Once she convinced herself there was nothing more menacing than dusty sheets, she turned her attention to the cardboard box on the floor. It hadn't been there when she'd stood at the window; she was sure of it. Camille pulled the box toward her. It was so old and brittle, part of it came away in her hands. She lifted the lid and found a stack of photo albums neatly packed in a row. Assuming the album on the left would be the oldest, she lifted that one first. The binding creaked when she opened it, exaggerated in the attic's silence, and Camille stopped. She didn't want to draw attention to herself.

Then she shook her head. That was a silly thought; there was no one else up here. Attics were just creepy as a rule.

The album's first page held a newspaper clipping. The dim lighting made it too hard to read, but there was no mistaking the photograph of the manor. Standing, Camille carried the album to the window, trying to angle it just right in the muted light from outside. That didn't work at all.

With a sigh, she realised she'd have to take the box downstairs if she wanted to read anything, though she didn't think she could carry much of its weight on her still-throbbing wrist. She returned the album, replaced the box's lid, and pushed the box toward the stairs with one hand. Her knees protested as she shuffled forward on them across the attic floor, but it would be worth it when she could examine her new discovery downstairs.

Once she got the box to the top of the stairs, she debated carrying the albums down one at a time, but the thought of going up and down that narrow staircase made her reconsider. It was so steep, she felt like she'd just tumble down it at any moment, regardless of whether she sat or stood.

Her skin prickled with the overwhelming sensation that someone was coming up behind her to shove her down the stairs. She spun around on her knees, but she was alone. The slight rush of air she'd just felt across her face had to be her imagination.

She just wanted to get this box downstairs. So, she moved down the first few steps, turned around, and tried to pull the box toward her with one hand while cradling her throbbing wrist against her chest. One hand wasn't enough. Gritting her teeth, she grabbed it with both hands now, ignoring how much her wrist protested, and dragged that box backward down the stairs one step at a time. After what felt like an eternity, she'd finally reached the bottom of the staircase, where she straightened and rubbed her wrist.

"What have you got there?"

Camille jumped and whirled around to see Ms McAllister standing in the doorway. "Um... I found these albums in the attic. Just wanted to take them back to my room to go through them. Ms McAllister just stared at her with tightly pursed lips. "I'll put them right back when I'm done," Camille volunteered.

The woman nodded. "No mind. I suppose they're yours now, anyway. Though I don't see what interest these old things could hold for a young person."

Camille didn't quite know what to say, but she felt herself flushing under Ms McAllister's intense scrutiny.

"I'll take the box to your room, Miss."

"Oh, no! That's fine. It's really heavy."

"Nonsense. I'm far stronger than I look. That thing looks like it's about to fall apart, anyway. I'm not sure you should be lifting it and trying to keep it together with that sore wrist of yours."

Camille blinked as the old woman stooped to pick up the box with very little effort and carried it back down the hall. For the life of her, she couldn't figure out how Ms McAllister knew she'd hurt her wrist.

BY THE TIME Camille had arranged herself on the window seat, the album close at hand, the clouds had unleashed a torrent of rain. The view from her bedroom had no become a grey and dreary world. Camille didn't mind. She enjoyed the rain and thought it the perfect weather for sifting through these old albums.

Opening the first one again, she took another look at the newspaper article. The manor looked majestic and commanding in the photo — the sweeping drive and the fountain in full working order. Arcs of water spiralled up around the centre statue of the woman, water pouring from the jug she held.

'*LeRoux Manor Revealed*' was the article's title, and when Camille found the date — 15th March 1817 — she found herself awed by how old this new house of hers really was. The article itself discussed the duration of this mansion's build and the upcoming party the LeRoux family would throw to celebrate its completion; they planned to invite all the townsfolk to join them, regardless of their social standing.

She turned the page to reveal another newspaper article, this one sideways and spanning across both pages.

'*Tragedy at LeRoux Manor*' was dated just a week after the previous article.

'*A day that was supposed to see a community come together to rejoice over the new beginning for the town instead became a day of fear and horror never seen before in Woodville.*

Celebration turned to tragedy for the esteemed LeRoux family, founders of the grand LeRoux Manor and estate. Witnesses stated that when the LeRoux's daughter Mena, age 6, failed to appear at the party, her father Caleb LeRoux, age 45, went to search for her. When he also failed to return, his wife Cecile, age 36, raised the alarm.

Attending guests and local authorities conducted an extensive search of both the manor and its grounds. The body of a mutilated cat was discovered a few metres into the woods bordering the estate. Its tag identified it as belonging to Mena LeRoux. Approximately two hundred metres farther into the woods, the body of Caleb LeRoux was found, facedown and with a knife embedded in his upper back.

Authorities maintain there is still hope of finding Mena LeRoux alive as search efforts continue into the night.

Cecile LeRoux and her son Pierre, age 10, reside in the manor at this time and ask for privacy and prayers as they grieve the loss of a husband and father, awaiting the return of their beloved Mena.

Police are asking members of the public to come forward if they have any information as to the whereabouts of Mena LeRoux.'

Turning the page, Camille found a family portrait of the LeRoux family. Judging by the extravagant dress Mena wore, she assumed the photo had been taken the day of the party.

She leaned closer to the album for a better look. The whole family looked so severe with their unsmiling faces staring back at her. This was just how people posed for photos back then, but it made it difficult to feel any sort of connection. They were distant relatives — complete strangers. Camille stared at Mena, who stood in front of her mother and beside her brother, a posy of flowers in her little hands. There was definitely a glint in the girl's eye — perhaps just the mischievous nature of a six-year-old.

Camille smiled. Then, as she flipped through the albums, her smile slowly melted into a frown; one article after the next documented the ongoing search and the dwindling hope that Mena LeRoux would be found alive.

Finally, she had to take a break and turned to stare out at the dismal weather. It seemed so cruel that a day that started with such joy and celebration for her ancestors would turn into a family's worst nightmare.

A loud creak startled her from her thoughts, and she turned away from the window and carefully looked first at the closed doors of the wardrobe and then the open bedroom door. The album fell from her lap to the floor with a thump.

Camille could have sworn it sounded like someone stood on a creaky floorboard right beside her, though she was well aware of the fact that old houses like this shifted and made their own sounds. Then she realised the wardrobe door was ajar. She stared at it; certain it had been closed only a moment ago. She remembered specifically that she'd closed it after getting dressed and double-checked the latch before releasing the handle.

With a shaky breath, she got up from the window seat and approached the wardrobe. Aside from haphazardly pulling her clothes out of the boxes and shoving them onto the shelves and racks, Camille hadn't paid much more attention to it than that. When she opened the doors, the left hinge definitely creaked, but she couldn't tell if it was the same sound that had startled her. But everything looked just fine. She ran her fingers across all her clothes hanging there, then noticed one of her sweaters had slipped halfway off the hanger. Camille reached back to feel for the other end of the hanger, then stopped. Was there a cold draft coming through the wardrobe?

Something clammy and freezing clenched around her wrist, and Camille screamed. She yanked her hand back so hard; she lost her balance again and fell backward onto the floor.

"Careful, miss," Miss McAllister stated calmly from the doorway. "You don't want to injure the other wrist as well."

Then Camille's mother pushed past the old woman and ran to Camille's aid. "Honey, what happened? Are you okay? I heard screaming."

"Someone grabbed me," Camille gasped. "In the closest."

"What?" Her mother helped her to her feet and glanced at the wardrobe.

"Now, now, miss," Miss McAllister added, heading into the room. "I think all that poking around in the attic and the dreary weather has your imagination running rampant." The woman approached the wardrobe and pushed the clothes aside to reveal the wooden back. "You see? There's no monster here, child."

"I'm not a child," Camille grumbled, staring at the open wardrobe.

"Perhaps Miss McAllister has a point, Camille. Why don't you come with me for a drive into town? We need a few things from the store, and the change of scene could do you some good. Maybe we should get that wrist checked out while—"

"It's fine, Mum. Just a strain."

"Well, I want to take a look at it before we go. If nothing else, you should wrap it and stick some ice on it for a while."

Camille nodded, letting her mother guide her from the room, though not without first casting a suspicious glance over her shoulder at Ms McAllister and the wardrobe. She could have sworn the woman dipped her head the tiniest bit, and a shiver ran up Camille's spine.

CHAPTER THREE

A RE YOU ALL right?" her mother asked as she navigated the slick roads through the rain. "I'd thought you'd be thrilled to get out of the house and check out a few new shops."

Camille turned from the window and smiled. "I am. I'm just tired. I didn't sleep well last night."

"The house kept you awake?"

"Something like that." Camille turned back to the window, unsure whether she should mention the woman from the garden. "Mum, could we maybe ask Miss McAllister to stay out of my room? She gives me the creeps."

"Camille. That's not very nice."

"Well, she does! She's always lurking and sneaking up on me."

Her mother sighed. "I think maybe you're letting the house get the better of your imagination. It's probably just a novelty for her to have new people in the house. I'm sure you can understand her curiosity about us. But if it'll make you feel for comfortable, I'll have a word with her about it."

"Thanks, Mum." She glanced out the window again and saw the library sign on the side of the road. "Hey,

Mum, would you mind if I checked out the library while you run your errands?"

Her mother shot her a quick frown, but she slowed down and pulled over along the side of the road. "Are you sure you're feeling okay? Not that I'm not thrilled by you wanting to read so much, but you've never passed on going shopping before."

"What are you trying to say?" Camille asked with a cheeky grin.

"Nothing. Nothing. By all means, go spend some time at the library. I'll come find you when I'm done."

Camille leaned over and gave her mother a kiss on the cheek. Jumping out, she pulled her hood over her head against the rain, then ran down the street to the library.

When she stepped inside, she just stood there for a moment, taking in the high rows of shelves and the musty smell of old books. Light filtered in from angled windows in the roof, revealing the rain-laden clouds above. It had been a long time since she'd been in a library, and something about the smell made her think of her childhood. With a smile, she approached the counter.

The librarian peered over her glasses with a slightly raised eyebrow. "So, you've decided to resort to the library?" she asked. Unsure if the question was meant to insult her or just state the facts, Camille just nodded. "Well, I'm Ms Liddell. Now, you won't find the internet here, either. We like to uphold a more traditional library." The librarian stepped out from behind the counter and with a curled finger gestured for Camille to follow.

The girl complied in silence, her curiosity mounting as they weaved through the surprising number of shelves, all heavily laden with books. They stopped at a small bookcase against the rear wall; on either side hung black and white photographs of the town over the years — LeRoux Manor featured in more than one. A sign hanging from the ceiling labelled this section as, '*Local History*'.

"Here you go. Everything we have on LeRoux Manor and Woodville is here. It's not the most comprehensive collection — I suppose we're not the most interesting place to write about — but I'm sure you'll find something of interest. Unfortunately, we don't allow these books to leave the library, but you can photocopy anything you like."

"Oh, I didn't bring any change with me..."

The librarian pursed her lips. "Since you're new in town, I'll give you some free credit on your library card. After that, you can just top it up as you need. That's about the extent of any technology I can offer you."

"That's awesome. Thank you."

"You're welcome," Ms Liddell replied with a small smile. Camille's gratitude seemed to have thawed her somewhat. "I already know your address, so I just need your name, and I can make one up for you while you peruse the collection."

"I'm Camille LeRoux."

Ms Liddell stared at her, her mouth fell open, and her glasses slid down her nose.

"Uh… is something wrong?" Camille asked, scuffing the toe of her sneaker back and forth across the carpet to mask her unease under the sudden intensity of the librarian's stare.

Ms Liddell shook her head, as though banishing her thoughts, and the woman's smile looked strained this time. "No, of course not. You just took me by surprise is all. We all thought the LeRoux line ended with Charles."

"No, he was my father's uncle. I've never met him, though."

"Ah… and are you the only girl of the family? I mean, do you have any siblings?"

"Nope. Just me and my parents."

"Interesting…"

"That I'm an only child?"

"Oh, no. It's nothing. I'll go make up your card up for you. Just come and grab me if you need anything."

Camille watched Ms Liddell walk away, her strange questions hovering after her. Now she really did feel like a stranger in a new town. She turned her attention to the shelves and read through the titles, unsure where to start. Running her fingertips along their spines, she whispered the titles to herself, waiting for one to call out to her.

Architecture of LeRoux Manor
LeRoux Manor: A Brief History
Woodville and Its People
Woodville: A History

She found herself drawn to *LeRoux Manor: A Brief History* and withdrew it from the shelf. Then she carried it to the small research table, sparse except for a single desk lamp, and sat down on the hard, plastic chair. Taking a quick look around the desolate space, she lifted the cover, and the book's thick spine cracked. Camille wondered how long it had been since anyone looked at it.

Unable to pass up checking out the photos before reading, she flipped through the book and gazed at the images of the manor when it was first built, with its immaculate gardens of bountiful flowers, majestic trees, and perfectly sculpted shrubbery. The large staff looked impressive lined up along the veranda of what Camille thought was the rear of the house. She couldn't help but admire its magnificence—at least, how it used to be. It was no wonder the town revered it so much. Turning the page, she found the same family portrait she'd seen in the album in her room, only this one was in colour.

Again, Camille found herself drawn to Mena, with her solemn expression overtaken by the mischievous twinkle in her eyes. It surprised Camille to see that Mena's hair was the same deep auburn as her own, only Mena's fell in curls around her shoulders while Camille's hung thick and straight down her back.

"What happened to you?" Camille muttered. Knowing she didn't have long before her mother would be ready to return to the manor, Camille took to photocopying as much as she could.

"DID YOU FIND what you were looking for?"

Camille jumped and spun around to see her mother behind her. "Mum, you scared me." She placed the last of the books back onto the shelf. "I'm not sure yet. I'll go through what I have when I get home. Can we come back if I need to? I can't take any of these books out of the library."

Her mother gave her a sideways look. but didn't dissuade her. "Of course we can."

Too impatient to wait until they were home, Camille sifted through the copied pages in the car and ignored the frequent glances she felt her mother cast her way. When they returned to the manor, she hardly lifted her head as she got out of the car and walked up the steps to the front door.

"Don't mind me," her mother called. "I'll just carry all the groceries myself!"

Camille turned. "Sorry, Mum. I was off in my own world."

Her mother smiled. "It's fine. Your father's coming around the side of the house. He can help me. It's just nice to see you taking such an interest in the place. I'd still like help with dinner, though, please. You have an hour."

Camille nodded and smiled at her mum, grateful for the time to dive straight into her reading.

She settled into her window seat, plugging her headphones into her phone, and placed the photocopies in her lap and the box of albums at her feet. The first few pages she read focused on the Mena's disappearance and the murder of the girl's father. It seemed to be the stand-out event of Woodville's history, though Camille couldn't imagine much of anything ever happening in such a small town. She found it both odd and quite sad that, with the size of the population at the time of Mena's disappearance, they never found her or Caleb's murderer. How awful it would have been for Mena's mother and brother to never know what happened to either of them.

After a bit more reading, she discovered the most popular theory seemed to be that a squatter had been living in the woods behind LeRoux Manor, and Mena had wandered into his territory. At best, he'd abducted her; at worst, she was murdered. When her father went looking for her, this trespasser had murdered him as well. The police believed the culprit must have been an outsider, as the whole town was present at the Manor and the only two unaccounted for were Mena and Caleb LeRoux.

Camille sat up straight as she read the next sentence; *the knife used to kill Caleb LeRoux was unlike any they'd seen before.* Other than the fact it was particularly large, no other description was provided. The report did state that the weapon had been wielded with such force, it was buried to the hilt in Caleb's back. The knife had entered between his left shoulder and his spine at an angle that suggested the culprit had raised the knife above his head before swinging it down. It was a catastrophic blow — one that would have killed him quickly.

Camille stared out the window and focused on the trees. The theory kind of made sense, especially with the way Caleb was murdered. But something about it still didn't sit right with her. How could a supposed stranger go unnoticed for so long in such a small town? Even with everyone up at the manor the day of the party, surely someone must have seen him in the days before or even after the murder. Camille felt there was more to the story, and she decided that discovering what really happened to Mena and Caleb was to be her new project.

With some reluctance, Camille joined her parent's downstairs for dinner. She sat quietly as they talked, absently pushing her food around the plate with her fork.

"Earth to Camille," her father said loudly.

She jumped again in her chair. "Sorry, Dad. I was just thinking."

"We can see that. What's on your mind?"

Camille straightened up in her seat, glad to have her opening. "Well, I decided I wanted to know more about this house — or manor, or whatever we call it — since it's been in the family forever and we know nothing about it."

"Have you found anything interesting?" her mother asked.

"Actually, yes. Did you know the LeRoux's threw a big party once this place was finished and invited everyone to come and see it? Rich or poor. Everybody in the whole town. It sounded like a big deal for back then."

"Yes, I dare say it was." Her father nodded thoughtfully as he tore of a piece of his roll and popped it in his mouth.

"And... during the party, Caleb LeRoux — the husband, the man who built this place — was brutally murdered. His six-year-old daughter Mena disappeared, and no one ever found her."

"What?" Her mother's knife clattered to her plate.

Camille nodded. "Yep. Mena went missing first, then her father went looking for her. He didn't come back either, so everyone at the party went looking for them. They only found Caleb, though. Well, his body."

"Phillipe?" her mother exclaimed.

Camille's father shrugged but kept his eyes on his food. "Well, yes, it's true. It's hardly a secret."

"And you didn't think I needed to know about it before moving here?" her mother asked, annoyance flickering across her face. Phillipe lifted his head and flashed a sheepish smile at his daughter while reaching across the table for his wife's hand.

"I honestly didn't think it would be an issue," he stated. She gave a slight shake of her head at his renowned nonchalance. Camille's mouth twitched in amusement, and she tried to hide it by taking another bite of her dinner. Her father was so laid back that he often didn't consider things might be cause for concern in others. "It happened a couple hundred years ago at least, and the murder was in the woods beyond the estate, not in the house."

Her mother took a moment, leaning back in her chair and sipping at her wine. "So, what else did you find out?" she asked her daughter.

"Well," Camille stated, putting down her fork, "nothing, really. Caleb's body was found in the woods, face down with a knife in his back. Mena was never seen again. The only lead—if you can call it that—was that everyone thought the murderer was a stranger to the area."

"How awful," her mother exclaimed. "Though I must say, that seems like a rather vague theory for the murder of such a prominent man at the time."

Camille nodded. "And what was so weird was that the knife in Caleb's back was described as something 'they'd seen before'. Like something that wasn't generally made at the time. Maybe that's what led them to the stranger theory."

"I can't believe I didn't know about this." Her mother turned to Camille's father again.

Clearing his throat, he gave a small smile. "It's honestly not something people advertise. Besides, Charles was my only living relative, and we hadn't spoken to him since Camille was a baby. Family history has never been in the forefront. I honestly had quite forgotten all about it until now."

"Why didn't you talk to him after I was born?" Camille asked. Her parents exchanged an unreadable glance at the sudden change of topic. "Come on, guys. I'm not a kid. I can handle it."

"Your great uncle and I had a falling out is all."

"You've told me that a hundred times. What was it about?" Camille prompted.

"Camille…" her mother started.

"No, it's okay," her father replied. "She's right. She's not a child." He turned to her and held out his hand with a solemn frown.

Suddenly concerned, Camille reached out and placed her hand in his. "What's wrong?"

"Well, when you were born, my uncle insisted quite… fiercely that we give you up for adoption."

"What?" Camille gasped and pulled her hand away.

"Of course, your mother and I never entertained the thought," he assured her. "Not for one second. The day you were born was the happiest day of our lives, and we wouldn't give you up for the world."

"Good to know…" Camille replied dryly. "So, what was his reason for wanting to cast me from the family tree before he'd even met me?"

"To this day, I still don't really know. And that's the truth. As soon as he found out we had a daughter instead of a son, he just wouldn't let it go. So, we cut all ties with him. Honestly, I'm surprised he left the Manor to us. Yes, I was his only living family, but I was sure he wouldn't want to give me anything."

"What else would he have done with it?" Camille asked.

"Oh, he could have left the estate to the town, for example. Left it as some kind of heritage museum. God knows the place has some history."

"Are you all right, sweetheart?" Camille's mother asked, reaching out and placing her hand on her daughter's.

Camille sat quietly for a moment, staring down at her plate. "I think so. I mean, sure, it's not a nice feeling to know someone wanted to give you away. But I didn't even know him. You guys wanted me, and that's all that matters."

"Good." Her mother gave her hand a gentle squeeze before releasing it.

"Something else on your mind?" her father asked, and Camille found herself pushing her food around on her plate again. She looked from one parent to the other, trying to gauge whether to tell them.

"Better out than in," her mother gently prompted.

"Well, our first night here, I saw something. Someone. I was sitting at the window seat in my room, and I saw an old woman standing in the gardens outside. She stared right at me. And before you say anything, it definitely wasn't Miss McAllister."

"Are you sure you weren't dreaming, honey?" her father asked. "There's no one else up here. Just us and the McAllister's. Unless of course you saw a ghost..."

"Phillipe! That's not funny," her mother scolded. Her father chuckled, raising his hands in defence against her playful slaps.

Camille couldn't help but smile. "She definitely wasn't a ghost. I mean, I could see her as clearly as I see both of you. Ghosts are supposed to be... I don't know. Less here, aren't they?"

Her father shrugged. "I couldn't say. I've never seen one."

"Have you seen her again?" her mother asked.

Camille shook her head. "Just that first night."

"Well, that settles it." Her mother wiped her mouth on her napkin. "You were just overtired from a long day of moving. That's all."

Camille returned her attention to her plate, more certain than ever that what she saw had not been her imagination at play.

CAMILLE SAT AT the window seat, the box from the attic in front of her. She pulled out another photo album and instantly felt a rush of enthusiasm sweep over her, lifting the sombre mood that had hung over her since dinner. She loved looking at old photographs, especially black and white ones of people long since passed. There was something magical about trying to work out who they'd been and what their lives were like.

The photos were well preserved, though many were discoloured around the edges. Looking closely, she was surprised to find the photos weren't of the LeRoux family but appeared to be of the staff. She ran her fingers over their expressionless faces, wondering if they'd liked working at the manor, if the LeRoux's had treated them well. She froze, her fingers hovering over the face of a little girl peering out from behind the skirts of one of the women. "No way..." she whispered, then rushed to the bedside table for a better look under the lamplight. The child looked about six years old and was the spitting image of Mena LeRoux, only despite the fact this was a sepia-toned photo, the child's hair was not the same auburn Camille had seen in the colour photo. Now, it was clearly a bright white. Scanning the handwritten entry at the bottom of the photo, Camille shook her head in disbelief.

'LeRoux Manor Staff – Solstice Day, 1867.'

With a frown, she rummaged through the first album she'd opened, hunting for the article on the LeRoux Manor party. Holding the two pages side by side, she compared the photo of Mena from the article to the girl in the staff photo. There was no mistaking it; aside from the hair, they were identical. "In 1867, you should have been fifty-six," Camille whispered. "Not six."

CHAPTER FOUR

CAMILLE STIRRED, FROWNING as she tried to hold onto the sleep she'd finally managed to grasp. It was no good. A loud thump made her open her eyes and wonder what could make such a noise. Listening intently, she tried to pinpoint where it came from, then it repeated. She looked up at the ceiling; it sounded like something had been dragged across the floor of the attic directly above her.

Camille lay there, staring up at the ceiling, part of her wanting to go investigate and the other half hoping to ignore it and go back to sleep. A massive yawn overwhelmed her, and she made her decision by rolling over and closing her eyes.

Just as she started to drift off again, another thump and drag sounded, this time even louder. Camille shot out of bed and hurried barefoot across the floor. When she scurried down the hall, she found the door to the to the attic stairs open just a crack. The faint glow from the stairwell globe-light sent a sliver of light out across the dark floor. She stared at; the lightbulb at blown the last time she used it.

Camille told herself her father or Mr McAllister had simply replaced it, and she crept forward to press her ear against the gap as she listened for any sound of movement from above. The noise had stopped, so she slowly opened the door farther, cringing at the loud creak echoing through the darkness. She paused, wondering if she'd alerted anyone to her presence, but the rest of the house remained completely silent.

As she made her way up the stairs, she briefly closed her eyes and tried to ignore the immediate claustrophobia. Once she'd reached the top, she was surprised to find a candle lit in the rightmost of the two windows at the other end of the attic. Its small flame burned brightly, flickering a dance of shadows around it. "Hello?" Camille whispered, though it was still quite loud. "Is anyone here?" She stood still, half wanting to hear a reply and half terrified that she would. When only silence met her greeting, she cautiously moved forward, placing one foot precisely in front of the other in the hopes of avoiding the creaking floorboards. If there was someone here, she didn't really want them to know exactly where she was. Then she had to admit it; Camille wasn't convinced she was alone.

In that moment, her spine tingled with the feeling that she was being watched. "Come out where I can see you. I know you're here," she called a little louder, but still, there was no response. Her stomach churned, sending a flurry of anxiety through her as she noticed all the sheet-covered items that had spread across the floor were now pushed aside, cluttering up along the walls and looming at her like a spectral audience. Her heart quickened at the thought of ghosts having done all this. "Stop being stupid," she muttered, though she still kept her voice low. "Mum's obviously been up here sorting through things."

Then she forced the memory of that dragging sound from her head. With a frown, she caught sight of a large trunk beneath the window and walked toward it. Kneeling, she marvelled at the carved wooden lid of intricate figures, all of which seemed to dance around a central figure. The chest's condition was amazing; it looked brand new, though she knew it couldn't be. With both hands, Camille tried to lift the lid, but the chest must have been locked. She ran her fingers over the keyhole with a sigh. Where am I going to find the key amongst all these things?

The scraping sound rose again without warning, and Camille jumped when she realised it was coming toward her. She turned in time to see a key skidding along the floor before stopping at her feet. Camille didn't move. The sound of her rapid breath echoed in her ears as she peered into the darkness for any sign of another presence. But there was no movement, not another sound. Camille slowly bent down and picked up the key, careful not to take her eyes away from the darkness beyond the candle's small circle of light. Holding it flat in her palm, she knew it was old, judging by the key's narrow barrel tipped at one end with three square prongs; the other end had a decorative series of loops turning in on and around themselves. She fumbled a bit as she inserted the key into the lock on the lid of the trunk. Finally, with a loud click, the lock turned. It took both hands to lift the heavy lid, and the hinges groaned in protest as she heaved it open.

The trunk's contents were hidden under what she thought was a knitted rug. She gently pulled it out, holding it up for inspection in the candlelight, and realised it was a shawl, hand-made in a fine, lacey knit. There were holes in a few sections, where either age or moths had gotten to it over the years. Without a second thought, she draped it across her shoulders and closed her eyes, pulling the material closer. Despite its thinness, the shawl provided any amazing amount of comfort and warmth.

The candlelight flickered across a piece of metal in the trunk, and Camille reached down to pull out an old hand mirror. The back and handle were decorated with a pattern of interweaving leaves and flowers, though the silver was tarnished with age. Turning it over in her hands, she stared at her reflection in the mirror. Then she turned her head from one side to the other, watching the flickering candlelight dance across her face. It made her look different—as though she were looking at someone else's reflection. Don't be ridiculous, she thought, then turned the mirror away. The minute she did, the mirror's surface caught another face in its reflection—the face of someone standing behind her.

Camille yelped and quickly clapped her hand to her mouth as the mirror fell back into the trunk. She turned on her heel and looked around the attic, her heart pounding as she swallowed thickly. She could have sworn she'd seen a young girl peeking out from behind the white sheets covering some piece of furniture up here. Once she'd inspected the hanging sheets with a thorough gaze, unable to see anyone truly there, Camille tried her best to convince herself it was just her imagination — a trick of the candlelight playing with the shadows. Yet before she could reach back into the trunk, she heard the girl's giggle, followed by the sound of small feet racing along the wooden floor. Camille spun around again, her eyes wide, but again, no one was there. Reaching up for the candle, she carefully pulled it closer across the windowsill, focused firmly on the attic in front of her.

"Come find me, Catherine!"

Camille almost dropped the candle at the sound of the little girl's voice. It's not real. She's not real. She squeezed her eyes shut, took a deep breath, and held it, hoping her mind would right itself, Five, four, three, two...

Camille awoke with a start, looking frantically around her room. Her mouth fell open in surprise when she realised she was sitting upright in her own bed. Hearing an odd squeak, like the protests of an old hinge, she looked up to see the old woman from the garden staring at her from behind the clothes hanging in her wardrobe. Pale white hands reached forward from the darkness and pulled the doors closed again.

Camille screamed, leaping from the bed and running out into the hall. "Mum! Dad!" she cried. When she reached the landing, she found them both already halfway to her room.

"What is it?" her mum asked.

"What happened?"

"The old woman!" Camille sobbed. "She was in my room." She pointed back down the hall and caught the look her parents exchanged. So, she grabbed her mother's hand. "She's in there. I'm not making this up."

"I know you're not, sweetheart," her father said. "We'll sort this out." Then he led the three of them back to her room. "Now, tell me exactly what happened." He walked to the windows, checking they were firmly closed before peering out through the grime.

"Well, I had a bad dream, and then —"

"You were dreaming?" he cut in, turning from the windows to look at her.

"Yes, but I wasn't dreaming when I saw her. I'd woken up!"

He seemed unconvinced, but he placated her anyway. "And where did you see her?"

"She was in there." Camille pointed at the wardrobe as she sat on the edge of her bed. Her mother took a seat beside her. Chewing on her lower lip, Camille watched her father approach the wardrobe and yank open the doors, pushing them apart to completely reveal the inside. Only Camille's clothes and shoes remained.

"I'm telling you she was right there."

Dragging the clothes aside to reveal the back of the wardrobe, her father banged along the interior. "It's solid. Nowhere for anyone to hide or escape from."

"Maybe she came out while I was running to get you," Camille replied, all too aware of how lame her argument sounded. Her father signed, returning the clothes to their places, then closed the doors.

"Maybe you need to move rooms," her mother suggested gently. "Closer to ours. It might help you to feel more settled. You're used to being in a room right beside us."

"That has nothing to do with it." Camille jumped from the bed; her fists clenched angrily by her sides. "I know what I saw. She was there, just like she was outside on our first night."

"Still, I think it would be best if you switched rooms," her mother replied. "At least until we can remove that old wardrobe and replace it with something a little more modern and less… intimidating."

"I'm fine where I am, thanks. I'd like to try and get some sleep now." She stormed around to the other side of the bed and climbed under the covers, turning her back to her parents. She heard her mother sigh as she got up from the bed, followed by her parents' soft footsteps as they left the room, leaving the door open behind them.

CAMILLE GROANED AS she woke up and rolled onto her back, gingerly rubbing her neck. It was stiff and sore after sleeping in the same position all night. I must have been more tired than I realised. Sitting up, she found her gaze drawn toward the wardrobe, the doors still firmly shut after her father's inspection the night before. Camille got out of bed and walked toward it, hardly noticing the coldness of the wooden floor beneath her feet. She opened the door and dragged the clothes to one side of the rail, reaching in to touch the back of the wardrobe. What if Dad missed something?

"Don't expect to find what you're looking for until you're meant to," came a voice from the doorway.

Startled again, Camille turned around to find Miss McAllister standing there, hands clasped formally before her as she watched.

"What did you say?" Camille asked, looking the woman up and down in surprise.

"I said your mother sent me up. Breakfast is ready." Before Camille could reply, Miss McAllister turned and went back down the hall, leaving Camille staring after her.

CAMILLE PULLED HER hair back from her face, securing it with a band as her mother draped plastic sheets over the window seats. "Can't we just get the window cleaners to do this?" she groaned.

"They're doing the outside. No sense in paying someone to do the inside when we can do it ourselves. This home will cost a fortune to clean up as it is. The outside of your bedroom was done first up this morning. You're welcome."

"Thank you. Do you realise how many windows there are in this house? Or that ninety percent of them are enormous?" Camille gaped.

Her mother chuckled. "Just as well you only have to help me do a few. School starts in a few days."

Camille sighed at the reminder, picking up the long-handled window-cleaner and giving it a dubious look. Then she scrunched up her face. "You know, I don't have to start school straight away. I mean, I wouldn't miss much initially, anyway, and I'd catch up quickly. I can stay here and help set the house up for a couple more weeks."

"If you stay home, you'll be helping me clean the windows," her mother replied with a smirk.

Camille stuck out her tongue and started cleaning the first of her bedroom windows.

"I know you must be nervous about starting a new school," her mother said, washing the window beside Camille's, "especially since it's your senior year."

"Honestly, I hadn't given it much thought until now," Camille lied. "I've been too caught up in the move and trying to get settled into this place." Her mother didn't reply right away, seemingly concentrating on the long strokes as she swept the window-cleaner from side to side, watching the grime give away with greater ease than they'd anticipated. "I think it would do you some good to get out of the house and make some friends. You've always loved school."

"I guess…" Really, her mother was right. She did love school.

Any new friends have got to beat creepy Miss McAllister always lurking in the shadows.

The conversation fell away as they focused on the cleaning. Though Camille wouldn't admit it, she found cleaning the windows kind of therapeutic. It was almost hypnotic watching the water turn black as it loosened the age-old grime from its resting place. As she dragged the wiper across the glass, she smiled in satisfaction to see the final dregs of dirt wiped clear and her own reflection clearly emerged in its place.

And there was the old woman's face again.

With a screech, Camille spun around, her window-cleaner clattering to the floor.

"Camille! Are you okay?" her mother asked. "What happened?"

Camille opened her mouth, but nothing came out. She could only point at the open bedroom door. "I... I saw her," she finally said. "The woman. I saw her reflection in the window. She was watching us from the doorway..."

Her mother remained silent, looking from her daughter to the doorway and back again. "Now, we went through this last night," she said softly, but it didn't hide the doubt in her voice. Camille held her breath as her mother casually walked to the other side of the room and peered out into the hall. "Hello?" she called. When there was no answer, she turned to her daughter with a reassuring smile. "No one there."

Camille scowled and watched her mother return confidently to the windows, feeling like she was a child being reminded that there was no bogeyman under the bed. Though as she picked up her cleaner, she noticed her mother's quick glance back at the doorway. They worked together in silence until their respective windows were clean.

"Will you look at that view," her mother exclaimed, standing back to more fully appreciate the sight.

Camille nodded. "I know. It was one of the reasons I chose this room. It's amazing. And that cleaning honestly didn't take as long as I thought it would."

Her mother laughed. "Does this mean you're willing to help me with the others?"

"Of course I'll help you, Mum. I might not enjoy it, but I'll help you."

"Well how about you help me with some of the windows today, and tomorrow, we'll head into town first thing and get all your school supplies."

Camille agreed with a smile and slung her cleaner over her shoulder.

CAMILLE LEANED AGAINST the kitchen bench, peeling carrots at half the pace it took her mother to prep the other vegetables. "I don't know about you, but I'm starving after today," her mother stated, scooping up some diced onion and garlic and tossing them into the hot saucepan with a few herbs. The smell wafted toward Camille, and her stomach rumbled in response.

"I know one thing for sure," Camille said. "My shoulders are killing me. My sore wrist was nothing compared to this. I might not be able to lift my arms at all tomorrow."

Her mother laughed. "That's a possibility. Give them a good stretch out in a hot shower before bed. It'll help."

"How are my two favourite girls?" her father asked when he walked into the kitchen. He placed a kiss on his wife's cheek before heading to the sink and washing his hands.

"You reek," Camille's mother said, wrinkling her nose. "What on Earth have you been doing?"

"Here I was, thinking that I smelled like the roses," he replied, flashing a wink at Camille. "I've been working with Mr McAllister to compile a comprehensive of just how much maintenance is required around here and where. As you can imagine, the list is a mile long, and some things have been let slide for a long time now."

"Who'd have thought?" Camille replied with a grin. "Do you even know their first names? Mr and Miss McAllister. It just sounds so formal and creepy."

"There's nothing creepy about showing respect. They come from a generation where it was considered rude to call an elder by their first names unless invited to do so. But no, I don't actually know their first names. They're slightly unusual folk, though, aren't they? I'll give you that much. Or maybe they're just very protective about this place."

"Well, I guess it's essentially as much their family home as it is ours," Camille's mother said. "More so. It's only a family home to you in name." She added a handful of vegetables to the pan.

"Yeah, you're right. It probably pays to remember that. Though sometimes, I get the feeling Mr McAllister is waiting for something. Or someone. Like he's receiving instructions or awaiting approval for someone. I can't explain it, but more than once, I've found his behaviour unnerving. To each their own I suppose! I do have some good news, though." Phillipe turned to his daughter. "The Wi-Fi is up and running." Then he grabbed a piece of carrot off the chopping board, tossed it in the air, and caught it with his mouth.

"Awesome!" Camille was halfway out of the kitchen before she looked at her mother, eager for permission to leave her mother with cooking dinner.

With a laugh, her mother waved her off. "You have an hour until dinner."

"What's the password?" she asked her father. He walked toward her, making a show of searching through his pockets before finally withdrawing a slip of paper and handing it to her.

"Thanks, guys."

CAMILLE REACHED INTO the second drawer of her bedside table, pulled out her laptop, and plugged it in beside her bed. She ran her hand over it, as though wiping away dust. Then she opened it, powered it on, and looked at the piece of paper in her hand. When she saw the password, she rolled her eyes - 'LeRoux19'. "Original, Dad," she said with a laugh.

The first thing she did with the internet was to jump straight onto her social media. Sure, she'd received messages from her friends since moving, but it wasn't quite the same as scrolling through photos and commenting. It made her feel more connected, almost like she was still there with them. Though knowing she had limited time until dinner, she only took a quick scroll through to satisfy her curiosity before she opened a new tab and typed in 'Woodville Highschool'. Before the move she'd refused to listen to anything her parents had tried to tell her about her new school. She hadn't even been ready to look it up before now. She slowly clicked from one page to the next, more interested in any pictures she came across than reading about the school itself.

She came to a map, and her fears of getting lost on her first day quickly vanished. The school grounds were half the size of her previous school—if that. The buildings themselves looked old but well-maintained — large brick buildings with angular roofs, surrounded by plenty of greenery and minimal concrete. Covered walkways connected the buildings to each other and were covered with thick tangles of vines laden with small purple flowers. Camille sat back, admiring how pretty it looked and knowing the photos must have been taken in spring. The school wouldn't look as pretty when she started in winter.

Scrolling down farther, she groaned when she saw a photo of the library. A large sign sat over the threshold — LeRoux Library. She'd hoped to search the school library's resources for any further information on LeRoux Manor, but now she wasn't so sure. With a sigh, she closed the laptop and headed downstairs for dinner.

CHAPTER FIVE

CAMILLE WATCHED THE manor grow smaller in the side mirror as her mother drove them out of the estate grounds toward town. The morning fog gave her new home an ominous look, hovering around the grounds as though trying to shield the manor from prying eyes. Ignoring the chill shooting through her, she turned to her mother. "Did you know my new school has a library named after us?"

Her mother smiled. "No, I didn't, but it's hardly surprising. I imagine we'll see more than one reference to the family name as we get to know the area better."

"Awesome..." Camille replied dryly.

"The manor and the LeRoux family have been the backbone of the town for a long time. It's a huge part of the history here. I know we didn't know your uncle, but you should still be proud to be a part of such a legacy," her mother explained.

"It's kind of cool, sure. But it's going to be hard enough as the new kid without being a LeRoux too."

"You'll be fine. You'll make friends in no time. Who knows? It might even be easier because you're a LeRoux."

"Yeah, they'll know all about the new girl who lives in the creepy house."

"It's not creepy…" her mother replied. Camille turned and looked at her mother, eyebrows raised. Her mother flashed her a quick sideways glance and laughed. "Okay, it's a little bit creepy. But that's only because it hasn't been looked after. Once we give it a good once-over, it'll feel much less intimidating."

"If you say so…" Camille replied, turning back to gaze out the window.

"Can you go to the bookstore and pick up your school order while I pick up a few things for your father from the hardware store? Then we'll go and get your uniforms. Or is your wrist too sore again after the windows?" Her mother slowed as she spotted an empty parking space amidst the row of cars lining the side of the road.

"It's achy, but I think it's fine," Camille replied. "I only need a few books." She watched impatiently as her mother parked the car, barely waiting for her to turn the engine off before she unclicked her seat belt and opened the door. I'll meet you back here." She slung her bag over her shoulder, jumped out of the car, and walked briskly toward the bookstore. She was surprised how cold the morning was and wished she'd worn something warmer. She still wasn't used to the change in climate.

When she reached the bookstore, she waited briefly for the doors to slide open and was instantly grateful for the warm air that greeted her. Camille stepped inside and stared, rubbing her hands together and waiting to warm up.

"Not bad for a small-town bookstore, right?"

Camille jumped and turned to find a girl about her own age standing beside her, wearing a polo shirt with the store's name on it. "Sorry," she replied with a smile. "I guess I just wasn't expecting it to be so... big."

The girl laughed. "Well, Woodville boasts the title of 'coldest town in England', so people like to stay inside and read a lot. You're new here, right?" The girl reached up to adjust her already immaculate blonde ponytail, her blue eyes warm and friendly.

"Is it that obvious?" Camille felt suddenly boyish and self-conscious next to the curvy, naturally beautiful girl in front of her.

"Only because we rarely ever get new people here. So, you're big news."

Camille pulled a face before she'd had time to censor herself.

"Oh, don't worry. Everyone's super friendly here. Well, most people. I mean, every town and school have their jerks, but for the most part, everyone's lovely. Plus, you're a LeRoux, so you kind of have an inherent respect happening."

"Oh," Camille replied, unsure how else to respond. "How did you know I was a LeRoux?"

The girl laughed. "Like I said, it's a small town. I'm pretty sure Miss Liddell, the librarian, let the cat out of the bag. Also, everyone was super curious about what would happen when Mr LeRoux died. The whole town thought he was the last of the family, so it was all very shocking," she said playfully.

Camille couldn't help but smile; the girl's enthusiasm was infectious. "Well, I'm Camille," she said.

"Oh! I'm sorry. I'm Grace Harker. We're both seniors at Woodville High, so we're bound to have some classes together. Speaking of school, you're here to get your books, right?" Camille nodded. "Great. I'll go grab them from the back for you."

"Is it okay if I have a look around first?"

"Sure thing. Just come up to the counter when you're ready, and I'll have them waiting for you." Grace smiled and walked off.

Camille looked around, unsure where to start. Her gaze rose up to the second-floor balustrade and a sign that marked the books there as the History section. So, she headed to the narrow staircase running up the side of the wall and took the steps two at a time. On the second floor, the wooden floorboards creaked under the carpet as she walked from one row of shelves to the next. Then she found a small section titled 'Local History'. Kneeling, Camille perused the titles, many of which she'd already seen at the library. Her eyes fell on a rather thick volume — Woodville: A Complete History. When she pulled it from the shelf, she turned it over and balked at the price. It would take a huge chunk out of her holiday savings. Yet as she opened the book and saw some the photos frequenting almost every page, she knew she had to have it. Disallowing herself the opportunity to even look sideways at another book, she hurried back down the stairs and to the front counter, heaving the extra volume onto the counter.

Grace chuckled. "Planning to brush up on some local history before school starts?"

"Something like that."

"I know you don't have your student card yet, but I'll give you the student discount."

"Awesome! Thanks." Camille was more than grateful to save a little more money.

Grace scanned the back of the Woodville book but didn't touch the textbooks. "The schoolbooks have already been paid for," she said as she pushed over a huge stack of books bound in string across the counter. She laughed at Camille's baffled expression. "Yeah, you can't carry all these on your own. Do you have far to go?"

"My mum's waiting for me at the car just up the street a little. I'll go grab her to help me."

"What? Don't be silly. I'll help you carry them out." Grace turned and called out to another staff member to come watch the register, then she picked up the stack of schoolbooks.

"At least let me carry the big stack," Camille offered.

"Don't worry about it. I actually carry books for a living, you know," Grace replied. She made carrying the entire bound pile look incredibly easy. Camille couldn't help feeling bad, but her aching wrist and stiff shoulders screamed at her under the weight of the one Woodville book she did carry. "My friends and I are meeting up after I finish work for burgers at Rick's," Grace added as they headed out the door. "It's a tradition we've had since we were in primary school. We always go the night before school starts up again. Even though we pretty much spend most of our time there, anyway. Do you want to come along? Meet a few friendly faces before tomorrow?"

"I don't want to change up your tradition…" Camille replied shyly.

"Oh, you wouldn't. It'll be nice to have someone new to talk to."

"Okay. I mean, I'll have to check with Mum first, but I'm sure it'll be fine."

Her mother looked up from where she leaned against the car, her eyebrows raised in surprise as Camille and Grace approached. She quickly opened the back door so Grace could offload the books.

"Mum, this is Grace. She works in the bookstore. Same year as me at school."

"Nice to meet you, Grace."

"You too, uh…"

"You can call me Allysha," Camille's mother replied with a smile.

"Nice to meet you, Allysha."

"Mum, Grace and some of her friends are meeting up later for burgers. Is it okay if I go?" Allysha glanced from one girl to the other. "I don't see a problem with that. So long as you're home by nine."

"Mum…" Camille groaned in embarrassment.

"It's fine," Grace said. "We all have to be home by then, anyway. First day of school tomorrow and all that. We can come pick you up around six, if that works. My mum's dropping me and Jayne off."

Camille smiled gratefully at her mother as she exchanged numbers with Grace.

"Well, I'd better get back to work. They'll be wondering where I am. Was nice to meet you, Allysha."

"You too, Grace."

"See you later, Camille." With a smile, Grace turned and hurried back toward the shop.

CHAPTER SIX

C AMILLE SMOOTHED DOWN her top for the twentieth time and pulled her hair away from her face and up into a ponytail. Then she scrunched up her face at her reflection and pulled her hair out of the ponytail again. While Grace had been nothing but friendly, Camille felt anxious about meeting the whole group.

What if they don't like me? They'll probably make fun of me for being a LeRoux. Or end up thinking I'm just a weird city girl. And I have an accent... they'll say I talk funny.

Forcing herself to stop thinking of every possible bad scenario, Camille took a deep breath and gave herself a final once-over. She boasted her standard look tonight — a dark-blue shirt dress over black leggings, an old leather jacket, and her favourite pair of boots. She shuffled her feet across the floor, making the charms hanging from the zippers of her boots jingle against each other. She looked at them in the mirror and found tears pricking her eyes in an unexpected spurt of homesickness. The two charms were of an emu and a kangaroo — the two animals featured on the Australian Coat of Arms. She wiped her eyes, reminding herself why she'd bought them in the first place. Emus and kangaroos can't go backwards—and neither could she. Taking a deep breath, she gave herself another full glance in the mirror. This'll have to do. She grabbed her bag and headed out the bedroom door. Of course, it completely startled her when she found Miss McAllister standing in the middle of the hallway just a few metres away, staring towards Camille's room.

"What do you want?" Camille snapped, not caring if she sounded rude. Miss McAllister raised an eyebrow, looked Camille up and down, then turned on her heel and slowly walked away. Camille stared after her with a frown. She felt bad for snapping, but the woman gave her the creeps with all this lurking about. Even when she couldn't see the woman, she always felt like Miss McAllister was somewhere nearby, watching her.

Once the woman was out of sight, Camille pulled her bedroom door closed behind her and dashed downstairs to the kitchen. Her mother stood at the bench, humming to herself as she prepared dinner. "I'm going to wait out the front for my lift," Camille stated, approaching her mother to give her a kiss on the cheek.

"What? You're not going to invite them in?" Allysha raised her eyebrows in mock surprise.

"You're hilarious, Mum," Camille replied. "I'll text you the address. The place is called Rick's, on Main Street. I'm pretty sure everything's on Main Street."

"Well, I won't have any trouble finding it then, will I?" Her mother laughed.

Camille waved goodbye and headed toward the heavy, wooden front door. When she yanked it open, she saw headlights rising over the hill toward the house. The car pulled around the fountain to the front door, and Grace eagerly jumped out of the car. Her hair was wet under her black beret and hung around her face; her work uniform had been replaced by tight, dark jeans with tears slashed across the knees and a billowy white shirt underneath a red felt jacket hanging just above her knees. Camille tried not to be self-conscious, but she couldn't help feeling like the gangly duckling next to the graceful swan.

"Hop on in. I'm so excited!" Grace exclaimed as she opened the back door for Camille. "I've told everyone you're coming, and they can't wait to meet you. That's Jayne in the back and my mum Isabelle in the front."

"Hello. Nice to meet you both," Camille said; she thought she sounded far too awkward as she climbed into the back.

"Welcome to Woodville," Isabelle said, turning to smile at her. "How are you liking it so far?"

"It's lovely, from what little I've seen. We haven't had much of a chance to explore just yet."

"I can't believe you actually live in there," Jayne exclaimed as she tried to peer past Camille for a better look.

"Jayne," Isabelle chastised. Grace laughed.

"Sorry. I didn't mean it in a bad way. I just meant that place is huge. Is it just you and your family in there?"

"Jayne…" Isabelle cut in.

"It's fine," Camille reassured her. "It's just me and my parents. I don't have any siblings. Oh, and there' s an elderly couple who are kind of like caretakers. They live here too."

"Wow," Jayne whispered, turning to look at the house through the rear window as the car turned back down the driveway. "Is it creepy inside?"

"Oh, my goodness, Jayne!" her mother barked from the front. Camille and Grace laughed together.

"Parts are a little creepy," Camille confessed. "Mainly because everything's old and not well looked after." She didn't want to give too much away, considering she didn't know these people very well yet. "I think once my parents have finished with it, it'll seem much more inviting."

"I'm sure your parents will do the manor justice, Camille," Isabelle stated, smiling at her through the rear-view mirror.

CAMILLE WAS THE last to step out of the car, suddenly anxious with a ferocious cluster of butterflies hurtling around in the pit of her stomach. She hadn't had to make new friends in a long time—nor had she ever worried that people wouldn't like her. Such a foreign feeling definitely pushed her beyond her comfort zone. She quickened her pace as the girls stopped and waited for her at the entrance. "You'll be fine," Grace whispered in her ear, giving her arm a squeeze as she led them inside. Camille smiled at her in gratitude before taking in the restaurant. It was set up like a 1950's diner, with booths and a jukebox, the staff in white uniforms with little peaked caps on their heads.

"This is awesome," Camille stated.

"Not too old-fashioned for a city girl?" Grace asked.

"No way. I love it."

"Then just wait till you try the food," Jayne announced. "It's brilliant."

Camille grinned and followed the girls to a booth in the back corner. Then her self-confidence faltered again when she saw two boys sitting in the booth, and she quickly looked around, hoping she'd find herself at another booth instead.

"Ladies, about time you rocked up. We were going to order without you," one of the boys said as he slid out of the booth and threw his arm across Grace's shoulders. He planted a kiss on her cheek.

"I told you we were picking Camille up first," Grace replied.

"I know. I'm just stirring." The boy winked at Camille and held out his hand. "Hi. I'm Jonathan Glasser, dutiful boyfriend and comic relief." He grinned and flicked his blond hair out of his face. "This dude is Lachlan Rivers. Ledge of a point guard and Woodville Academy's pride and joy."

Lachlan also slid out from the booth and extended his hand. He seemed the opposite of Jonathan, with dark, short-cropped hair and piercing blue eyes. Camille was a little taken aback by the intensity of his gaze when she shook his hand and was mortified to feel the heat of a blush move up her neck and into her cheeks. "Uh, point guard... Basketball, right?" she asked, unsure of what else to say, her mouth suddenly feeling dry and she hoped the others couldn't see her instant crush. Lachlan nodded but didn't say anything at all.

"Righto, Camille from Australia," Jonathan declared. "Let's sit, and you can tell us all about yourself over some food." He pulled Grace into the booth beside him. Lachlan slid in opposite Jonathan, nodding his head in Camille's direction. But before she could follow, Jayne dove in beside him, casting an irritated look at Camille who was left hovering at the end of the table. She felt ridiculous, and with Jayne's unmistakable 'back off' vibes, Camille slid into the booth alongside Grace.

"Pretty much everything we do revolves around these blokes' stomachs," Grace told her with a laugh. Seemingly oblivious to Camille's embarrassment, or the territorial glances Jane was flicking in her direction, despite the friendly smile on her face.

"I don't know if the girls told you, Camille, but the food here's brilliant," Jonathan stated.

"So I've heard," Camille replied and picked up the menu, partly to actually read it, and partly to avoid meeting his gaze. Still at the mercy of the butterflies in her stomach—now aggravated by her growing attraction, she found she had no appetite, yet she didn't want to offend her new friends by not taking part in their tradition. "So, what's good here? Or is that a stupid question?" Camille asked, smiling when they laughed.

"It's kind of a stupid question," Jonathan said, "but as you're new, we'll let it slide. I think we should start you off slow. Ease you into the Rick's experience. Try the classic cheeseburger and chips. And a vanilla milkshake. You won't regret it."

"Sold," Camille replied, lowering the menu. She was grateful for not having to decide on her own.

A woman approached them on roller skates and pulled a notepad and pen from the front pocket of her apron. "Hey, guys," she said before looking down at Camille. "Welcome to Rick's. I'm Amy. You're new here, yeah?" Camille just nodded. "And you've just moved here?"

"Yeah, they've moved into LeRoux Manor," Jayne added.

Amy's eyes widened in awe. "Wow. Creepy. I'd heard the rumour but didn't know if it was true. That's cool."

"Uh, yeah. Something like that."

"How come we don't get the friendly 'Welcome to Rick's' bit, Amy?" Lachlan asked, and Camille smiled at him, grateful for the deflection. He glanced at her and offered a small nod.

"Because you lot are part of the furniture. Now, what can I get you?" They put in their orders as Amy frantically jotted it all down before flashing them a smile and gliding away.

"You can't just announce to everyone that Camille's moved into LeRoux Manor," Grace said to Jayne, who looked up in surprise.

"Why? It's not like it's some kind of secret. I'm sure the whole town knows by now anyway." Jayne folded her arms.

"It's fine, really," Camille added, not wanting any friction on her behalf.

"In this town, everyone knows everything," Jonathan said. "Though obviously, being your new friends, we're allowed to ask you questions about it, aren't we?"

Camille smiled, more focused on the fact that he'd referred to them as her friends. "Sure. I don't know if I can answer too much, but go ahead."

"Is it creepy?" he asked.

"I already asked that!" Jayne announced.

"Well, I wasn't there, was I?" Jonathan retorted.

"It's a little creepy sometimes, but I think it's just because it's so big and old. I'm still getting used to it," Camille lied with a half-smile. This was starting to sound like her go to soundbite.

"So, no cool ghost stories or anything?" he asked, sounding quite disappointed.

"Nope," Camille said. "Not one." She toyed with the edge of her napkin, then looked up. Lachlan stared at her intently, and she quickly returned her gaze to the table, fearing he'd see the lie in her eyes.

"You know, there was a murder there," Lachlan stated.

Grace scoffed. "You can be so morbid sometimes."

Camille smiled nervously again, unsure whether Lachlan was trying to unnerve her or just knew his history. "It's okay," she said. "I know all about it. The murder of Caleb LeRoux and the disappearance of his daughter on the day of the manor's grand opening."

"Doesn't that creep you out?" Jayne asked, hugging herself against an imaginary shiver and shifting closer to Lachlan, glancing up at him as though hoping he might put a reassuring arm around her.

Camille watched them for a moment, feeling a pang at the thought that the two of them might be an item. Lachlan, though, seemed oblivious to Jayne's attention.

"Not really. I mean, it was so long ago, and it didn't happen in the actual house." Camille shrugged. Grace saved her from any further investigation and skilfully deflected the conversation toward filling Claire in on their holiday shenanigans and local gossip.

Before long, Amy returned with their food. Camille marvelled at how the woman balanced all that food on the trays while skating around. If it was Camille doing it, she wouldn't last two minutes. When everyone tucked into their burgers, the comfortable silence made Camille even more grateful to be here. The boys grunted and groaned in appreciation as they ate. Camille savoured each bite, conceding that this was the best burger she'd ever tasted.

For the rest of the evening, LeRoux Manor thankfully wasn't mentioned again. Camille had more than enough time to think about it once she returned home. For now, she was grateful for the change in conversation. The group filled her in on all the best places in town, where all the kids hung out beyond school hours, and what the teachers were like.

"Just a heads up," Jonathan said. "Mr Ostervic will likely corner you the first chance he gets, regardless of whether you're in his class or not. He's a bit... eccentric. Especially when it comes to LeRoux Manor."

"He's not that eccentric," Lachlan added.

"Of course you would defend him. You're the teacher's pet." Jonathan threw a chip at his mate.

Lachlan picked it up and ate it. "What can I say? I'm good at everything." He spoke so dryly; Camille couldn't tell if he was boasting or joking. The others laughed, and she couldn't help sneaking a glance at him, only to find him already looking at her again. She felt herself blushing again and futilely tried to push him from her mind.

Both a jock and good at school? This guy can't be for real.

ON THE DRIVE home, Camille was surprised to find herself yawning.

"Looks like you had a good time," her mother said.

"Yeah, I did. It was nice to meet some people before school tomorrow."

"Your new friends seem nice."

"I think so. They're all so different. Like, it's hard to see what they have in common. I mean, Lachlan and Jonathan have basketball, but aside from that, the only common ground might be that they've known each other all their lives."

"That's how it works sometimes, sweetheart. Those can be some of the strongest friendships, I think." Camille yawned again. "Straight to bed for you," her mother stated as they pulled up into the driveway.

"No arguments here," Camille replied. She leaned over and kissed her mother on the cheek before getting out of the car.

She inspected her reflection in the bathroom mirror, trying to see herself through Lachlan's eyes, wondering if he liked her too. Quickly feeling ridiculous, she pulled a face at herself and left the bathroom, flicking off the light on her way out. A strange hum wafted down the hall toward her, and she paused to listen. Then, smirking at her own paranoia, Camille realised it was her mobile vibrating against her bedside table, and she hurried back to her room to pick it up. Grace had sent her a facetime request, so she accepted it before remembering she still stood there in her pyjamas.

"Hey," Grace whispered, though it sounded forced and fairly loud. "Sorry to call so late. I just wanted to check in with you and see how you found tonight."

"No worries. I was just getting ready for bed," Camille whispered back, wondering why, as there was no way her parents would hear her talking from their bedroom. "I had a really good time. Everyone was really nice."

"Are you sure? You seemed a little unnerved by Lachlan."

Camille smiled. "He's fine. I just wasn't sure how to take him. I mean, he doesn't say a lot."

Grace nodded. "At least not compared to the rest of us. He's just super intense with everything he does. He takes overachiever to the next level. But he's also a really great bloke, once you get to know him."

"Jayne seems keen on him…"

Grace laughed. "Yeah, you picked up on that, did you? She's not exactly the subtle type, our Jayne. She's been in love with him for so long, we tend to not even notice anymore."

"What about Lachlan? Does he notice?"

Grace scrunched up her face. "He doesn't seem to be interested, but that could just be because he's so focused on his schoolwork and his basketball. Who would know?

Lachlan keeps most things pretty close to his chest. Why? Are you keen on him?" She shot Camille an exaggerated wink.

"Hardly!" Camille felt herself flush at the thought. "I only met the guy tonight."

"If you say so," Grace replied, clearly not prepared to let the idea go. "I'll drop it if you show me what your room looks like. I imagine it's brilliant."

"Well, not quite yet. There's still a lot to do." Camille turned the phone around and slowly scanned the room—starting with the four-poster bed, now with a black and silver bedspread and black crepe drapes covered in tiny, starlike specs of silver. Moving the phone toward the windows, she heard Grace gasp. "Holy crap. Those windows are epic!"

Camille smiled and recalled her own reaction to seeing them for the first time, though now the moonlight flowed freely through the clean glass instead of so much dust and dirt.

Camille smiled and recalled her own reaction to seeing them for the first time, though now the moonlight flowed freely through the clean glass instead of so much dust and dirt. She moved the phone around the room—over the deep-green wallpaper with the shimmering silver detail that, in its cleaner state, made Camille think of tiny snail-trails across the grass. Next, she moved quickly past the wardrobe and the doorway, then spun the phone around toward herself.

Grace screeched, and Camille fumbled to keep from dropping the phone. "What?" she asked, panicking. "What is it?"

"The door!" Grace demanded. "Go back to the doorway!"

Camille turned toward the doorway and peered into the dark hall, her heart pounding in her chest. She overheard Grace's father telling her to get off the phone and get to bed. The call terminated, Camille closed the door, and she Camille stared down at the phone in her hand, wondering what the hell had happened. Calling Grace back to clarify might get her new friend in trouble, so Camille plugged in her phone and set it on the bedside table before climbing into bed. As she reached over to turn off the light, her vibrating phone made her jump. Then she read the text from Grace.

'Sorry, can't talk. Got in trouble for making too much noise.'

'What happened?' Camille quickly texted back.

'Some woman was standing right there in the hallway. Scared the piss out of me.'

Camille lowered the phone and looked at her closed bedroom door.

'Was probably Miss McAllister lurking again,' she sent. 'She does that a lot.'

Still, Camille put her phone on the bedside table again and slowly swung her feet off the bed and onto the floor. Determined to catch Miss McAllister in the act, she tiptoed toward the door, careful to avoid the squeaking floorboards. When she reached the door, she grabbed the handle and yanked it open. There was no one there. Her phone vibrated again, and Camille closed the door, walked back to her bed, and read Grace's next message.

'Does Miss McAllister have white hair pulled back into a bun and wear a high, white-lace collar?'

Camille froze, her eyes flying back to the door before flicking towards the closed wardrobe and back to her phone.

'No. No, she doesn't.' Camille couldn't write anything more.

CHAPTER SEVEN

CAMILLE PULLED HER coat tighter against the icy morning, regretting not having taken her father up on the offer to drive her the whole way to school. But she'd wanted to speak to Grace before they got caught up in all the first-day mayhem, worried that she may have driven off her new friend before setting foot through the school gates. She jogged across the road when she saw Grace waiting for her in front of the bookstore. Grace gave her a little wave before quickly shoving her gloved hands back in her pockets.

"Hey," Camille said as she stepped in beside her, smiling with relief.

"Hey. So, who was lurking outside your room last night if it wasn't McAllister?" Grace asked as they walked. "I thought you said they were the only other people in the house. Was it a ghost?"

"Wow. Straight into it!" Camille replied, trying to smile though she wasn't really joking.

"Sorry," Grace said. "I was just thinking about it all night. She kind of freaked me out."

"Freaked you out? How do you think I felt being told there was someone outside my room?"

"I'm sorry. I didn't mean to scare you. It just gave me a shock."

"What exactly did you see?" Camille asked, wanting more clarification even though she knew deep down Grace had seen her mystery woman.

"It's hard to say, exactly. It was so quick. I only really saw the top half of her with the hallway so dark. She just clasped her hands together in front. Really pale against the long black sleeves. Buttons up the front of the dress. At least, I'm assuming it was a dress, with a high collar. Like a white lace or something around the neck. White hair in a bun. I don't even recall much about her face. But she was... glaring at me right through the phone. Like she could actually see me. That's all I saw."

For a long time, neither of them said anything else as they walked.

"So... you've seen her before?" Grace prompted.

Camille nodded. "A few times. Only the first time was really clear. It was my first night at the manor."

"Ugh..." Grace shuddered. "That is so creepy. And totally cool."

"How is it cool?"

"Well, it's like a ghost of LeRoux Manor's past seeking out the modern generation to connect with us. I mean, it's clearly a ghost, right?" Whatever fear Grace had had, it was rapidly replaced by enthusiasm for her theory.

"Yeah, I guess so. She looks so real, though, doesn't she?"

"What did you expect a ghost to look like?" Grace asked.

Camille shrugged, "Honestly, I have no idea. I guess I always thought they'd be more... I don't know. Transparent?"

"Hmm... Who do you think she is?"

"No idea. I haven't seen her in any of the pictures I've found so far."

"Have you had a look in the book you bought yet? There's bound to be something in there."

Camille nodded. "Good idea. I haven't had the chance to have a proper look at it yet. I'll check it out as soon as I get home." They put the topic of the woman on hold as they met Jayne, Jonathan, and Lachlan at the front of the school.

"Ready for your first day?" Jonathan asked as he reached for Grace's bag.

Camille smiled with as much confidence as she could muster. "Sure. Starting senior year in a new school at the wrong time of year, and as the town freak, no less... This is going to be awesome." Her new friends laughed, and Grace reassuringly slipped her arm through Camille's, leading her toward the gate.

"Welcome to senior year, my friends!" Jonathan declared as they entered Woodville High together.

"ARE YOU GOING to tell the others what happened last night?" Camille asked Grace as they left their double period of Advanced English.

"It's not really my place to tell them. I mean, it's your house. Your family history. We don't keep secrets, but I know you just met us. I get it if you need some time to get to know us better before telling everyone. On the other hand, some fresh perspective might be a good thing."

"Hmm..." Camille's parents hadn't believed her when she'd told them. What if her new friends thought she was crazy? But Grace was the one who saw her, she reminded herself.

Grace led her to a table outside where the others were already waiting for them at a picnic table under a beautiful old tree. "How's your first day of school treating you?" Jayne asked, though she eyed Lachlan instead of looking at Camille.

"Pretty good," Camille replied. "Just trying to learn my way around the place."

"What class do you have after lunch?" Grace asked as she sat beside Jonathan. Sitting on the bench opposite her, Camille pulled the folded piece of paper from her pocket and opened it up. "Uh, double history."

"Same as me. We can sit together if you like," Lachlan suggested quietly.

When Camille looked up at him, she caught Jayne's gaze darting frantically between her and Lachlan. "Uh, sure. Thanks." Then she looked away. Something lightly tapped her shoe, and she found Grace staring at her with a raised eyebrow and the slightest hint of a smile. Camille took a deep breath and slipped her timetable back into her pocket. "There's something we thought we should share with you guys..."

"We?" Jayne asked, scowling at Lachlan.

"Me and Grace." She couldn't help but smile as Jayne visibly relaxed.

"Last night after dinner," Grace started, "I Face-Timed Camille…"

"I was showing her around my room, and she… saw someone in the hallway."

"Someone who shouldn't have been there." Both Grace and Camille looked expectantly at the group.

"Wait. What do you mean someone who wasn't supposed to be there?" Jonathan asked. "Do you mean like someone broke in?"

"Not exactly," Camille replied.

"Woah… Are you saying you saw a ghost?" Lachlan leaned forward in his enthusiasm.

"We think so," Camille said. "I didn't see her. I was too busy looking around to show Grace my room. But Grace got a good look."

"She was old-fashioned-looking," Grace explained. "But so vivid. At least from what I could see, which was just from the waist up. I thought there really was someone standing there in the hallway."

"That sounds…" Jayne whispered.

"What did she look like?" Lachlan demanded. "What exactly happened?"

Camille and Grace did their best to recount the brief experience. "I also saw her that vividly my first night in the manor," Camille added. "I'm pretty sure I saw her a few other times. Like in my wardrobe. Sometimes, I think I see her out of the corner of my eye or in a reflection."

"Bloody hell, that's intense," Jonathan stated with a shake of his head.

"I knew there was something paranormal going on in that place," Lachlan added. "Why the wardrobe?"

"I have no idea. Weird, right? My Dad checked it and reckoned there's no way anyone could just disappear in there, but I know what I saw."

"Well, if she's a ghost, then of course she could," Jonathan stated.

"Seems like a pretty random object for a ghost to be attached to," Jayne said, obviously quite eager to participate.

"You're telling me…" Grace replied kindly.

"Have you experienced anything else?" Jonathan asked.

Camille paused, looking down at her hands. "Before I saw her the last time, I had this weird dream. Only it felt so real. I was up in the attic, and I found an old trunk. It was locked, but then out of nowhere, a key skidded across the floor toward me. There was something about the trunk… when I opened it… it felt like déjà vu. Like it belonged to me or something. I know it was only a dream, but I just haven't been able to shake it."

"Have you looked for the trunk?" Grace asked. "Maybe the dream was trying to tell you something."

Camille looked up in surprise. "No, I haven't. I didn't actually think that it might be real."

Grace shrugged. "You never know."

"That would be so cool if it was…" Jonathan added.

"You should document it," Lachlan suggested. "Everything you see and experience. Like a blog or something. It would be awesome."

Camille glanced at him, wondering why he seemed so enthusiastic about her experiences at the manor when he'd barely said two words about anything else.

"That would be pretty cool," Grace agreed. "Part of the blog could focus on trying to work out who the woman is and what she wants. They say ghosts haunt places for a reason, right?"

Camille shrugged. "I guess so." Suddenly, she felt reluctant about all of it. It was one thing to tell her new friends, but did she really want to put it out there for the whole world to see?

"At least have a think about it," Grace said. "You don't have to decide right away." Her smile clearly indicated she loved the idea.

"Yeah, I'll think about it," Camille replied with a small smile, grateful when the boys changed the subject to that afternoon's basketball practise.

"I HEAR WE have a LeRoux in our class!" exclaimed Mr Ostervic as he entered the classroom, dropping his bag on the desk and facing the students. Camille slid down into her seat, feeling the hot flush of mortification rush from her chest up into her face.

"I told you…" Lachlan whispered with a grin.

"Camille LeRoux, raise your hand, please." Mr Ostervic scanned the room, looking for the new face. Camille slowly raised her hand as all eyes turned on her. "Don't worry. I won't do anything embarrassing like make you stand up and introduce yourself. Though I will say it's exciting to have a young LeRoux in our midst."

Camille mustered a small smile as she lowered her hand and cringed in her seat. Lachlan chuckled softly beside her, the unexpected sound a welcome distraction from her embarrassment. It sent a flutter of nerves through her. "Now," Mr Ostervic continued, turning to the whiteboard behind his desk and picking up a marker, "it's the first day of your senior year and the perfect time to give you your major assignment." The glass groaned. Stepping aside, Mr Ostervic revealed the project on the board: 'Family Tree'.

"Is he serious?" Camille whispered to Lachlan, but he didn't respond. He just stared at the board. She noticed his tight grasp on the pen in the palm of his hand, and she frowned with equal parts worry and intrigue.

"I want a comprehensive family tree, starting with your immediate family and working back from there for as far as you can. I appreciate some of you won't be able to travel as far back as others, but I expect your full efforts on this. The project will make up fifty-percent of your final grade." A second groan swept over the classroom, and Mr Ostervic smiled at Camille. "Now, given the enormity of the task, you will work together in pairs. To make it easier for you, the person you're currently sharing a desk with will be your research partner for the duration of the assignment." Camille snuck a sideways glance at Lachlan. Jayne's going to kill me.

CAMILLE FELT FORTUNATE that she hadn't faced a single class without at least one of her new friends alongside her. Yet she couldn't help but feel a little nervous sitting beside Jayne. She wasn't looking forward to telling her she'd been partnered with Lachlan for their history assignment. She'd been friends with the group for five minutes and certainly didn't want to rock the boat.

"We should totally use this time to do a little research on your blog," Jayne whispered conspiratorially.

"I haven't said I'm going to do one yet," Camille replied. She was finding fewer and fewer reasons not to.

Jayne dismissed her protest with a wave of her hand, then typed the words 'LeRoux Manor' into the search engine. Unable to hide her curiosity, Camille leaned over as much as she dared so she could see the results. "This can't be right…" Jayne whispered.

"What?" Camille whispered back, now completely invested.

"There's hardly any hits. An announcement about Mr LeRoux's death, and some generic information about the Manor and when it was built and all that. But that's pretty much it."

"That seems odd. Maybe try a different search," Camille suggested. "What about 'LeRoux family'?"

Jayne typed it in and sighed. "That isn't much better. Nothing interesting at all. No offense."

"None taken," Camille replied, searching the screen. "How about 'murder at LeRoux Manor'? That's bound to pull something up."

"Good idea." Jayne typed quickly, then slumped back in her chair. "You can't be serious..." The search had returned zero hits.

"That's impossible!" Camille explained a little too loudly, garnering herself a pointed look from the teacher. She ducked her head and lowered her voice. "I've seen the newspaper articles. How does the net have nothing about it?"

"That's it," Jayne whispered, her eyes still on the teacher. "Now you have to get the information out there. It's a conspiracy!"

Camille shot her a sideways glance. While she didn't agree with the conspiracy theory — yet — she did think it bizarre to fine no information online. "Okay. I'll do it."

CHAPTER EIGHT

C AMILLE LUGGED THE heavy new book toward the window and laid it before her as she sat cross-legged on the seat. She smiled in satisfaction at the cracking spine when she opened the book. She loved new books.

A gust of wind surged against the window, making the glass rattle slightly. Camille looked out at the manor grounds and the woods beyond. The wind weaved through the trees, swaying the branches left and right as though both taunting and beckoning to her. Forcing herself to turn back to the book, she was tempted to skim through it to look at all the pictures. Then she reminded herself that if she wanted to be well-informed for her blog, she needed to read every word from start to finish. At this rate, aside from what she'd found in the attic and the few pages she had from the library, the book might be her only decent resource on the manor.

Flicking over the two pages of contents, she stopped on the first page laying out the LeRoux family tree. She placed her finger at the top and scrolled down. With a whoop of excitement, she held her finger under the name at the very bottom of the tree, right beneath her parents, who were linked together by a single line indicating their marriage. Camille looked back up at the top of the tree to Caleb LeRoux, married to Cecile Lecuyer. Beneath them was Pierre and Mena. Her eyes widened in surprise as she saw she shared Mena's birthday. As she took another glance down the tree, her smile turned into a frown. Returning to the top for a third time, she slowly scanned each line until she returned to her own name.

Camille leaned back against the cushions and stared out at the woods, as though the answers to her confusion were hidden amongst the trees. According to the family tree, she was the only female descendent of the LeRoux family since Mena. How is that possible? With a sigh, she uncrossed her legs and got up from the seat. She'd have to question her father about it at dinner.

"SO HOW WAS your first day of school?" her mother asked, smiling as she took her place at the table.

"Pretty good, actually. It definitely made a difference already knowing Grace and the others. Turns out I had at least one of them in all my classes."

"That's a stroke of good luck," Her father stated, then filled his mouth with steaming roast beef.

"It's a small school, so probably not that unlikely, really," Camille replied with a shrug.

"My daughter, the optimist." Her mother chuckled.

"I prefer the term realist." Camille smiled and started eating.

"So, what interesting things did you learn?" her father asked, piling his fork up again.

"Dad, it was only the first day…"

"So? There was nothing to learn at all?" He winked at his wife.

Camille rolled her eyes. "Actually, now that you mention it, one of my major assignments for the year is on the family tree. I've found a couple interesting things about that already."

"Do tell." Her father's smile lacked any amusement.

"Well, first, during computer lab, Jayne and I decided to search for information on LeRoux Manor. Nothing came up, aside from just stock-standard location, et cetera. No information about its history, about what happened to Caleb and Mena. Nothing. Don't you think that's weird?"

"Maybe," her mother said. "I mean, don't they say you can find anything on the internet these days if you know how to look for it? Maybe you need to try refining the search."

"I don't think you can get much more specific than 'LeRoux Manor'. You want to know what else is weird?"

"Sure," her parents replied in unison, busying themselves with their meal.

"The book I bought on the manor had our family tree in it—"

"Are we on it?" her mother asked sharply.

"Yes! Which is pretty cool, I have to admit. But that's not what I wanted to tell you. I looked over it, and not only do Mena and I the same birthday, but I'm the only girl born into the family since her."

"That's interesting," her father stated, not looking at either of them. "Clearly, you should have been a boy."

91

"Ha, ha, Dad. You're hilarious. Seriously, though, don't you think that's bizarre? I mean, what are the odds of only two girls being born in two hundred years?"

"Sure, it's unusual," he said, "but genetics is a tricky thing. Some families have a lot more men than women, and vice versa. It doesn't mean anything. That family tree doesn't have all the information. What about the unlisted pregnancies that didn't reach full-term? The girls that could have been born but never were?"

Camille stared at her plate. She didn't want to think she was reading too much into the family tree, but it was hard to ignore her father's logic. Maybe she was letting Grace's enthusiasm for the manor cloud her judgement. "How come the family tree starts with Caleb?" she asked. "He obviously had parents."

"I don't know about his parents, sweetheart," her father said. "But my guess would be that the family tree starts with him because he built the manor. And that's what the book's about, right? Honestly, I've never delved into the history of our family. I prefer to look forward, not back."

"Maybe reading the whole book will answer some of your questions," her mother added gently.

"I hope so," Camille said. "So, can I please be excused? I have some reading to do." Her parents nodded, and she rose from the table headed into the hall. Her mother's voice wafted toward her from the dining room.

"Phillipe, is that why Charles was so against us having a daughter?"

Camille stopped short when she heard the question, straining to hear her father's response.

"Honestly, I don't know. Dad never talked about the family after his falling out with Charles. We were kids when it happened. And Dad wasn't… well, he was never very open about discussing most things. I can't imagine that's the reason Charles was so upset. What a crazy notion, right?"

"Not much crazier than him wanting us to put Camille up for adoption and try again for a boy," her mother said.

"I just find that hard to believe. The whole thing's ridiculous."

There was a pause. "Still, I have to agree with Camille. No girls born to a family in two hundred years? It's definitely strange."

Camille had heard enough; the thought of a connection between her uncle's obscene wishes and the family tree made her sick to her stomach. Taking the stairs two at a time, she promised herself she'd get to the bottom of it. She was halfway down the hall to her room when someone stepped out in front of her and made her jump.

"You really should learn to leave things alone, Miss," Miss McAllister drawled, her stern gaze fixed firmly on Camille.

Camille took a deep breath and collected herself, annoyed that she'd let the old woman surprise her again. "Well you should stop lurking in hallways," she snapped. "It's creepy." Then she moved around the woman, fighting the urge to turn back; she had a feeling

Miss McAllister was staring after her. Instead, Camille closed the bedroom door behind her and waited, listening for movement in the hall. When she was met with nothing but silence, she slowly backed away from the door and went to her place on the window seat. Stretching her legs out in front of her, she set the book in her lap and started with Chapter One.

SHE AWOKE WITH a start and banged her arm into the window. The book went clattering to the ground. Her alarm beeped incessantly, and she reached out with her other arm to turn it off before she realized the alarm wasn't there. She'd fallen asleep on the window seat.

With a frown, Camille swung her sleep-heavy legs over the edge of the seat and stumbled toward her mobile still vibrating and beeping on her bedside table. Once she'd turned it off, she stretched her neck a little, wincing at the stiff soreness there. She couldn't believe she'd fallen asleep at the window; the first day of school must have taken more out of her than she'd thought. Camille smiled, realising it was the first time since moving into the manor that she'd awoken feeling well-rested. She couldn't wait to hear her friends' thoughts on her interesting ancestry.

CHAPTER NINE

Y OU'RE DRIVING ME crazy," Grace exclaimed as they left maths class together. "I can tell you're holding something back!"

"What? How?" Claire laughed. "You've known me for five minutes."

"I can tell, because you have the world's lousiest poker face. You've been fidgeting and staring off into space all day."

"Yeah, I do want to share something, but I think I'm going to wait until lunch hour. Just so I can tell everyone at the same time… I think I need the group's input."

"Oh! I do love a good intrigue!" Grace stated with a dramatic wave of her hand. They weaved through the throng of students on their way to the table under the tree. Jonathan and Lachlan were already there, stuffing their faces as though they hadn't eaten in days.

"Hey," Grace greeted as they approached and took their seats. The boys only grunted in response; their feeding frenzy clearly interrupted. Grace rolled her eyes at Camille as she pulled a container of grapes from her bag and offered a few. Camille smiled, took a couple grapes, but still couldn't look away from the boys' ravenous eating. "I know…" Grace whispered loudly.

"It's like watching a horrid accident. You just can't look away." Camille could only nod.

"You should see how they eat after a big game," Jayne said, taking a seat beside Grace.

Grace let out a disgusted snort. "So true. It's totally disgusting. They're the same after training too."

"So why do you hang out with us then if we're so disgusting?" Jonathan asked, wiping his mouth with the back of his hand.

"Well, because you also happen to be cute," Grace replied.

"Lucky for me, then." Jonathan winked.

Lachlan brushed off his hands and looked up at Camille with a nod of greeting. Camille smiled back, not sure if this was his version of a friendly greeting or his way of reacting to her intrusion on their group.

"So, Camille made a discovery last night..." Grace piped up.

"Uh... okay." Being put on the spot made Camille suddenly nervous. "It's probably not that big a deal, come to think of it."

"Come on. Don't bail on us now," Grace prompted. "Tell us what's on your mind." Clearly, she didn't plan on letting it go.

Camille flicked quick glances at each of them before diving in. "So... you all know — or knew about my Uncle Charles, right?" They nodded. "Well, when I was born, he wanted my parents to put me up for adoption."

"What?" Grace and Jayne exclaimed in shock.

"That's messed up." Jonathan looked at Lachlan, who gave his solemn nod of agreement. "After that, my parents cut all ties with him, and I never met him. I only found this out after we'd already moved here. We're the last living LeRoux's, so the manor was left to my dad. But what's really interesting is that last night, I found a family tree in a book about the manor. If it's accurate, turns out I'm the only girl born into the family since Mena LeRoux."

"The girl who disappeared the same day her father was found murdered, right?" Lachlan asked.

Camille gaped at him. "Uh, yeah. The day the manor opened the property with a huge party."

"Wait, didn't that happen over a hundred years ago?" Jayne asked.

"1817," Lachlan answered. "So, two hundred years ago."

"So, no girls in two hundred years?" Grace asked slowly, as though trying to work out the odds in her head.

"I mean, obviously, most of the men married, so there are women in the family. Just not born into it. Until me, I guess."

"That doesn't even sound possible," Jonathan stated.

"That's exactly what I said," Camille replied. "I mean, it could be nothing, but it just seemed like too much of a coincidence to me."

"I definitely think that's something," Lachlan said. "There has to be more to it." He leaned forward on his arms and gazed intently at Camille. "You're going ahead with the blog, aren't you? This is an epic way to start it." Camille didn't have to look at Jayne to feel the heat of the girl's stare. "Uh… yeah. I will. But I haven't done anything about it yet."

"Let me know when you do." Lachlan tapped his hand on the table. "I want to see what you come up with." Then he turned to Jonathan. "We have maths. You… you coming?"

"Yeah. You know what he's like if we're late," Jonathan replied dryly. He stood from the table and slung his bag over his shoulder.

"Keep us updated," Lachlan called over his shoulder as they walked off.

"We'd better get going to P.E.," Jayne announced, shoving her things into her bag a little too forcefully. Grace gave Camille a small smile, as if to say, 'Ignore it.' The three girls headed together toward the gym.

Lachlan's words played over and over in Camille's mind, despite her best intentions of blocking them out.

"I can't believe your uncle asked your parents to give you up," Grace said softly, shaking her head. "What kind of person does that?" Camille shrugged. "I'm sorry. That's pretty insensitive to keep talking about it, isn't it?" Grace placed a concerned hand on Camille's arm.

"Not at all. Like I said, I'd never met him. Sure, it's not a great feeling, knowing he wanted me out of the family. But my parents never gave it a second's thought. That's all that matters."

The girls finished their walk in silence. When they entered the gym, they went straight to the bleachers to sit down. Grace leaned forward to look at Camille, who sat on the other side of Jayne. "So, are you going ahead with the blog thing, then?"

"I think I need to," Camille said. "Even if it's just for myself. I need answers. I just have absolutely no idea how to set up a blog. Not even a website."

"Jayne's a genius at computers, aren't you?" Grace announced, glancing up at her friend.

"I'm all right." A small smile tugged at Jayne's mouth. "I can set one up for you, at least."

"That would be awesome. Any chance you guys are free after school?"

"I have to work at the bookstore," Grace replied, pursing her lips in disappointment.

"I'm free," Jayne offered. "If you don't mind that it's just us."

"Of course not," Camille said. "That would be brilliant!" That got her the first genuine smile from Jayne since they'd met.

"Hey, you guys could bring your laptops to the bookstore and work from there. That way, I can still be in on the action," Grace suggested.

"You think setting up a blog is action?" Jayne laughed.

"You know what I mean. What do you think?"

"Sounds good," Camille replied. "I'll just need to let my mum know."

"Same here," Jayne agreed. Then the teacher blew his whistle.

CAMILLE STOOD UNDER the steady flow of hot water, smiling as the smell of her green-apple conditioner filled the bathroom. They'd worked for a good couple of hours setting up the website and the blog just the way they wanted it. Jayne had done an amazing job, and Camille was thrilled with the finished result. She'd used a distorted photo of the manor for the homepage and had edited it to include swirling fog and haunting music. The creepy, mysterious feel they'd created was perfect, all without making it look cheesy. Jayne had shown her how to manage it, and while the site was still bare at the moment, Camille looked forward to filling it with all the information she planned—hoped—to uncover. Jayne had even set her with a first task—to enter the LeRoux family tree in its entirety. Of course, she'd said simply taking a photo and uploading it wasn't good enough. It had to be done manually, and that would take a while, but Camille didn't mind. She wanted to familiarise herself with her ancestors, to build connections with the family she'd only known in name.

They couldn't have all been like Uncle Charles.

Turning off the shower, she grabbed her towel, then stepped out into the cool bathroom. Grateful for the slightly warmer bathmat, she shuffled it toward the mirror just to keep her feet off the freezing bathroom floor. When she looked up at the mirror, though, her hand shot out to clutch at the towel rack, and she almost tripped over the bathmat in surprise.

Written into the steamy fog coating the mirror was a name—Caroline. Camille spun around and looked behind her, but the bathroom door was still closed. She glanced back at the mirror, and her mouth dropped open. Every part of her froze as the image of that ghostly woman flooded her mind. She struggled to rationalise.

Think. Think!

Before her shower, there hadn't been anything on the mirror at all. Looking back at the door again, she envisioned Miss McAllister sneaking in to do this. But that couldn't be right. She'd rolled another towel and stuffed it up against the bottom of the door to keep the steam in and the draft out. It was only a little effective, but that towel remained exactly where she'd placed it. No one could have opened the door.

Wrapping herself in the fresh towel, she kicked aside the rolled one on the floor and fled the bathroom. The cold floor no longer bothered her as she dashed to her room. Then she snatched her phone from off the bed and hurried back to the bathroom to take a photo. She stopped so suddenly that she almost slipped and fell. The mirror was wiped clean.

She could only stare at it, unable to move, knowing she'd been gone just for a few seconds. Am I going crazy? Snatching her clothes from the bench, she stormed out of the bathroom. The hall creaked behind her, making Camille jump, and she turned to see Miss McAllister walking away from her down the hall.

"Miss McAllister," Camille called, "were you in the bathroom just now?"

The woman turned slowly, her face as cold and unreadable as the bathroom floor. "No, Miss. I was not."

Camille glared at her, trying to determine if she believed the woman. Someone Miss McAllister's age surely couldn't move faster than her. "Who's Caroline?" Camille asked. Miss McAllister's stony expression fell away, and her already pale skin blanched around her widening eyes. "Who is she?" Camille's pulse raced. She'd gotten an actual response from the woman; this couldn't have just been her imagination after all.

"The past belongs to the past," Miss McAllister said. "Leave well enough alone if you know what's good for you." Then the woman turned on her heel and scurried off down the hall.

Too stunned and confused to move, Camille stared after her until her pounding heart settled a little. Now the cold made her shiver, so she returned to her room and closed the door. She absently threw on her clothes, then climbed onto the bed and opened her book. Turning it to the LeRoux family tree, she meticulously scanned the thing row by row, name by name, looking for a Caroline. When she reached the bottom without having found it, she leaned back against the cushions and frowned at this dead end. There was no Caroline in her family tree. Who the hell is she, then?

Camille grabbed her laptop, opened the browser, and typed in 'Caroline and LeRoux Manor'. It came as no surprise that the search proved less than helpful. Sighing, she picked up the phone and texted Grace.

"You won't believe what's just happened..."

CHAPTER TEN

PLEASE TELL ME you've updated your blog with Grace's sighting and the mirror incident?" Jayne pleaded.

"Without any evidence to post, people will just assume I've made everything up," Camille replied.

"Some people are going to think that whether you have any evidence or not," Grace argued. "You know. Don't believe everything you see and all that. But we know it's real. Besides, isn't the point of the blog anyway? To document everything?" She tore off a piece of her sandwich and popped it into her mouth.

"I'm with Grace," Jonathan agreed around a mouthful of chicken wrap. "Most people just think LeRoux Manor is super creepy, so I doubt anyone would actually be surprised to hear there's a bunch of weird stuff going on there."

"Well, that's awesome..." Camille replied with a rueful smile. "I'll be the blog girl who lives in the creepy manor."

"That's the spirit!" Jonathan exclaimed. Grace gave him a playful nudge in the ribs.

"Have you considered the possibility that you've been looking into the wrong family tree?" Lachlan asked quietly.

Camille frowned at him. "What do you mean?"

"Well, you said Miss Mc Allister definitely reacted to the name Caroline. Her family has lived in the manor for as long as the LeRoux's have. So maybe Caroline isn't related to you. Maybe she's related to the McAllister's." Camille raised her eyebrows in admiration of his theory.

"Boy wonder strikes again!" Jonathon shouted, slapping his mate on the back.

"That's not bad at all," Grace said. "You could be onto something, there."

"Maybe there's something about them back at the manor," Camille suggested, "either in the book or the attic stuff."

"Maybe, yeah. Or, if you want to go to the library and see what we can find, that might help. I'm not working today."

"Definitely," Camille said.

"I can't," Jayne added, dropping her gaze in disappointment. "I have to babysit. Won't be done until after dinner."

"I'm keen," Lachlan offered. The girls looked at him in surprise, but he just kept eating.

"Uh, sure..." Camille said, feeling Jayne's stare burning into her.

"Yeah, I'll leave you lot to the library," Jonathan said. "Not really my thing. But I expect an update if you find anything cool." Grace rolled her eyes at him.

"Same here!" Jayne added, clearly not wanting to be left out.

"What's everyone got for the last two periods?" Jonathan asked.

"IT here," Camille answered while Jayne nodded in confirmation.

"We have bio," Grace told the boys, obviously referring to them and herself.

"What would I do without my personal assistant?" Jonathan grinned and stood from the table.

"I think you'll find you're my assistant." Grace dumped her bag in his hands. He kissed her on the head, then slung her bag over one shoulder while his own hung from the other.

"Cool," Camille said. "We'll meet you out front after school." They waved each other off before walking in separate directions. By the way she stomped next to Camille, Jayne was obviously annoyed she couldn't join them after school. Camille thought it best they walk in silence until she could think of a way to remedy the situation.

They entered the IT classroom, and took their seats, and found a different teacher sitting at the desk. Once everyone was seated, he finally spoke, his bushy grey eyebrows joined in an unfriendly frown. "I'm substituting today. You can have a free work session to work on what you want, but I don't want to see any nonsense or rowdy behaviour."

Jayne and Camille glanced at each other with raised eyebrows. The teacher returned to whatever he was reading, and Camille leaned over toward Jayne. "If you don't have anything you want to work on," she whispered, "would you mind helping me finish off the post for my blog?" Jayne's eyes widened, and she nodded eagerly.

Camille was relieved to find she had to do very little — Jayne was clearly in her element — and watched in awe as her the girl expertly uploaded images and rearranged text.

"Okay, we're ready for a preview to see how it all looks before it goes live."

"Live?" Camille asked.

"As in publish it so everyone else can see it. Aren't you supposed to be the high-tech city girl?" Jayne laughed.

Camille gave her a rueful smile. "Tech I love, so long as it works. It's the how anything works I know nothing about. You, on the other hand, are so good at this stuff."

Jayne gave a nonchalant shrug, but her proud smile gave her away. "I'm okay. Better than most. Who knows? Maybe I'll make a career out of it."

"I really think you should." Camille leaned in for a better look at Jayne's handiwork. The page started with a photo of Camille Jayne had taken from her Facebook page. Beside that was a brief introduction chronicling Camille's move to LeRoux Manor and her interest in finding out the truth about the manor's history. On the next page, Jayne had uploaded the LeRoux family portrait from Camille's phone. Below the photo was the LeRoux family tree Camille had typed up, with a change in the font to better suit the site. The final page detailed Camille's strange experiences in individual journal entries, ensuring they were properly documented while also giving some character to the blog.

"Are you happy with it?" Jayne asked.

"Are you kidding me? I love it. It's awesome. Thank you so much."

"You can do the honours, then." Jayne moved aside.

Camille smiled as she moved the mouse over the 'Publish' button and clicked.

"You remember how to add new posts as we discover more information, right?"

Camille nodded. "I think so. But if I get stuck, I'll let you know." Jayne smiled, and Camille hoped the ice between them had finally thawed, opening the way for them to become friends.

CAMILLE DIDN'T KNOW why she felt a wave of butterflies in her stomach when she saw Lachlan and Grace waiting for her at the school gate. Grace saw her first and waved. Camille returned the gesture before deflecting her gaze to the ground. She felt so awkward under Lachlan's intense stare as she approached. After what felt like an eternity, she finally reached them, feeling the heat in her cheeks and hoping they'd mistake the blush for a chill from the cold air. She made a point of rearranging her scarf for good measure.

"About time, LeRoux," Lachlan said, pushing himself away from leaning against the wall. "We were starting to think you weren't going to show."

"Sorry. I think I accidently took the scenic route from the computer lab."

Grace laughed and hooked her arm through Camille's. "You'll know this place like the back of your hand before you know it." They made their way toward the centre of town, Grace seemingly happy to take over the majority of the talking for the three of them. Camille tried to focus on what she her friend was saying rather than worrying about the fact that Lachlan walked half a step behind them. Finally, Grace led them into the library, and Camille welcomed the warmth.

"Hi, Ms Liddell," she said to the librarian as they walked past the front counter.

"Good afternoon." Ms Liddell offered only the smallest smile as she peered at them over her glasses, her hands resting on the book lying open on the desk. When they reached the first bookshelf, Camille looked back to find the librarian still watching them and fought off the urge to shiver.

"Where did you say all the Woodville stuff was?" Grace asked, and Camille pointed toward the back wall. They went there first, and Grace scanned the shelves. "Wow. Not a lot here, is there?"

"There isn't really a lot to write about aside from the manor," Lachlan started. "Beyond that, we're just like any other small town, I expect." They each grabbed books from the collection and carried them to a table.

"What's the best way to go about this?" Camille asked.

"How about we start by checking contents and indexes for any reference to the McAllister's or any other servants at the manor," Lachlan suggested. So, they each grabbed a book from the small stack and got to work. It wasn't long before they realised their search was going to be more difficult than they thought.

"Can I help you with anything?" Miss Liddell asked. All three of them jumped at her unexpected and silent approach.

"Uh, not sure..." Camille stammered. "We're looking for some specific information but not having much luck."

"What information would that be?"

"We're trying to find more information about the manor staff," Lachlan stated confidently. "We know the McAllister family have worked there since it was first built, so we were hoping to find some kind of family tree or employment records. Do you know if either of those exist?"

Miss Liddell only stared at him in response. He shifted under the intensity of her gaze, then looked at Grace and Camille.

"Uh, Miss Liddell?" Grace asked.

The librarian turned her attention to Grace, as though she hadn't done anything strange, then said, "I'll be right back." The woman turned and walked away; her footsteps soundless on the carpeted floor.

"What was that about?" Camille whispered.

"I have no idea," Lachlan replied, gazing around the library.

Grace frowned. "That was super weird..." Camille nodded.

"I don't really care," Lachlan said with a shrug, "as long as she has something that'll help us. I guess we can put these books away."

It took about ten minutes—enough time for them to wonder if Miss Liddell was actually coming back—for her to reappear. In her hands was a densely packed manila folder, bound together with a piece of string, like an old-fashioned parcel. She placed it on the table between them.

"What's that?" Camille asked.

"Everything I have on the manor that isn't already published. It was donated to the library. From a private collection, so to speak."

"You mean, someone was actually interested enough to research the manor?" Grace asked.

"Something like that," Miss Liddell replied. "A professor was very interested in the history of the manor... I think it was about twenty years ago now. Possibly longer. I was only a library assistant then, but I recall him being quite charming. Some of his theories were a little too fanciful for my liking."

"Fanciful how?" Camille queried.

The raised her eyebrows. "He had a rather distasteful fascination with the paranormal. The man was here all the time, writing up his findings and theories. Then one day, he just stopped coming. Shortly after that, I received this. It was quite the scandal."

"I didn't know a donation to a library was considered a scandal," Grace said with a frown.

Miss Liddell stared at Lachlan again for a moment. "Well, he simply up and vanished. We never saw or heard from him again. I do remember the letter that came with the folder was very strange. Dated a few weeks before he disappeared, yet the package didn't come to us until at least a month after. I suppose none of that really matters now. Everything he researched is in the folder. Please be careful with it." Then she walked away and left them to it.

"Curiouser and curiouser…" Camille whispered.

"At least she came up with the goods." Lachlan pushed the folder toward her. "It's your family's home. You should open it."

Camille gave him a small smile as she placed her hands on the folder. She wasn't sure why, but it felt a lot different than opening a book. This felt more personal. Carefully, she untied the string, and Lachlan and Grace leaned closer. The folder was worn around the edges, and Camille gently opened it to reveal a stack of papers haphazardly thrown together.

"Well, this'll be fun to sort through," Lachlan stated.

Camille exchanged a questioning look with Grace, unsure if he was serious or joking. Then she picked up the first few papers and flipped through them. "Looks like everything's dated, so that's something." She placed the A4 hand-written pages back in the folder. "How about I split this pile into three?"

"Sounds good," Grace replied, and Lachlan nodded. Camille grabbed the first stack and handed them to Grace. The next stack went to Lachlan, leaving Camille with what remained in the folder. Grace glanced quickly through her pile. "At least his handwriting's neat."

"It might be easier if we try to sort everything into chronological order first," Lachlan suggested, reaching for the first pile.

"If you say so." Grace pulled her stack toward her.

Camille took the last stack and marvelled at how a professor could be so disorganised.

They searched through the donated research in silence until Camille lifted a page to reveal a journal, "Hey guys, check this out."

"Awesome," Lachlan exclaimed. "Open it. Maybe it's got the professor's name."

Camille opened the journal and immediately found the legible name written on the first page. "Professor Robert Rivers."

"Woah, what?" Grace stood from her chair and walked around the table to peer over Camille's shoulder.

"What? Camille asked. "Do you know who that is?"

"Uh, that's Lachlan's surname." Both girls looked up at him.

His eyes were wide, and he seemed to have paled even more, if possible.

"Lachlan?" Camille prompted.

He swallowed thickly. "My uncle. I never met him, but I know he was obsessed with the manor. My father was really messed when he disappeared. Mum said he's never been the same since. I guess that's why I've always kind of been so interested in it. But I never imagined finding his work. Or that he'd done so much research on the place." He eyed the journal with a slight scowl.

Camille lowered her gaze. "I'm really sorry to hear that." "Thanks," he said quietly, his eyes still fixed on the journal with an expression Camille thought was part intrigue and part fear.

"Here." She pushed the journal toward him. "You should have it."

Lachlan only nodded in response, reaching out for the journal and pulling it toward him. He sat there for a moment, one hand on the cover while the fingers of his other hand tapped on the table. Camille and Grace exchanged a quick look, and Camille wondered whether this had been such a good idea after all. Finally, Lachlan opened the journal and ran his fingers over his uncle's name. "How about we leave the journal for last and look through these papers for anything on the McAllister's?" he suggested, closing the journal and pushing it to the side.

"Uh, sure. Whatever you want to do," Camille replied, taking a quick look at where the journal sat, all the more intrigued to learn of its contents. Instead, the three of them focused on their individual piles of paper.

It was a slow process; everything was hand-written and at times hard to read. It seemed if the professor was particularly excited about something, his handwriting became almost unreadable. Yet Camille found herself enjoying the process of reading and deciphering, trying to pull anything relevant from the professor's thoughts. Despite the less-than-ideal way they'd come into possession of the professor's work, she felt herself forming a connection to her new home and its past.

"I found it," Grace cried, then ducked her head when she seemed to remember where they were. "I almost gave up, but this has to be it." Lachlan and Camille moved closer and huddled around Grace for a better look. It wasn't set out like the LeRoux family tree in her book; it was a page of dates with entries beside each, and it was the exact information they'd been after.

THE MCNALLY FAMILY TREE

YEAR	NAME	NOTES
1807	Anne McNally	McNally family comes under the employ of LeRoux family.
1817	Anne McNally	McNally family move with the LeRoux family into the new manor. Year of Mena's disappearance and Caleb's murder.
1827	Anne McNally & Dougal McFarland	Marry
?	Catherine (McNally?)	Possible cousin to Anne McNally
1829	Watson McFarland	Born
1849	Watson McFarland & Caroline Felding	Marry
1850	Sybil McFarland	Born
1874	Alice McFarland	Child adopted by Caroline
1877	Sybil McFarland & Alaric Stafford	Marry

1880	Mary Stafford	Born
1910	Mary Stafford & Malcolm McAllister	Marry
1911	Thomas McAllister	Born
1940	Thomas McAllister & Lucy Grey	Marry
1942	Robert McAllister Margaret McAllister	Born – Twins

"Look," Lachlan said, pointing at the page. "Here's the McAllister's down the bottom, born in 1942."

"And there's Caroline." Camille pointed to the entry higher up on the page. "1849. Watson McFarland married Caroline Felding."

"Woah, 1849... So she married into the McAllister family, then," Lachlan stated.

"Looks like it." Camille's enthusiasm faltered for a moment when she spotted another name on the list. She pointed to the line for 1817, the year the manor was completed and the LeRoux family tragedy unfolded.

"He's listed Catherine—cousin of Anne McNally?"

"So?" Lachlan shook his head. "Anne was the first in the family to work at the manor. Maybe he just didn't know if Catherine had worked there too."

"She did," Camille replied.

"How do you know?" Grace asked.

"It sounds silly, but the dream I had… the one in the attic with the trunk… I heard a little girl say the name Catherine. It can't be a coincidence." Grace and Lachlan just stared at the page.

"I think there might be more going on here than we thought." Lachlan leaned back in his chair and lifted his arms for a stretch.

"Let's focus on one mystery at a time," Grace suggested. "So, Caroline married into the McAllister family tree in 1849, but it doesn't say how old she was. A year later they had a daughter. Sybil."

"What about this?" Lachlan pointed to a side note. "Caroline adopted a girl in 1874 named Alice."

"That seems odd…" Grace murmured. "By then, Sybil would have been twenty-four and Caroline would've had to at least be in her forties."

"Yeah, this is weird," Camille added. "Maybe Alice was a relation or an orphan she took in?"

"Maybe," Lachlan replied. "We might find the paperwork for it in all this."

After another exhaustive scan through the pages, they found nothing.

"Does Woodville have a registry?" Camille asked. "I'll search the net when I get home."

"Worth a shot," Grace agreed. They turned to Lachlan, who seemed to have been too busy flicking through his uncle's journal to hear them.

"Lachlan?" Grace nudged him.

"Huh? Oh, sorry. I just saw the last entry."

"Don't you know you're not supposed to skip to the end?" Grace joked.

"What does it say?" Camille asked, shifting to the edge of her seat, her hands clasped on her lap beneath the table. She couldn't say why, but she suddenly felt anxious.

Lachlan gave her a quick glance before returning to the page. "Well, it says that in order to further his research, he'd convinced Charles LeRoux to allow him a limited stay at the manor. On the condition Charles could review his research before it left the house."

"That's it? That's the last entry?" Camille asked.

He nodded. "So we know he went to the manor and was never seen again."

"We don't know for sure that was the last time he was seen," Grace cut in. "Just because it says that was his plan doesn't mean it happened. There's no proof he was at the manor. He could have left town before then."

"Look at all of this, then," Lachlan replied, scowling. "Do you really think he'd just leave it all behind and pass up on the opportunity to his obsession right there, at the source?"

Camille and Grace exchanged glances. "All I'm saying," Grace said, "is we don't know for sure that he was there. At least, not yet. We have to keep an open mind."

"If you say so. I have to go." He didn't look up at either of them as he stood and placed the journal in his bag, "I'll see you tomorrow." It was almost as an afterthought before he turned and walked away.

"What the hell?" Camille whispered.

"I know, right?" Grace answered in equally hushed tones before returning to her pile of notes.

Camille stared after Lachlan, wanting to go after him but not wanting to face the questions and innuendos from Grace if she did.

"I didn't know much about your uncle," Grace said. "I don't think anyone did. Which makes me wonder why a man as private as Charles LeRoux would agree to let someone stay at the manor. Especially someone with the intent of investigating."

Camille leaned back in her chair. "You're right. It doesn't make much sense. Maybe he knew there was something going on there and wanted to get answers."

"Maybe we'll never know," Grace added. "Did you find anything in his stuff that indicated he'd seen the old woman?"

"Honestly, I have no idea. I haven't been over that side of the manor yet. I'm not even sure my parents have. I think they're leaving it until last, out of respect. All I know is that he kept to a small part of the manor and left the rest of it untouched."

"Might be worth having a look," Grace suggested, and Camille nodded silently. A chill ran up her spine.

CHAPTER ELEVEN

CAMILLE KNEW SHE was dreaming. She could tell straight away, because the scene before her had a strange ochre hue to it. She watched a woman walking across the manor grounds. Everything was lush and perfectly manicured, and even in her dream-state, Camille longed to run barefoot along the grass. Forcing herself to focus, she turned her attention to the woman again. She was a fair distance away, yet Camille could see enough to know she was a woman roughly in her forties and couldn't possibly be a LeRoux—not with the way she dressed. Her skirt was long and black, coming up high to the waist, and her white shirt billowed at the shoulders before cinching at the wrists. The apron hanging from her neck and fastened around her waist, though, gave away her station.

The woman didn't appear to be in any great hurry. In fact, she seemed sad, melancholy, her gaze focused on the ground directly in front of her rather than ahead. Camille wanted to reach out to her, to ask her if she was okay, but she apparently was only meant to watch in this dream. The woman placed her hands on her belly, and a quick sob escaped her, filled with yearning and pain. As though sensing someone watching her, she picked up the pace and, to Camille's surprise, headed straight toward the woods. She only went in far enough so as to hide herself from anyone on the grounds, then she sat on a moss-covered log. The woman buried her face in her apron and wept. Camille felt the woman's distress and longed to comfort her for reasons she couldn't understand.

She blinked, suddenly feeling dizzy as she found herself farther in the woods, the crying woman only just visible ahead through the trees. She felt her hand squeezed, and she looked down to find a little girl at her side. Her hair so blonde it was almost white, tied halfway up with a dirty lavender ribbon and peppered with twigs and leaves. She looked like she'd taken quite the tumble through the woods. The girl stared straight ahead, and together, they walked toward the woman.

The sound of their feet crunching on the leaves and sticks below them made the woman look up and wipe frantically at her face, as though she feared discovery. The woman peered through the trees, trying to see who approached. Camille paused and without looking down released the child's hand before gently urging her forward. Still hidden behind the trees, she saw the woman's expression morph into surprise and joy.

"Why, hello, there," the woman said. "My, you are a mess, aren't you? Why don't you come over here so I can get a better look at you?" The woman held out her hands, but the girl stopped. The woman lowered her hands and smiled. "Well, now. You look like you have been through quite the ordeal. Where are your parents?"

"I don't know," the little girl whispered. "Daddy didn't want me anymore. He thinks I'm naughty."

The woman's smile faltered in a shadow of disbelief, but she quickly dismissed it, and the smile returned. "Well, he's clearly mistaken. Why don't you come on up to the house with me, and we'll get you fixed up?"

"Has everyone gone home now? I hate crowds. Adults are so boring."

The woman looked down at her, scowling a little in confusion. "There are no guests at the manor at present, if that's what you mean. Just the family and servants, as it is most of the time. What's your name?"

The girl turned and studied the treetops towering overhead. "I don't remember," she said firmly, yet her lower lip trembled.

"Now, now." The woman stood, stepped forward, and placing her hands gently and tentatively on the girl's arms. "It's all right. I'm sure it will come to you once you've had the chance to rest awhile. For now, how about I call you... Alice? I do love that name."

The girl lowered her gaze from the trees and looked at the woman. "Me too." She stepped forward and wrapped her arms around the woman's legs in a tight hug. Then Camille finally saw the little girl in full—a child in a party dress that was now torn and dirty. Camille's heart pounded as the familiarity dawned on her, and she had to remind herself it was just a dream. This wasn't real.

"Now that we have that settled, my name is Caroline," the woman said. "Let's go back to the manor, get you into a nice hot bath, and put some food in your belly." She held out her hand, waiting for Alice to reach for it in her own time, and led them back toward the house. Alice turned and looked over her shoulder, as though she knew Camille was watching. A devious smile tugged at the corners of her mouth, and those crocodile tears quickly dried up, forgotten.

CAMILLE AWOKE WITH a start, trying to catch her breath as she fumbled for the bedside lamp. Light flooded the room, and she leaned back against the pillows, panting. The girl in her dream was Mena. She'd looked over the girl's portrait enough times that she would recognise her anywhere. Only in the portrait, Mena's hair was auburn, like her own. And according the family tree, Mena should've been in her fifties when Caroline was an adult, not a child. She remembered the photo she'd found of Mena with the staff, thinking it was even less likely now that this second girl was just a look-alike.

What the hell is going on? Camille suddenly felt overwhelmed with fatigue, and even though she wanted to get up and write down every detail of her dream, she felt herself being pulled back into slumber.

A chill passed over her, and Camille reached for the covers. When her fingers failed to find them, she felt herself rousing into wakefulness with an uncomfortable hardness under her head and shoulders. She opened her eyes and blinked. This wasn't her bedroom.

Clambering to her feet, Camille shrugged off the lingering sleepiness like a heavy coat. Faint light barely filtered through the small windows at the far end of the room, and she realised she was in the attic. She frowned down at her feet, as though they could somehow reveal to her a plausible explanation as to how she'd gotten here. Then she saw the envelope beneath her toes and bent to pick it up. It looked old, and perhaps it had once been white but was now brown and felt thin and frail in her hands. Walking toward the window, she hoped for a better look, but the dawn light wasn't strong enough yet for her to read the faded writing on the front. The large writing in the centre and the smaller script in the upper left corner made her think it was most likely a letter. Keeping her eyes fixed firmly on the floor, Camille hurried toward to the staircase. Ignoring her racing heartbeat, she descended the dark stairs as quickly as she dared.

ONCE SHE WAS back in her room with the door closed firmly behind her, Camille flicked on her bedside lamp and sat on the edge of the bed. The exposed sheets felt cold under her pyjamas, and she wondered how long she'd been up in the attic. The thought brought with it a wave of panic at the uncertainty, but she shook it off and held the letter under the light. It was addressed to a Mrs Jane Fielding. Camille carefully opened the envelope, which had been unsealed long ago, and withdrew the folded paper. With even greater care, she unfolded the pages, worried they'd fall apart at her touch. The letter was handwritten in perfect, slanting cursive and dated 1st November, 1874.

My Dearest Mother,

The most extraordinary occurrence befell me yesterday. My prayers have been answered, though not in the way I had expected, and I had to get word to you as soon as I could.

As you know, I have been melancholy for quite some time now, as it has pained me greatly that I've not been able to conceive another child. You've told me time and again over the years to hold true to myself – that we all have a path to walk, whether or not we understand the journey.

Well, Mother, I think my path was revealed to me yesterday. I was having one of my melancholy spells upon reflecting that our most beloved Sybil would be a mother herself in a few short years, gods permitting (things seem to be quite serious between her and her beau, Aleric). I became overwhelmed at the memories of her infant years, so overcome with longing to be blessed with another but also knowing that I would soon be past my time to conceive. I needed fresh air, and I ventured out for a walk in the woods while the LeRoux family were out, all the while wondering what my purpose was now that Sybil was grown. Surely it wasn't my sole purpose to serve the LeRoux family – not that they haven't been good to me, but what would I do if I had no other purpose? Did I have to wait to become a grandmother before I felt happiness again?

No word of a lie, Mother, I had sat in the woods for not ten minutes when a young girl appeared in front of me. Oh, my! She looked such a fright. I hate to think how long she'd wandered the woods on her own and with no idea how close she was to the manor.

I call her Alice, for she is still quite confused and unable to recall her own name or what happened to her. The lack of food and water wouldn't help, I suspect. When I asked her of her parents, she said she knew not of them, only that her father didn't want her anymore because he thought her naughty. The poor child! I know what you're thinking, and of course, I notified the authorities after first speaking with Mistress LeRoux. She has been so kindly toward me. She said Alice can stay with me until we determine her kin. I do not know how, but I am certain she has none. Alice can't be any older than five or six years old, yet there is a wisdom in her far beyond her years. I know in my heart that she was sent to me – or more so, that we were sent to each other.

Sybil is quite put out and thinks I am being ridiculous, as though I endeavoured to take in some stray animal found in the wild, not some defenceless child. Watson, on the other hand, simply said it warmed his heart to see me smile again.

Oh, Mother, I really do hope the child may stay with me. I know you are too unwell to travel, but I do hope the two of you can meet.

Your loving daughter,
Caroline x

Camille lowered the letter and stared blankly across the room. It took her a moment to make sense of all the questions flooding her mind. The girl in her dream, the girl in the letter – Alice – was Mena. She had no doubt about it. The look that Mena had shot her in that dream made Camille think the girl knew exactly who she was – and where she was. But she was too smart, even at her young age, to say otherwise.

You're being ridiculous! It was just a dream.

And yet, Camille just couldn't shake the feeling that it was so much more than that. It felt more like a memory, but how could she explain why Mena's hair was now white? Or why she was still the same age as the day she'd vanished from LeRoux Manor almost sixty years prior? Camille massaged her aching temples, wondering how on earth she was going to explain the latest experience to her friends. When she looked down again at the letter resting on the bed beside her, she seriously considered keeping it to herself. All she knew for certain was that, for whatever reason, she' d been given a glimpse into the past—and she honestly didn't know if she could expect anyone to believe her. It was all happening for a reason, she knew, but for the first time, she questioned how much she really wanted to know what that reason was.

CHAPTER TWELVE

"HEY," GRACE SAID, nudging Camille in the side. "Earth to Camille."

Camille looked up from where she'd been doodling in her workbook as the teacher cleared his throat in annoyance. She waited for him to return to his lecture before she turned to Grace beside her. "Sorry. I'm not really with it today."

"Is everything okay? Did something else happen?" Grace whispered.

Camille paused, pretending to watch for the teacher while she pondered what to say. "No. I'm just tired. I haven't gotten a lot of sleep lately." Grace nodded, but her frown made it clear she didn't buy the excuse for a second. Camille returned to her doodling, the steady drone of the teacher's voice drifting through one ear and out the other. All she could think about was the letter and the look on Mena's face in the dream as Caroline led her back to the manor. None of it made any sense. It was impossible. Yet she couldn't shake the feeling that it was more than just a dream. Still, Camille needed more answers before she discussed it with the others.

As the teacher turned to write on the board, Grace leaned over and whispered, "I'm working tonight at the bookstore. Yes, even Woodville does late-night shopping on Thursdays. Lachlan's keen to hang out and do some research. Do you want to come? Jayne will be keen too, and Jonathan will come if the rest of us are."

Camille nodded. "Sure. I have to go home first, but I'll get Mum or Dad to drop me over. What time?"

Grace shrugged. "I start at four and won't finish 'til nine, so whenever you want is fine. Just bring your laptop and the professor's research."

"Okay. I'll get there when I can."

CAMILLE RAN HER fingers over the edge of Caroline's letter. If her friends found out she'd kept it from them, she knew they'd be annoyed, especially after how invested they all were. With a final look, she folded up the letter and gently eased it back into the envelope. Feeling guilty about keeping the secret, it seemed that showing them the letter would be a fair compromise, but she would decide whether to tell them about the dream when the time came.

Camille stifled a yawn, walked toward the wardrobe, and opened the doors. She pulled a pair of jeans off the shelf and threw them over her shoulder, then reached out for a shirt off the rack and stopped. A black item she didn't recognise caught her eye, hanging slightly over the edge of the bottom shelf. Bending down, she grabbed the item and held it out. It was the shawl.

This can't be happening...

There was no denying the shawl was the same one from her dream; it even had the same holes in the delicate knit. Her hands trembled as she examined it, and she couldn't stop shaking her head. The instant sound of her phone ringing on the bedside table startled her enough that she dropped the shawl. For a minute, she stared at it on the floor, as though it were a snake intent on biting her, and her phone kept ringing. Sidling away from the shawl, worried it would somehow disappear if she took her eyes off it, she hurried toward her bedside table and picked up the phone. Jayne was calling her. Camille fought the urge to ignore the call and finally answered it.

"Hey," she said. "What's up?"

"Uh, Camille? Have I got you at a bad time?"

Camille sighed. "No. Sorry, Jayne. I'm just in a rush trying to get ready."

"That's why I rang. My mum has a shift at the hospital tonight and won't be able to pick me up later. We're wondering, if we pick you up and take you to the bookstore, would your parents mind dropping me home?"

"Definitely. That should be fine."

"Awesome. I'd be right miffed if I had to miss out."

Camille smiled at the relief in Jayne's voice. "What time do you think you'll be here? I'll wait out the front for you."

"Give us about half an hour?"

"No worries. I'll see you soon." Camille hung up and slipped the phone into her bag on the bed. Then she slung the bag over her shoulders and with slow steps walked back to the shawl lying on the floor. She gingerly picked it up, wanting to tell herself it was just a coincidence, but after her dream the night before, she was starting to believe more in the theory that somehow, she was being shown these things for a reason. She didn't know whether it was the house, or the old woman, or both — or neither. But they'd only lived in the house a week and the ... activity ... was increasing with each day.

Now, even as she held the shawl, she felt her initial fear fading away. Something comforting about the worn piece of clothing tugged at her, like an early-childhood memory she couldn't quite reach but still made her feel safe. She folded up the shawl and gently tucked it into her bag.

Camille closed the bedroom door firmly behind her and walked down the hall toward the staircase. Halfway there, she heard her parents' laughter wafting through the house, and she followed the sound until she found them in one of the ground-floor rooms.

"Oh, hello, sweetheart. How was your day?" her father asked, approaching her to place a kiss on her forehead

"Okay."

"Just okay?"

Camille walked past him and went to kiss her mother, who sat on a long, antique lounge. "Yeah, nothing interesting to report. But we're all meeting at the bookstore to work on our assignments together."

"Why the bookstore?" her father asked, sitting on the second identical lounge.

"Grace has to work tonight, so this way, she can still pitch in."

"I wonder how much actual paid work she'll get in with you lot there distracting her," her mother said with a smile.

Camille rolled her eyes. "It'll be fine, Mum. We won't distract her while she's busy. At least this way, she can still sort of join in."

"I'm just stirring," her mother reassured her. "Do you need a lift into town?"

"No thanks. Jayne's mum is picking me up. But would it be okay if we took her home?"

"Not a problem." Her mother covered a yawn.

"I can pick them up, hon," Camille's father said. "You look exhausted."

"I am, but it's an accomplished exhausted. I can't believe how nicely this room is cleaning up."

"It looks great, Mum." Camille scanned the room. Between the two antique lounges with their teal upholstery sat a long, wooden coffee table gleaming with fresh polish and topped with a runner that matched the lounges. On one side of the room were three of the same beautiful windows Camille had in her own room, only these didn't have window seats. On the right-hand wall stood an impressive fireplace, with lion heads carved into the stone on either side of the mantle. It too looked freshly scrubbed and cleaned. Spanning the length of the left wall was a floor-to-ceiling bookshelf crammed with books.

"What do you call this room?" she asked.

"I think they originally would have called this a sitting room or a parlour," her mother replied.

"It's very lavish."

"Well, the LeRoux's were a very well-to-do family, despite their tragedy."

"Is it okay if I take a look at these books when I have some time?" Camille asked, longing to drop everything and look at them now. "Of course. I suppose you could say they're yours now."

"Awesome. Okay, well, I told Jayne I would meet them out the front. I'll text you later when we're ready to be picked up, if that's okay, Dad?"

"Sure. Go enjoy your research with your friends."

Camille said good night and walked out into the foyer. She caught Miss McAllister; half hidden as she peered out through the staircase balustrade. They stared at each other for a few moments, and Camille fought the urge to say something horrible. Instead, she declared, "Good evening to you, Miss McAllister!" The woman scowled and retreated. Shaking her head, Camille continued to the front door and opened it just as the car lights rose up over the bend toward the house.

In the car, Camille politely answered Jayne's mother's friendly questions, but her mind kept returning to the letter and the shawl. Stifling a yawn, she realised how tired she was, as though with each passing day in the house, more of her energy seeped from her. The idea popped into her mind that it almost felt like the house was taking her energy from her on purpose—that in order to show her the past, it needed energy from the present. She knew if she voiced this concern, either her friends or her family would tell her she was being silly, that she just needed sleep. She tried to convince herself of the same.

As they walked into the bookstore, Grace waved at them from behind the counter where she was serving customers. Then she gestured toward where Jonathan and Lachlan lounged on a set of couches, a tray of coffees on the table before them.

"Took you girls long enough," Jonathan joked as Camille and Jeyne joined them. "I was almost tempted to crack open a book."

"Impatient to get started on more research, then?" Jayne asked with a raised eyebrow.

Jonathan scoffed. "Hardly. But I can't leave you lot to your own devices while you have all the fun without me, can I?"

"Did you bring your laptop?" Lachlan asked Camille. She nodded, frustrated by the warmth she felt rushing into her cheeks under his gaze.

"It's surprisingly busy in here tonight," Jonathan said. "I think I heard that one of the staff called in sick. But Grace has a break in half an hour, so she said to just get started without her and she'll pop over when she can."

Camille reached into her bag to pull out her laptop, her hand momentarily resting on the shawl before she quickly brushed it aside. She would need to wait for Grace to join them if she was going to say anything at all.

As she stifled another yawn, Jonathan pushed the tray of coffees towards them. "You look like you could use this."

Camille gave him a grateful smile. "Thanks."

"Oh, is one of those for me too?" Grace asked as she approached. Then she perched on the edge of the couch beside Jonathan.

"Of course!" He passed a coffee up to her before wrapping his arm around her.

"Jonathan said you didn't have a break for another half an hour," Jayne stated.

"I switched when I saw you guys arrive. I wanted the goss before you got started."

"So do I," Jonathan stated. "Lachlan told me you found some of his uncle's research."

"Since when are you interested in research?" Jayne scoffed, then took a sip of her coffee.

"Historically... never. But this is different. This is someone we know. Well, we don't technically know him. You know what I mean. What are the odds that Lachlan's uncle disappearing is connected to the manor?"

"I'm at least keen to try getting to the bottom of it," Lachlan replied. "It can't be a coincidence. Don't laugh... but I think this is all happening for a reason."

"And what reason would that be?" Jonathan asked.

Lachlan shrugged under everyone's gaze. "I don't know, but there has to be one. With everything Camille's going through on top of my uncle's research... it just can't be for nothing."

"You're quiet," Grace said to Camille. Camille nodded but still hesitated with her hand on her bag, inadvertently drawing the group's attention to it.

"What is it?" Lachlan asked. He stood from the couch and approached Camille's lounge to hover right there beside her. Camille lifted her bag onto her lap to make room for Lachlan to sit next to her, trying to ignore Jeyne's sharp breath.

"Is everything okay?" Grace prompted.

Camille looked at her hands. "Things have… escalated a little."

"Escalated?" Lachlan asked.

Camille looked up at Grace and Jonathan, feeling the intensity of Lachlan and Jayne's stares on either side of her. Taking a deep breath, she said, "You're going to think I've lost the plot this time for real. But a few things have happened at home the past couple days."

"So, tell us," Lachlan said. "We won't think you've lost it. Whatever it is, it's clearly worrying you." He lifted his arm and rested it on the back of the chair. Camille had to force herself to ignore the sensation of his arm resting against her hair.

"Well, it started with a dream I had last night. Only it wasn't a dream so much as it was a glimpse into the past. At least, that's how it felt. Like it was something that had actually happened."

"What was it about?" Jayne asked.

"Caroline. I didn't know it was her at first. Not until she introduced herself."

"She introduced herself to you?" Jonathan asked.

"No, not exactly. It was like I was there, watching. And then I was a part of it." Camille explained the rest of the dream to them, emphasising the impression she'd had that Mena had known exactly who she was and had lied about it.

"Okay…" Jonathan said. "So that's intense. But it's just a dream, right? Like you said, when Caroline worked at the manor, Mena would have been in her fifties. If she'd even been alive. Not still a little girl."

"I know. It doesn't make any sense. But then... well, there's something else." Camille paused, and everyone stared at her in anticipation. "Okay, when I woke up from the dream, I wasn't in my bed. I was lying on the floor in the attic."

"What? Like you sleep-walked?" Grace asked.

Camille shrugged. "I guess, if I got all the way up there. The weirdest part is that when I woke up, I found this right next to me." She reached into the bag and withdrew the letter.

"Woah, that looks old..." Jayne exclaimed. "Can I read it?"

Camille nodded and handed it over. Then she grabbed her coffee from the table and focused on that instead. Jayne read it aloud, then handed it back to Camille. The group sat in silence for a few seconds until Jonathan let out a low whistle.

Lachlan took a deep breath. "So—"

"Wait," Camille interrupted, deciding to bite the bullet. "There's one more thing. You guys remember the other dream I had, right? The one about the trunk and the mirror and the shawl?" They nodded, urging her to continue. "Well, just before Jayne came to pick me up, I found this in my wardrobe. It was just folded neatly on the bottom shelf." Reaching into her bag, she gently pulled out the shawl and held it out for everyone to see.

"That's pretty much exactly as you described it," Grace said, standing from the arm of the couch for a closer look. "Even the holes"

"This is crazy..." Jayne reached out to touch the frail fabric.

"You're sure it wasn't there before?" Lachlan asked.

Camille nodded. "The wardrobe was definitely empty when we moved in."

"Damn. I have to get back to work so Kylie can go on break," Grace said. "I'll come back over when I can." She gave Jonathan a quick kiss and Camille a reassuring albeit sympathetic smile before dashing off toward the register.

"I believe you," Lachlan stated, looking Camille straight in the eye. "I know something's going on in that house."

"We believe you too, don't we, Jonathan?" Jayne jumped in, though Camille couldn't help but wonder how much of the girl's support was genuine and how much was just following Lachlan's lead.

"I don't know what's going on," Jonathan said. "But I have to admit there's a tonne of weird stuff, and it seems to be centred around you."

Camille gave them a grateful smile. "Good, because I'm starting to feel like I'm going crazy."

"Who wouldn't?" Jonathan said.

"Have you said anything to your parents?" Jayne asked.

"Not really. When I told them about seeing the old woman, they just put it down to an overactive imagination and a nightmare. I haven't bothered telling them anything else."

"Well, you have us," Jayne said. "Now we just have to work out what the hell's happening."

"I think it's clear someone or something is trying to tell you something," Lachlan said. "It's like the longer you live in the house, the more these things are revealed. Like you're somehow giving it the energy it needs to show you."

"That's exactly what I was thinking on the way over," Camille said.

"It sounds like something out of a damn horror movie," Jonathan added.

"Do you have a better theory?" Lachlan demanded, sounding on the verge of anger.

Jonathan sighed and leaned back into the couch, looking up at the ceiling. "Honestly, no. I just can't believe we're legitimately sitting here talking about messages from the past and ghosts and haunted manors."

"Tell me about it," Camille said. "I don't think this is what my parents meant when they said moving halfway around the world would be an adventure."

"Regardless of the how, what's the why?" Lachlan said. "What have we learned?"

While Camille now understood where Lachlan's intensity about the manor came from, she found it confusing. She couldn't tell if his interest was solely in the manor, or whether his enthusiasm might have been fuelled a little more by how he felt about her. Telling herself she was being silly; Camille forced that last possibility as far back in her mind as she could and focused on what Lachlan was saying rather than what he might or might not have been thinking.

When no one answered his question, Lachlan dove in himself. "Okay, so we know Caroline's important to the manor. She took Mena in as a daughter, only she didn't know it was Mena. So, she called her Alice instead. Mena should have been in her fifties, not a little girl. Obviously, we can't explain that bit now, so let's just leave it as it is."

"Then we have the shawl from her dream. Right here in front of us. It's obviously connected to Camille, but we have no idea how or why. Most likely, it's something else to do with the manor..." Jayne said.

"Don't forget the old woman," Camille added. "She's been finding me from the moment we moved in."

"It's got to be because you're a LeRoux," Jayne added. "That seems pretty obvious."

"And your similarities with Mena," Lachlan said. "She was the last girl born into the family until you, Camille." Jayne nodded. "It's true," Jayne added, and Camille wondered if she'd only imagined the other girl's reluctance. "You fit right in, like you've always lived here."

"See?" Grace said. "That settles it. A birthday sleepover at the manor. That is, as long as your parents won't mind."

"I'm sure we can find the room." Camille joked.

"This is going to be so awesome!" Jayne squealed.

"What's awesome?" Jonathan asked as he and Lachlan approached the table. "Aside from our basketball skills, that is."

"We're going to have a sleepover at the manor tomorrow night!" said Jayne. "Well, maybe." She glanced at Camille. "If Camille's parent's say it's okay."

"Can we come?" Lachlan asked and took the only spare seat available, which was next to Jayne.

"Oh… so you've always dreamed of going to a girl's sleepover party?" Camille joked.

Lachlan laughed in a rare expression of amusement, and she found herself revelling in the way his blue eyes brightened above his smile. "Not exactly. Though I have always wanted to spend a night in the manor."

"I'd have to agree with that." Jonathan casually draped an arm around Grace's shoulders and picked up a menu with the other, eyeing it hungrily. "I'm pretty sure no one in this town can say they've spent time in the creepy LeRoux Manor."

"Except me," Camille said.

Jonathan winked at her. "Exactly. So why should you have all the fun?"

"Yeah, you're part of the group now, remember?" Grace added with a laugh.

"Okay, okay!" Camille raised her hands in mock defence. "I'm not sure how my parents would feel about boys staying the night… But it's not like we don't have spare rooms."

"We'd be on our best behaviour," Lachlan declared, raising his hand as if swearing a vow.

Camille smiled at him and pulled her phone out of her bag to text her mother. "All I can do is ask, right?" She figured it was a question better asked via text, so her parents could think about it, rather than saying no on a call if she put them on the spot.

"Hi, guys. Congrats on the win." Amy skated up to their table. "What can I get for you?" The girls placed their orders, and Camille's mouth fell open when the boys listed their seemingly endless order.

Seeing her expression, Jayne laughed. "We did warn you."

Camille smiled back at her, relieved that Jayne didn't seem to resent her for Lachlan's attention. At least, the thought of spending the night at the manor seemed to cool whatever resentment was there.

THE GUYS WERE in high spirits after their basketball win, and Camille found herself enjoying the carefree evening full of wisecracks and laughter. It was a nice change from conversations focusing on the manor and its mysteries. For the first time since moving to Woodville, she felt like a normal, carefree teen surrounded by good friends. She realised she now liked the thought of calling this new place her home; it almost felt like she'd always lived here.

Before she'd had the chance to fully register the thought, she felt suddenly lightheaded and queasy. She lowered a half-eaten chip to her plate and stared down at the table, forcing herself to take long, slow breaths.

"Camille? Are you okay?" Jayne asked from the opposite side of the table.

Camille didn't trust herself to speak for fear she might be sick. All she could manage was a slight shake of her head.

"Let her out." Grace nudged Jonathan out of the booth, half a burger still in his hand. "I'll get you some cold water," Grace offered as Camille slid out of the booth.

A loud rushing flooded Camille's ears, and a wave of nausea hit her like a kick in the stomach. Tumbling to the ground, she clamped her hands over her ears, but that only seemed to make the noise louder. She had a brief thought of being trapped beneath crashing waves, the water swirling and whirling over her head. It felt as if she were about to fall through the floor itself. Squeezing her eyes shut, she willed the sensation to pass. At first, her friends' voices sounded far away, but one by one, she heard their cries of concern.

Grace and Lachlan helped her to her feet, and the rushing stopped. The sudden silence left Camille stunned and completely confused.

"What happened?" Lachlan asked.

Camille looked at each of them in turn. "I have no idea."

"Are you okay?" Grace asked.

Camille swallowed and nodded. "Just... feeling a bit lightheaded."

"Here, sit back down." Lachlan moved out of the way so she could sit on the edge of the booth.

Then Amy skated toward them. "Is everything okay?"

"Yeah, we're fine," Camille replied before anyone had a chance to say otherwise. Amy gave them a dubious look but took off again for her other customers.

"Are you sure you're okay?" Grace whispered.

"Yeah, I feel fine now. Just tired. That was so weird."

"Maybe eating something will help."

Camille gave her friend a small smile and absently picked up another chip.

CHAPTER THIRTEEN

D O YOU REALLY think you're up to having all your friends over?" Allysha asked.

Camille avoided meeting her mother's concerned stare, focusing instead on getting the pillowcase on the pillow, like it was the most technical task she'd ever attempted. "Yeah, I'm fine, Mum. Just tired. It's been a big week."

"Exactly my point. Which is why I think the sleepover would be better suited for another time."

"Really, Mum. I'm actually looking forward to it. I think it'll be good for me. And it's my first birthday in Woodville. Kinda depressing if I didn't do something, don't you think? I feel lucky that I made friends already and that they want to hang out with me on my birthday."

Allysha sighed. "Fine. But I meant what I said about the boys sleeping in this room and not with you girls. And I want the doors left open."

Camille couldn't help but smile. "Oh, come on, Mum. You don't have to worry. Trust me."

Camille set up some cushions around the floor of her room and placed all the research she'd collected in the centre. Sure, it wasn't the most exciting way to spend her birthday weekend, but she hoped her friends would be happy to pick up the research where they'd left off. She couldn't explain it to herself, let alone to the group, but she felt like she was running out of time.

Looking around her room, she tried to pick out a few ways to make it more comfortable for them all. There were a number of rooms in the manor better suited to studying, but she wanted to keep what she could away from her parents. She wasn't sure how they'd react, especially after the way they'd taken her reports of seeing the old woman. It was enough for them to know she and her friends were working on an assignment. As for Miss McAllister ... well, Camille certainly didn't want her to know what they were up to.

As though on cue, a loud creak came from the doorway. Camille jumped and turned to see Miss McAllister at the door.

"Your mother asked me to let you know your friends are here," the woman stated, her distaste more than evident in her sneer. Camille could only stare at her while her heartrate slowed to normalcy again. Miss McAllister glanced quickly down at Camille's research setup, then gazed at Camille again before a deep frown further darkened her expression. Without another word, the woman turned and walked away.

Camille waited a few moments to be sure Miss McAllister was gone before she left the room. Then she shut her bedroom door behind her.

"This place is insane!" Jonathan exclaimed, gazing around the foyer. "I mean that in a good way."

"Well, then, I thank you, Jonathan," Allysha replied. "I think."

Camille descended the stairs two at a time. "Hey guys."

"This is seriously awesome," Jayne said.

"Yeah, I can't believe we're actually standing inside the manor." Lachlan looked around as though trying to drink in every minor detail.

"Well, I'm just glad you're all so happy to see me." Camille laughed.

"Of course we are!" Grace replied, giving her a hug.

"I'll leave you lot to it," Allysha said. "And I'll bring up some afternoon tea a bit later. Camille, I'll let you advise your friends of the house rules."

Camille rolled her eyes. "Yes, Mum... Come on, guys, My room's up here." She led them up the stairs, smiling at their hushed exclamations as they pointed at one thing or another. "It's not a church, guys. You can talk normally." Ushering them along, she realised she'd already taken her new home for granted; the things her friends pointed out to each other had either gone unnoticed or had received no more from her than a passing thought.

She stopped at the room next to her own and opened the door to reveal two single beds freshly made up. "This is where you guys are sleeping."

"Sweet." Jonathan stepped inside and flopped down on the closest bed. "Ah... this is the life."

"Don't even think about it." Grace stormed in, grabbed his arms, and forced him to sit up. "You're not here to sleep."

"I thought this was sleepover..." Reluctantly, he got to his feet.

"A common misconception about sleepovers..." Grace corrected, and the girls laughed.

"You're a cruel mistress." Jonathan wrapped his arms around his girlfriend and yawned. Lachlan walked to the bed beside the windows and set down his bag. When he opened it, he removed the journal, then looked up at Camille. He was clearly as eager to get stuck in their research again as she was.

Camille led them on to her room and pushed open the door.

"Holy crap. This has got to be the largest bedroom I think I've ever seen." Jayne slowly wandered around the room.

"Yeah, your phone did not do this room any justice," Grace said, taking it all in with wide eyes.

"I'm just glad to see it's not all pink and girly." Lachlan grimaced, looking entirely uncomfortable with his hands shoved into the pockets of his jeans.

"Hardly," Camille said, suddenly hyper-aware that he was in her bedroom. What the hell had she been thinking? "Uh, well, everything I have is there on the floor, including the albums I found in the attic."

"Neat." Lachlan took a seat on a cushion next to where Jonathan was already making himself comfortable. When the girls joined them, Lachlan added the journal to the pile.

"Find anything interesting in that journal yet?" Jayne asked.

He shook his head. "Not really. I mean, it's interesting, but none of its really that helpful."

"I don't feel like we're really getting anywhere." Grace sighed.

"So, what do we actually have so far?" Jayne asked as she attempted a semi-discreet shift of her cushion toward Lachlan's.

"Well, we know Caroline is an ancestor of the McAllister's and that she adopted a girl who looks exactly like Mena," Camille said. "But we don't know how that's possible or why Miss McAllister looked so horrified when I mentioned Caroline's name... after I saw it in the mirror."

"And we now know that my uncle was researching the manor before he vanished," Lachlan added.

"Does your family actually know what happened to him?" Jonathan asked.

Lachlan sighed. "All I know is what Mum and Dad told me. That he just vanished one day, and they never heard from him again. He stopped calling, stopped coming over. When they reported it to the police, nobody really took it seriously. They asked some questions and a had a little look around, but if they found anything, they seemed to write it off as my uncle just wanting to escape a small town."

"They didn't even pick up that he was interested in this place?" Camille asked.

"Why would they? Your great-uncle was a recluse, and everyone thought he was... unwell. I don't think the police ever had a reason to come looking much closer. They wouldn't have gone to the library like we did. We know that was the last time anyone saw or heard from him. When he delivered his research to Ms Liddell

"What else do we know?" Grace asked.

"Maybe not that we know for certain," Jayne said. "Anybody still think there might be a connection between the manor grounds and some kind of ancient paganism?"

"I still definitely want to look into that some more," Camille said, and the others nodded. "And then… we also know I've seen the old woman. More than once. I've had those weird dreams, and then I found the letter. And the shawl."

"I do have an idea," Lachlan said, looking up at Camille. "But you can totally say no."

"What is it?"

"Maybe we can check out your great-uncle's rooms? You said he only lived in a small section of the manor, right? We might find something there."

Camille chewed on her bottom lip as her friends cast her expectant glances. "I'm actually all for it," she said. "I just need to work out what to say if we run into my parents."

"We could just say we wanted a tour of the manor," Jayne suggested. "It's not like we'd be lying."

Camille nodded. "Well, I think I know where he was staying…"

"You mean you haven't been in there yet?" Lachlan asked. "How's that even possible?"

She shrugged. "I guess it just felt wrong to go have a look. Not just because he's dead. I mean, he didn't want me in the family in the first place, you know?"

"That's totally fair," Grace added. "We don't have to if you don't want to."

"No, we should. It makes sense to at least have a look, especially if we find more about the manor or the old woman."

"Does this mean I have to get up?" Jonathan asked from his nest of cushions on the floor. Grace rolled her eyes, and he groaned like an old man as he pushed himself to his feet.

"Lead the way," Lachlan said softly, and Camille gave him a small smile before taking them out of her bedroom and into the hallway.

Camille led them past the staircase and across to the opposite side of the manor. She cast a quick glance at the door to the attic, picking up the pace as she led her friends past that, too. Jayne sneezed as they weaved through the west wing, still untouched—at least to Camille's knowledge. She ignored her friends' tourist-like fascination, instead focusing her thoughts on how her great-uncle had lived in such conditions. Everything looked coated in dust, and the strong, musty smell made her certain a window hadn't been cracked in well over a decade. She really hoped she wouldn't have to help her parents clean it out. A nervous anxiety spread through her the closer they got to her great-uncle's quarters. She had no idea why she felt that way, but if it wasn't for her friends, she would have turned around and gone right back to her room.

"I think this is it through here," she announced, her voice hushed. Then she turned the bronze door handle and slowly opened the door, cringing as it creaked on its hinges. Camille hesitated, really not wanting to step inside, but then she felt Grace's hand on her back. The girl peered eagerly over Camille's shoulder, and with a deep breath, Camille walked into the room. The flurry of nerves in her stomach intensified with every step.

They found themselves in a sitting room with a large lounge turned away from the window and hidden away beneath thick drapes. Beside the lounge was a matching armchair, a plaid rug draped across the arm. A book lay face-down beside a pair of tortoiseshell glasses on a small, rectangular coffee table, as though her great-uncle might return at any minute and continue where he left off. Slightly to the side and behind the armchair was a trolley packed with books, which Camille assumed had been brought up from the library. She walked across the thick burgundy carpet, the dust from her movements tickling her nose.

"Look." Lachlan pointed to the small fireplace behind the chairs. Above it hung a white sheet clearly covering something hanging there on the wall. With feigned bravery, Camille walked toward it and pulled down the sheet, sneezing at the thick puff of dust. When she lifted her head again with watery eyes, she found a large mirror there over the mantle, with a decorative, gold-filigree frame. The glass had been shattered at some point but remained in place.

"So... he accidently broke a mirror and decided to cover it up?" Jayne asked as she moved around the room.

"Maybe..." Camille studied the bare mantlepiece, which prompted her to take another look around the room. "It's all so... impersonal. No photos, no keepsakes, nothing. If it wasn't for the rug and his book and glasses, you'd never know anyone lived here."

"My guess is that's exactly how he liked it," Lachlan said as he picked up the book on the table. "Through the Looking Glass. Seems like an odd choice for an old man."

"Don't knock the classics," Grace added. When walked toward him and took the book from his hands, gently opening the cover. "Oh, wow! This is a first edition." Then she placed the book back on the table and turned her attention to the book cart.

Camille walked to the far wall, where a small, modest door stood ajar in the centre. She tried to peer through but couldn't see a thing. She swallowed thickly; her previous bravado evaporated.

"Here, let me," Lachlan whispered in her ear. A pleasant shiver ran down her neck. He reached around her and gently pushed open the door to reveal her great-uncle's bedroom — large but as dark as the sitting room, with the drapes firmly shut over the windows. The enormous, wooden four-poster bed was raised on a small platform with three steps all the way around it. On the far side, the thick, decorative curtains hung from the bed's posters, sealing it off from the world. Only the side facing the door had been drawn back and secured with a tasselled cord. Lachlan strode to the far side of the room, where more sheets hung over something facing the bed. He yanked the sheets down, having the foresight to cover his nose and mouth beforehand. Beneath the sheet was a wardrobe as large as the one in Camille's room, though the wood was more of a mahogany than the near-black of her own. This one, though, had a mirror on the front of each door — both of them shattered.

"Okay, so clearly your great-uncle broke these, right?" Lachlan asked.

"Looks like it. It was only him and the McAllister's living here."

"Woah, more smashed mirrors?" Jonathan exclaimed as he walked into the room, closely followed by Jayne and Grace.

"It smells funny in here." Jayne scrunched her nose in distaste as they all hovered around the wardrobe.

Camille stared at her fractured reflections in the glass, and a wave of panic swept over her. Turning on her heel, she stormed out of the bedroom, through the sitting room, and out into the hall.

"Camille!" Grace called right before she grabbed Camille by the arm. "Are you okay? What happened?"

"Nothing." Camille tried to catch her breath and shove the rising waters of panic back down. "I just started to feel a bit claustrophobic and needed some air."

Grace nodded with a frown of concern as the others joined them.

"I don't think there was anything in there at all that could help us," Jayne stated.

"Yeah," Lachlan said. "If anything, it's just led to more questions."

"You mean like why are all his mirrors broken?" Jonathan asked, half-joking.

"That would be it." Lachlan turned to Camille, placed his hand on her shoulder, and looked at her intently.

"Are you okay?" She could only nod, not trusting herself to speak, feeling paranoid that they could all see the effect he had on her. He gave her a small smile and released her. "Do you think it's worth asking Miss McAllister about the mirrors?"

Camille shook her head. "I'm sure she'll just tell me to mind my own business or keep my nose out of where it's not wanted or some other platitude."

"She really doesn't like you very much, does she?" Jonathan asked with delayed observation.

Camille found herself laughing in spite of it. "No, I don't think she does. She's watched me like a hawk ever since we moved here. It's like I'm a naughty child she's got to watch in case I touch something I'm not supposed to and break it."

"Have you considered the possibility that maybe the opposite it true?" Grace frowned, though her eyes glinted with enthusiasm for her developing theory.

"What opposite?" Lachlan asked as Camille just waited for the answer.

"Well, what if the reason Miss McAllister has watched you closely is more to do with her trying to protect you?"

"Huh?" Camille squinted in disbelief.

"Think about it. You said she watches you like a hawk. But what if it's in a protective way and not in animosity? We know she's lived here her whole life. If anything's going on in the manor, I'm sure she's well aware of it. You said the McAllister's only maintained your great-uncle's living quarters while he was alive, right? So, she would know about the mirrors. She was probably the one who covered them up for him in the first place."

"So, what are you saying?" Lachlan asked slowly, processing the theory himself.

"Maybe Miss McAllister is trying to protect Camille from whatever's going on in this place. From the old woman. From whatever made Camille's great-uncle smash the mirrors. From... everything."

Camille looked back towards her great-uncle's rooms. "But why? It doesn't make any sense. My great-uncle didn't want me in the family, so why should she care if I'm in some kind of danger or not?"

Grace shrugged. "I honestly haven't thought that far into it. I just think it's an angle we should consider."

"If she wants to protect me, why doesn't she say something to me beyond cryptic warnings?" Camille asked.

"Maybe it's not that black-and-white?" Jayne offered with wide, eager eyes. Jonathan absently wrapped his arms around Grace's waist.

"You could be right," Lachlan said, and Jayne beamed. "Maybe she thinks if she was more direct, you'd think she was crazy. Or at best eccentric take her seriously and would just do the exact opposite of what she's warned you against."

Camille chewed on her lower lip as she mulled it over. He had a way of making it sound plausible, and yet she couldn't seem to give the theory any weight. "Maybe," she finally said, not wanting to discuss it any further. "But that still doesn't lead us any closer to the answers we really need. We already know she won't tell us anything."

Lachlan sighed. "Back to the books, then?"

She nodded and led them back through the house toward her room, unable to clear Grace's theory from her mind.

CHAPTER FOURTEEN

S O, WHAT DO you want me to start with?" Jonathan asked.

Camille opened the folder and separated the notes that had already been sorted by day from what hadn't. She handed the unsorted pile to Jonathan. "If you could start by putting these in chronological order, that would be great."

"I think I can manage that." He took the pile from her.

"Lachlan, if you want to keep reading through the journal, see if anything jumps out?" He nodded and reclaimed the journal from the pile.

"I'd love to go through the old albums from the attic," Jayne offered, and with a smile, Camille shoved the box toward her.

"The sorted notes or the huge book?" Camille asked Grace.

"The book for me, please."

Camille grabbed the pile of notes and eyed her window seat as she made herself comfortable on the cushions. She figured it probably wasn't fair to sit up there while her friends were all on the floor.

It didn't take long before she was submerged in the mystery of the manor, poring over one page after another. She rubbed her eyes, already sore from reading, and she looked up. The room had darkened a surprising amount without their notice, thanks to the storm clouds approaching the manor grounds. Camille got to her feet and had a quick stretch, barely garnering a reaction from her friends, and went to turn on the lights.

"Check this out," Lachlan said, and Camille hurried back to their circle. He held the journal open to show them the same symbol as the basketball uniforms drawn across the full length of the page.

"What does our school logo have to do with the manor?" Jonathan asked.

"It must mean something." Grace held up the book she was reading and showed them a close-up photo of the weathervane from atop the manor. There was no mistaking it was the same symbol.

"So, it's not just some cool design someone came up with for our school," Jonathan half-joked.

"Doesn't look like it," Lachlan replied dryly. "The journal says it's the combination of two symbols. The first is the lemniscate. The mathematical symbol for infinity. The second one, where the snake head comes from, is uroboros. Wholeness and infinity."

They sat in silence, looking at each other.

"Okay, am I missing something?" Jonathan asked. "It seems totally weird, but I have no idea what this actually means." He sighed in frustration. Camille shrugged. "Neither do I, but it's not a coincidence. I'd bet on that much. Does the journal say anything else about it?"

Lachlan scanned the next few pages. "Not a great deal, but it says that the combination of the two symbols was extremely powerful and rare. He'd found two other references to it. One where it was carved into a large standing stone at Dover, facing out to sea. The other was in France, engraved on a stone plaque at Calais, which he believed was facing the direction of the other."

"Okay, this is just getting weirder," Grace stated.

"Well, we know the LeRoux's came from France," Camille said, "so we have the connection between the two countries. As for the symbol found on a standing stone, I think it's safe to assume it was there a long time before Caleb LeRoux and his family came over."

"I think they're connected, though," Grace added.

"This is interesting." Lachlan pointed at the journal. "It looks like when the manor was built, the LeRoux's owned the whole of Woodville. Not just the manor land."

"That's probably not that unusual for back then," Grace said, "but it explains why the LeRoux's have always been a big deal."

"True." Lachlan nodded. "But it proves the link between the family and Woodville existed way before the manor."

"And it says here," Grace announced, pushing the heavy book into the centre of the group, "Caleb LeRoux and his family were living in this house before and during the manor's construction. That house now makes up part of the high school."

"Does it say how long they lived there before the manor was built?" Camille asked. Grace shook her head. A huge clap of thunder sounded, and they all jumped. "Bloody hell." Camille turned and looked out the window with wide eyes at the dark afternoon.

"So, I think it's probably bad timing, but I found something creepy," Jayne stated.

"Cool! What is it?" Jonathan asked.

"There was a thin notebook at the bottom of the album box, and it's filled with old newspaper clippings about mysterious animal mutilations and local pets going missing from around Woodville."

"Ew," Grace replied. "When was that from?"

Jayne flicked back to the start of the notebook. "Looks like the first article is from 1874. But what's really weird is there's a child's drawings all over it." She held it up for them to see, slowly turning the pages. The faded drawings covered the pages in an array of colours — rainbows, flowers, and animals.

"The drawings are around the articles," Lachlan added. "Pretty safe to assume they were done after they'd been stuck into the book, right?"

"Oh, gross." Jayne clapped a hand over her mouth. "Do you think it was a child killing the animals?"

"No way," Jonathan said, his voice heavy with disgust. "I bet the kid just came across the book and used it to colour in after the fact."

"Wait a second." Camille scrambled for the McAllister Family Tree. "1874. That was the year Mena — Alice — arrived at the manor and was taken in by Caroline." The group stared at each other in silence, the recent findings hanging over them as heavily as the rapidly approaching storm. "What else do the articles say?" Camille asked Jayne, realising she'd asked it barely over a whisper; she wasn't sure she really wanted to know the answer.

They waited as Jayne flipped through the articles. "Well, in 1877, a whole lot of animal bones were found in the woods that border the manor. They launched an investigation and apparently found old human bones arranged in what they believed to be a 'ritualistic nature'."

"Anything else?" Camille asked, only half listening. While Jayne read out the articles' highlights, Camille experienced the strangest combination of déjà vu and not feeling wholly present, as though she weren't really there with her friends in her bedroom. She'd never felt anything like it, and though it passed quickly, it left her unnerved and anxious. "Sorry, what was that?" she asked.

Jayne looked up at her briefly before rereading the article. "It says no one was charged, and the and the investigation quickly wrapped up. The LeRoux family had the woods' heritage listed and included them as part of the estate, making them private property."

"That's not half suspicious…" Jonathan scoffed.

"Hmm…" Camille frowned. "Why do I feel like it had to be Mena? I mean Alice. Or whatever we're calling her."

"That's just wrong," Jonathan declared with a scowl. "She was just a little girl then. It couldn't have been her."

Another clap of thunder crashed outside. Then the clouds opened, and heavy rain pummelled the windows. The ferocity with which the raindrops hit the glass panes made Camille think of tiny fists beating against them in protest, trying to make her and her friends stop what they were doing.

Lachlan's next words pulled her away from the image. "My uncle wrote that the LeRoux's' wealth grew static after Caleb's passing. They didn't have any significant financial growth after that, like all their money just... stopped coming in. Then in 1874, it all came flooding back again."

"That's weird, right?" Jonathan asked.

"Well, again, that's the same year that Alice was adopted by Caroline and the animal problems started," Camille said. "I'd say that's more than weird."

"You're still convinced Alice is actually Mena?" Lachlan asked.

Camille nodded. "I know it sounds crazy and makes no logical sense. I know if Mena was alive in 1874, she should have at least been in her fifties, not still six years old. But I know it's her. I mean, just look at the pictures. You can't deny it."

Her statement was punctuated by another thunderous crack from the storm, making them all jump. They stared at each other in momentary surprise before Jonathan chuckled. "Talk about creating an atmosphere..." Camille opened her mouth to respond but was silenced by the bedroom light flickering overhead.

"Uh... how likely is it that this place loses power if this storm keeps up?" Jayne asked nervously, staring up at the ceiling light.

"I have no idea," Camille said. "This is the first storm we've had here. But I'm sure it's be fine. If it makes you feel better, I'll go ask my parents where they keep the flashlights." Jayne gave her a relieved smile.

"I'll come with you," Lachlan stated, and the Jayne's smile disappeared just as quickly.

Camille tried to avoid looking at her as she got to her feet. The room lit up in a brilliant flash of lightning, shortly followed by another booming roar of thunder shuddering through the house.

"We'll be right back," Camille reassured them, then she and Lachlan stepped out of the circle. As soon as they did, the room shook around them. Camille tried to keep her balance as she stared at Lachlan in surprise; his expression mirrored her own as the shaking intensified. "Is this normal for your storms here?" she yelled over the noise. Lachlan shook his head as he reached out for her hand. As soon as their fingers touched, they were hurled apart by a sudden, unseen force that sent them both sliding across the wooden floor in opposite directions. Jayne screeched, she and Grace grabbed a hold of Jonathan, and the three of them huddled together, looking back and forth between Lachlan and Camille.

Lachlan pushed himself to his feet and strode resolutely toward Camille. He held out his hand again. She hesitated for a moment before reaching up for him. This time, he grasped her hand tightly, and the subsequent thunderclap roared so loudly, it sounded like it came from within the room. Then he pulled her to her feet and pressed her against him. She didn't have time to register their closeness as the lamp flew off the bedside table, hurtling toward them and shattering at their feet.

"What the hell is going on?" Lachlan yelled. Camille couldn't reply but looked to where her friends huddled together on the floor. She gestured for them to stay where they were, then stepped away from Lachlan with his hand in hers. Before they could move any farther, the floor shifted violently. She lost her balance and tumbled to the floor, almost pulling Lachlan down with her and crying out at the bite of broken glass piercing her skin.

Lachlan lunged toward her and almost fell himself. "Are you okay?" he asked, helping her to her feet as they braced themselves against each other to keep their footing. Camille looked up into his eyes and suddenly felt oblivious to the mayhem surrounding them — and the filthy stare Jayne shot her way. Swallowing thickly, she nodded, not trusting herself to speak. There was a final clap of thunder, sounding weakened as it ebbed away, and Lachlan and Camille gazed at each other.

"Camille, you're bleeding!" Jayne cried out, and Lachlan stepped back to get a better look.

He swore under his breath and lifted her hand to reveal the jagged cuts running down the length of her arm. It made her wince. He Lachlan stared at her intently, as though trying to determine what caused the pain.

"Her leg," Grace declared, pointing.

Camille's eyes widened when she looked down to see it for herself. She could only see blood seeping through her shirt at her ribs, but from the outside of her thigh protruded a slim shard of glass from the shattered lamp. Reaching down, she made to pull it out, but Lachlan grabbed her wrist and moved it away.

"I don't think you should do that. At least not until we have a first-aid kit or something. We don't know how deep it is."

Camille nodded "So we'll add first-aid kit to the list with the torches, then?"

"I don't think you should be going anywhere —"

"It will be way quicker for me to go than for me to try giving any of you directions through this place."

"I'm not keen on the idea," Jonathan offered, "but I think she has a point." Another clap of thunder shook the windows. They all stared nervously around the room, waiting for the next crazy thing to happen. When it didn't, they relaxed just enough to return to the task at hand.

"Maybe we should all go together?" Jayne offered.

"Probably best if you lot stay here," Lachlan replied. "In case that earthquake or whatever it was kicks up again. It's a lot safer in here than wandering around the manor." Jayne didn't reply, staring at Camille's hand still in Lachlan's. Camille let go of him and took a step to the side.

"Uh, you all saw that lamp, didn't you?" Grace asked. "And you want us to stay here?"

Camille looked from Grace to Lachlan, uncertain what to do. "I just don't want anyone getting hurt."

"Hey, I think the storm's passing," Lachlan said as a large clap of thunder rattled the room again.

"Yeah, it sounds like it…" Jayne replied.

"Did that not sound a little less fierce?" he asked with a shrug.

"Look, guys. Maybe they're right," Grace said. "This is freaky, but at least in here, we can see the four walls, and I'm pretty sure there's nothing else that can smash. They're just leaving for a few minutes."

Jayne stared at her with wide eyes. "Grace—"

"We're all a little scared," Grace continued. "How about we push Camille's bed against the wall? If the three of us sit there and waited with all these cushions, wouldn't that make you feel better?"

Jayne sighed and shakily got to her feet, her eyes on Lachlan as she feigned instability, but his attention was already back on Camille.

"Do you really think you're up for this?"

Camille nodded. "It's not far, and these look worse than they are. I promise."

"Okay. Let's get this over and done with, then."

As another bout of thunder shook the room, the lights flickered off. Jayne and Grace screamed before the lights turned back on, pulsing as though threatening to turn off again at any minute.

Lachlan offered his arm, and Camille leaned on it for support. "Let's go."

"Be careful," Grace said. "And hurry back."

CHAPTER FIFTEEN

L ACHLAN LED THEM back to the staircase, and Camille was more than happy to let him take the lead. Another deafening roar of thunder rattled the walls, and without thinking, she stopped and gripped his arm tightly. He looked down at her, then gently removed her hand. Camille felt herself flush with embarrassment just before Lachlan slid his fingers between hers and led them down the stairs. She grabbed his arm with her other hand, partly for support and partly because she just liked touching him.

They took it slower than she would have liked, but Camille had underestimated how much it would hurt to walk down the stairs. When they reached the sitting room, she reluctantly released Lachlan's hand. Her parents sat together on the long lounge under the warm glow of the free-standing Tiffany lamp beside them. Her mother's head rested in her father's lap; her face hidden from view behind the book she was reading. Her father had his headphones in to watch something on his tablet. He smiled at whatever it was, then looked up and saw them standing there. The smile slowly slipped away, and he pulled his headphones out of his ears. "What is it, Camille?"

Allysha lowered her book, and upon seeing her daughter's expression, she quickly sat up. "Camille? Lachlan? Is everything okay?"

Camille glanced at Lachlan, who also seemed to notice the immaculate state of the room, but he said nothing. "Wow, this room must be built like a bunker I can't even hear the thunder in here." she said, half to Lachlan and half to her parents.

"What are you talking about, honey?" Allysha swung her legs off the couch to sit fully upright beside her husband.

"The storm. Actually, it felt more like an earthquake. Or both. Just now. My whole room was shaking. It broke my lamp, and I hurt my…" Camille glanced down at her arm. There were no cuts. She pulled her shirt out away from her body to find it clean, and the leg that had filled her with such pain only moments before was now glass-free. She looked up at Lachlan and found his mouth agape and his eyes as wide as hers.

Her parents exchanged a glance before turning back to them. "I think if there'd been an earthquake," her father said, "we would know about it, sweetheart. I'd say it's more likely the house is just a little unsteady in the storm. That thunder's right overhead. Sure, the manor's big, but it's still going to shake a little."

Lachlan stepped forward as if to say something in Camille's defence, but she grabbed his arm and gave it a little tug. "You're probably right. I guess this place still creeps me out a bit."

"That's understandable." Allysha stood from the couch. "It'll take more than a week or two to get used to,

I'm sure. I think it's a good time for a cup of tea. Would you like me to bring you guys up anything?"

"Uh, no thanks, Mum. I thought we'd just grab some torches or something, though, if that's okay. Jayne's worried about losing power in the storm, and it's freaking her out."

"Not a problem at all," her mother said. "We have plenty. Your father made sure of that." Allysha walked past her daughter and gave Camille's shoulder a comforting squeeze. "Come with me into the kitchen."

Camille looked at her father, who winked at her before replacing his headphones and returning his attention to the tablet show. She exchanged a quick glance with Lachlan, then turned and followed her mother.

Loaded up with both torches and candles—and a strict reminder on the safety of said candles—Camille and Lachlan silently weaved their way back through the manor.

"Okay, seriously, what the hell just happened? You were injured. I saw it," Lachlan hissed.

"Your guess is as good as mine."

He shook his head but continued in silence until they got to the foot of the stairs. "Do you really think it was just the storm making your room shake like that?" he asked.

"No way. That definitely felt like an earthquake to me. I've never felt the floor move under me in a storm. Then again, I've lived in Woodville for five minutes. Maybe that's just how intense the storms are here, and

I'm just blowing it out of proportion. What do you think?" Camille stared at her feet as they started slowly up the stairs.

"I've lived here all my life, and I've never seen anything like that. It's odd, and you'll think I'm mental, but it kind of feels like the house — or the estate or whatever — was trying to make us stop."

Camille risked a quick look up at him. "Stop our research?"

Lachlan nodded. "And stop... you know. Us getting closer." Camille pressed her lips together to hide the smile as he coyly ducked his head and cleared his throat, lengthening his stride.

"I know what you mean, though" Camille stated, changing the subject. "If we were anywhere else, I'd be calling the whole thing crazy and would just forget about it. But I already know there's way more going on here than we thought. Jayne's gonna flip though if we tell her the earthquake apparently only happened in my room..."

"Maybe we shouldn't say anything. I mean, you're right, and it won't just be Jayne that flips. She'll definitely be the most vocal about it. Until we can work out what's going on, maybe we just don't tell them."

"I don't think they'll be worried that much about an earthquake when they see that all the blood and the cuts on me are suddenly gone."

Lachlan stopped and grabbed her arm. "Are you sure you're really okay?"

Camille lifted her shirt high enough to reveal the side of her ribcage. "Like nothing happened."

He reached out and gently rubbed his thumb over her skin. "Good as new…" Herr face flushed at his touch, and she let her shirt fall back down. Lachlan cleared his throat. "There's no lying to them, but there's no explanation, either."

"Awesome." They continued up the stairs.

Camille smiled ruefully, sneaking another glance at him before quickly turning away. "Bloody hell!" She almost tripped over the next step when she found Miss McAllister standing at the top of the staircase, watching them. Lachlan swore beside her as he dropped a torch and quickly fumbled to pick it up.

About to say something smart, Camille quickly thought better of it when she saw the old woman's expression. Gone was her usual sneer of distaste, replaced by a deep frown darkening her eyes. That frown didn't carry the usual disapproval, either. This time, it looked like both concern and fear.

"What's going on?" Camille asked. The woman said nothing. Lachlan had regained his composure beside her and stared up at Miss McAllister.

"Do you know what happened in my room just now? What happened to me?" Camille asked, moving up a step as though approaching a startled animal. Miss McAllister opened her mouth slightly, glanced at Lachlan, and closed it again. Camille's eyes flickered toward him before settling on Miss McAllister one more time. "You do know something, don't you?"

Miss McAllister took a hesitant step forward but stopped as her brother appeared from the shadows on Camille's left. He walked toward her, either unaware of

Camille and Lachlan on the stairs or ignoring them altogether and bent to whisper in his sister's ear. Camille and Lachlan exchanged a bewildered glance. Then Mr McAllister straightened, his back still toward the staircase, and his sister just kept staring down at them.

An icy chill ran up Camille's spine; something about seeing the two of them together unnerved her. It was almost like déjà vu, and yet she knew that wasn't possible. Then the anxiety crept back in when she realised the McAllister's' odder-than-normal behaviour confirmed there was something more going on in the manor. Somehow, that unspoken confirmation brought hot flushes of terror washing over her. Camille wished she could just drop the candles and torches and grab a hold of Lachlan. She knew it would make her feel better, but she didn't want to startle Miss McAllister and ruin whatever chance she had left of getting a response from the woman.

After what felt like an eternity, Miss McAllister turned around without a word and led her brother back into the shadows.

"What the hell was that about?" Lachlan murmured.

Camille looked at him, her unease still strong despite the McAllister's' departure. "I have no idea."

They hurried back to her room to find Jonathan, Grace and Jayne crouched together on the window seat, gazing out at the storm. None of them seemed bothered by the flickering bedroom light overhead. The minute Camille stepped through the doorway; the lights went out. It was still fairly early in the evening, but the heavy storm clouds completely blocked out whatever sunlight remained. Lightning flashed through the sky, and her friends jumped, glancing around the room. Jayne screamed just before the lightning disappeared, and Lachlan fumbled to turn on a torch. "It's okay," he said quickly. "It's just us."

"Please tell me you have torches," Jayne added with a sob. "This place is freaking me out!"

Lachlan walked toward them, torch in hand, and Camille dumped her armful of torches and candles on the bed. "Here you go," he said, handing Jayne his torch. "We brought plenty. And a bunch of candles too."

Camille set to work lighting the candles. Then she placed them on the bedside table and spaced them out on the floor around the room.

"It's okay." Grace placed a reassuring arm around Jayne's shoulders. "Just a bad storm. It's not like you haven't seen one before."

"Not in a haunted house, I haven't."

"No one said it was haunted…" Camille realised her words only fell on deaf ears as Jayne turned toward Lachlan and buried her face in his chest, the torch forgotten. A pang of something like jealousy shot through Camille, but when his eyes met hers, she had the strongest feeling he was trying to tell her something. The intensity of his stare made her flush hot again, so she cleared her throat and pretended to double-check the candles.

"And it's not just the storm," Jayne said through a few sniffles. "It's the weird earthquake and the lights and—"

"You did want to spend the night here..." Jonathan said with a shrug. Both Jayne and Grace shot him annoyed looks. "What? She did."

"What... what happened to those cuts you had?" Jayne asked, momentarily side-tracked as she pointed at Camille.

"Uh, so... I have no idea what happened, to be honest. I was kind of in a lot of pain when we left the room, but by the time we reached my parents, it was like nothing had happened."

"This isn't happening!" Jayne screeched, burying her face in Lachlan's chest.

"Look," Camille said, trying to ignore the way Jayne clung to Lachlan. She sat on the edge of the bed next to Grace instead. "I'll admit it's been pretty scary. I can't explain what's going on any better than you guys can. But the storm seems to be passing, and once it does, I'm pretty sure we'll all be a little more level-headed. So how about for now, we just try to ignore it and wait it out?"

"Sounds good to me." Jonathan tossed the cushions off the bed and led Grace toward them. He flopped back onto the floor, pummelling the cushions around him and making himself comfortable. Grace waited for him to finish before she sat down beside him. "While you too were gone," he added, "I was thinking about something."

"About what?" Camille asked, grateful for the distraction. She forced herself not to look at Jayne still clutching Lachlan to her.

"What if your uncle did come here... but never left?" Jonathan asked Lachlan.

"What do you mean?" Lachlan gently unlatched Jayne's arms from around his waist and guided her back to their circle, where he then sat between Jonathan and Camille. Pouting, Jayne was forced to sit between Grace and Camille, who was now hyper-aware of being on obstacles in Jane's path to Lachlan. But her heartbeat picked up at the same time, knowing she sat so close to him again.

"Well, we know that he'd planned to come to the manor and spend some time here," Jonathan continued, completely oblivious to the additional drama unfolding before him. "It was a huge opportunity for him, so there's no way he would've passed it up, right? But what if we don't just assume he left after that? Like I said, what if he came to the manor... and whatever happened to him happened right here?" Everyone else stared at him in surprise. "What?" He leaned back on his elbows. "I can chill and pay attention at the same time." That brought a few chuckles before the mood dampened again.

"So, you're saying you think he died here?" Lachlan asked with a frown.

"Yeah. I mean, I know it's a shit scenario to consider, since he was your uncle. But it makes sense to me. We know he couldn't have helped himself if he had the opportunity to stay here. And we know no one ever saw him again. Maybe he found something here that got him... you know."

"Or maybe someone just didn't like having a houseguest," Jayne added.

"Charles was an old man," Camille said. "And he was seriously unwell. Physically. I can't see him killing anyone."

"Your family also didn't know him that well," Jayne said. "We probably know as much about him as you do."

Camille tilted her head in concession.

"It might not have even been Charles LeRoux who did it," Grace added. "Assuming there was a murder."

"What are you saying?" Camille asked, shuddering as though an icy hand had brushed against the base of her neck.

"Well, he wasn't the only person living here, was he?"

The room fell silent again at that, with only the sound of thunder and the rattling windows to cut up the tension.

A much louder crack of thunder trembled through the room, and Jayne leapt to her feet. "That's it! I can't stay here in this murder-ghost house!"

Camille and Grace jumped up on either side of her. "You're okay," Camille said. "Nothing's going to happen to you. It's just a theory, and it was a really long time ago. And there aren't any ghosts here. Just a storm. It'll pass."

"Don't let it get to you," Grace added, rubbing Jayne's back. "Once the storm's over, you'll have a good laugh about this. I promise."

"And if you still want to go home after that, I know Mum or Dad wouldn't mind driving you back into town. I just don't think it would be very safe to head out right now."

"They're right, Jayne," Lachlan added. "Come sit back down. We might as well pass the time doing something constructive, right?"

Jayne glanced at him, then gave him a pitiful nod and reluctantly sank to the floor, shifting her cushion to be as close to his as she could get.

"Okay, so what do you all think about my idea?" Jonathan asked.

"I guess it sounds plausible," Lachlan replied. "Not that I really want to think about him dying here... Look, to be honest, I never knew the guy. But he was still my uncle. And I'd still like to know what happened to him. For my family's sake. For my Dad. But I can't see any way to prove or disprove your theory."

Jonathan shrugged. "Yeah, you've got me there."

"So, where do we go from here?" Grace asked. "It feels like we've just hit another dead end."

Camille was only half listening. Because she thought she heard something else between the claps of rolling thunder. Something that shouldn't be there.

"Camille?" Grace asked. The others stopped talking and eyed her warily.

"Camille?" Lachlan said.

She lifted a hand to silence him and cocked her head, listening intently. "Can you guys hear that?"

"Hear what?" Jayne asked, her eyes shifting anxiously around the room.

Camille wanted to scream at the storm when the sky rumbled again overhead, but she waited for the noise to die down so she could keep listening.

"Wait. I think I just heard something." Lachlan got to his feet again. "It's like a scratching, scrapping sound, right? Is that what you heard?"

Camille nodded. "I thought it was all just in my head." She got up too, and the others just stared at her in bewilderment.

"I don't hear it, dude," Jonathan said. "How can anyone hear anything over this storm?"

"Where is it coming from?" Grace asked.

"Not sure…" Lachlan glanced at Camille, and she shrugged.

Then the sound came again, and she walked past her friends toward the opposite side of the room—and the wardrobe. Pausing, she listened for it again, but the noise had stopped. Just as she was about to give up and return to the cushions, there it was. Looking up at Lachlan with wide eyes, she nodded.

He hurried to join her and pulled his phone out of his pocket. "To try recording it," he said.

"Hey, I want to hear it too." Jonathan forced himself to his feet and pulled Grace with him by the hand. Jayne quickly followed.

Huddling together around the wardrobe, they listened for the sound. Camille wished the storm would hurry up and pass so they could work out what the hell that noise was without being interrupted. The next time the scratching caught her attention, she almost jumped at how much louder it was.

"Yeah, I definitely heard that," Grace said. "What was it?"

Originally, Camille had thought it came from the wardrobe. But this time, it seemed to be in the wall beside it. She took a step closer and placed her hand on the wall.

"Great. So now there are ghosts in the walls too," Jayne muttered, folding her arms.

"Hardly," Lachlan said. "It's probably an animal that got in trying to escape the storm." He turned away from Jayne and placed his hand on the wall. Camille met his gaze and realised he didn't believe his own words for a second. That part terrified her. She knew, deep down, that it wasn't an animal, either. The memory of hearing the voice beyond the wall behind her bed came back to her and made her shiver.

"Wait! Did you hear it that time?" Jonathan asked, startling Camille out of her own recollections.

"Yeah. But that sounded like it came farther down the wall." Lachlan stepped around Camille to stand on her left.

"Wait, what?" she asked.

"Listen." He gently grabbed her arm and pulled her closer to the wall. Hesitantly, they both placed their ears against the plaster, facing each other.

"You two are nuts…" Jonathan forced a laugh that fell completely flat. The sound repeated, much louder with their ears against the wall. Camille and Lachlan jumped at the same time.

"How is it getting louder?" Jayne asked.

"Maybe it's not," Grace suggested. "Maybe the storm's just getting quieter." Her theory was punctuated by an enormous triple-clap of thunder reverberating through the whole room. Camille felt it through the wall too.

The scrabbling, scratching sound rose again. "I think it's moving…" Lachlan looked down the wall, following the sound with his phone. It sounded like it was moving in a straight line across the wall, remaining at about chest height.

"What kind of animal would move like that?" Jayne asked, taking a step back so she was half-hidden behind Grace.

"None that I know of," Lachlan replied.

"Where is it going?" Grace asked as the sound reached the corner of the wall before turning to travel toward her bedroom door. Camille and Lachlan hurried to follow it and stopped with it at the doorway, peering out into the dark hall.

"Jonathan, can you grab a couple of those torches please?" Lachlan asked.

"I really don't like this…" Jayne's voice quivered.

Lachlan shushed her and didn't turn around even as Jonathan handed him a torch. Camille looked back to see the hurt in Jayne's eyes and did her best to give the girl a reassuring smile.

"Wait. Did you hear that?" Lachlan pointed right— across the hallway. "I think it's moving that way on the other side. We're getting closer." He flicked Wendy blinked three times before opening her eyes as wide as she could. on his torch and stepped out into the hall with Camille right behind him.

"Can we wait here?" Jayne asked, but Grace grabbed her by the hand and pulled her along.

When Camille reached the light switch, she realised the power must be out everywhere now; she flipped the switch on and off, but nothing happened.

Lachlan ran the beam of his torch along the wall and over the closed door closest to him. "What's this room?" he asked.

"Another bedroom. We haven't really been in any of these rooms much. Just mine, the one you're staying in tonight, and the bathroom. Mum's been focusing on the main floor first."

Lachlan nodded absently, and the sound rose quite loudly again, dragging along the wall in front of them before starting across the wooden bedroom door. Camille reached out, quickly twisted the knob, and shoved open the door. They swung their torches across the room, ignoring Jayne's whimpers of protest behind them. There was nothing here but dusty, sheet-covered furniture.

"Wait, it's still out here!" Grace said. Camille and Lachlan hurried back into the hall. The sound moved faster, forcing them to almost jog if they wanted to keep up down the hall.

The sound reached the corner at the end of the hall and without pause continued into the adjacent wall across the landing. Then it disappeared again down the hall of the opposite wing. "This is so wrong..." Camille muttered.

"What's down there?" Lachlan asked, picking up the pace.

"Just more rooms." She frowned in realisation. "And the door to the attic." Lachlan shot her a quick look. She wasn't surprised at all when the scraping sound ended at the door to the attic stairs.

"Wait." Lachlan grabbed her arm when she reached for the door. Then he lifted his phone to remind her he wanted to catch whatever it was on audio and stepped in front of her.

"Do we really have to go up there?" Jayne asked.

Camille paused with one step on the staircase and turned around. "No, of course not. You can wait here." Before she took another step, a loud creak came from the darkness above them.

"Shh…"

"I didn't say anything," Camille whispered without turning around.

"Neither did we," Grace added, her whisper laced with fear.

Camille slowly turned her head to look at her friends, hoping one of them was playing a prank.

"Who—"

The attic thumped above them, like someone was running across the floor toward the staircase. The footsteps raced with increasing speed right toward the top of the stairs, then thundered down them toward the landing. Camille felt the thick churn of air as something rushed past her. Her panic and confusion made her leap back, but she lost her footing and fell down the few stairs to the hallway floor.

"Camille!" Grace jumped toward her. "Are you okay?"

Camille took her friend's outstretched hand and accepted the help back to her feet. "Yeah, I'm fine."

"What the hell was that?" Jonathan peered up the attic stairs before looking up and down the hall.

"You guys heard that?" Camille asked with equal parts surprise and relief.

"We sure did." Lachlan paused his recording and lowered his phone. "Shame we couldn't see anything, though."

"Maybe your phone picked up something we didn't catch," Jayne suggested, stepping toward him.

"You know, like in the movies."

"That's not a bad idea." Lachlan lifted his phone again and opened the clip. "Woah. I think I actually have something." He looked up at the others with wide eyes, and curiosity got the better of Camille. She hurried to his side for a look. It's just the last part when you fell," he told her then pressed play again. Something flashed across the screen at the moment Camille tumbled backwards, but nothing was clear.

"I don't know, man," Jonathan said. "That could just be a trick of the light or some dust or something."

"Can you replay it in slow motion?" Jayne said, leaning toward Lachlan and his phone.

He altered the settings as she suggested and played the footage back in slow motion. "Woah..."

Camille heard the hush followed by the footsteps as clearly recorded as if they'd come from a real person. The minute she fell backward on camera, a young girl rushed past her, grinning. The screen flickered when the child's hair flashed from black, to white, to black again. Even creepier was the moment the apparition looked right at the camera and giggled. That was also plainly audible, though none of them had heard it the first time. Then she was gone.

"Give us a look," Jonathan asked, and Lachlan handed him and Grace the phone.

"Okay, call me officially freaked out," Grace said.

"What, only now?" Jayne obviously tried to make a joke, but it sounded more like she was on the brink of hysteria. "So, do you think… I mean, was that…"

"Yeah, that was Mena," Camille said.

"Shit," Lachlan whispered. "I can't believe we actually got something."

"Isn't that what you wanted?" Camille asked.

"Yeah, of course. I just didn't think we would actually get something concrete. This is an actual, legitimate apparition sighting. We have to get this up on your blog."

Camille sighed and turned away from him.

"Are you still planning on checking out the attic?" Grace asked, taking Jonathan's hand.

Camille looked at Lachlan; his bravado was gone now. "No. I think we should call it for tonight." She led them back to her room, ignoring the fact that Lachlan had started recording again. As they turned down the corridor of her wing, the light flickered on just long enough for them to catch a glimpse of something on the wall.

"Did you guys see that?" Jayne asked.

Camille nodded before realising it was still dark. "Yeah. I have to admit, I'm not super keen to raise my torch for a better look."

"We'll do it together." Grace stepped up beside Camille, pulling Jonathan with her. Lachlan stood on Camille's other side, his phone ready, and Jayne took her place as close to him as she could get.

"Okay. One, two, three." They raised their torches. Jayne and Grace screamed and dropped theirs, leaving Camille and Jonathan to scan the wall alone. Camille barely heard Lachlan swear beside her as he took it all in via the phone.

"That wasn't there before, was it?" Jayne whimpered.

Camille couldn't answer as she passed her torch over it again. Scratched into the wall before them were the words 'Get them out.'

"Who else thinks it's a good idea to take that advice?" Jayne asked.

A loud crash echoed down the hall. Light spilled across the floor from the bathroom, flickering off and on every few seconds. Camille took off toward it.

"Camille, wait up!" Lachlan tried to run after her while also recording everything on his phone. Camille stepped into the bathroom and found the large bathroom mirror shattered and shards of glass all over the floor. She leaned over a piece large enough to see her reflection—only something didn't feel right. In the broken mirror, she saw herself as she was now and herself as an old woman at the same time. Her eyes widened in horror when a thick black thread appeared from nowhere in the mirror and sewed her reflection's mouth shut in three ugly X shapes. Camille's reflection moved when she did not, trying to shake the thread off lips that weren't hers. When Camille reached out, though, her reflection did the same, shaking her head faster and faster until the movement became a blur. A high-pitched screech filled the bathroom.

"Camille?" Grace grabbed her arm. The shriek cut off abruptly, and Camille realised the sound had come from her.

"Can you see that?" She pointed down at the glass.

"See what? Our reflections?" Grace asked as Lachlan stepped into the bathroom behind them.

"That's all you see? Just our normal reflections? Nothing weird?"

Grace shrugged. "Nope. I just see you and me. Admittedly, we've both looked better. But other than that, it's just us."

Camille dared to take another look and gave her friend a small smile through the glass, her heart still pounding.

"I think we need to get your parents," Jayne said from the doorway.

Camille nodded, giving her reflection a final glance before turning and leaving it behind her.

They huddled together as they moved along the corridor and around to the staircase, focusing their torches on the stairs. Once they reached the bottom landing, the five frightened teenagers hurried into the sitting room, where the light was still on without any hint of having lost power. Her parents were in the exact same positions as when she'd last seen them, only they'd fallen asleep—her mother's head resting in her father's lap, the book forgotten and on the floor. Her father leaned back against the lounge; his mouth slightly open while his show kept playing on his tablet.

"Mum?" Camille approached them, leaving her friends hovering at the room's entrance.

"Dad?" She raised her voice and frowned when neither of them answered. Even shaking her mother by the shoulder didn't wake her. Her father didn't respond to it, either. A wave of fear washed over her, and she placed her fingers on her mother's neck, then quickly her father's. Tears of relief stung her eyes.

"Are they okay?" Grace asked.

Camille nodded. "I think they're still just sleeping, but... I don't know why they won't wake up."

"Hey! Mr and Mrs LeRoux!" Jonathan yelled, stepping toward them and clapping his hands.

"Jonathan!" Grace waved him back toward her.

"What? We want them to wake up, don't we?"

Camille shook her parents again while Jonathan drummed up quite the racket, but still, nothing happened. "This is madness," Camille muttered. A sob escaped her.

"Hey, we'll be okay." Jonathan draped his arm over her shoulders and led her back to the others. "I'm sure we'll be laughing about this crazy night in the morning."

"Yeah, we just have to get through the night," Lachlan added, but he didn't sound convinced. "Storms do weird things. We just have to wait it out."

"Where?" Jayne asked.

"This is going to sound crazy, but I think we should see the rest of the night out in the kitchen."

"I don't think that sounds any crazier than anything else that's happened tonight," Jonathan said. "Plus, the kitchen means, you know, food and stuff." Grace gave him a playful nudge.

"The kitchen? Probably not the most comfortable room in this place," Jayne said.

"No, it's not," Camille conceded. "But I think it's the only room where I haven't had any sort of strange experience."

"That's good enough for me." Grace nodded. "But we still need to go back to your room first."

"What? Why?" Jayne stared back and forth between them; her eyes wide.

"All our things are up there. All the research, the laptop. At the very least, we should bring those cushions down in case we can manage to get any sleep."

"Good luck with that…" Jayne muttered.

"Grace is right, though," Camille added. "We could probably push the single mattress from the boy's room down the stairs too. But I'll need a hand. The sooner we get up there and back, the better."

"I can't walk past that wall again…" Jayne whimpered.

"Jonathan and I will come," Grace announced. "Lachlan, you can stay here with Jayne." She grabbed her boyfriend's hand and pulled him from the room. It took all Camille's willpower not to look at Lachlan before she left too.

Camille scowled in the darkness and flashed her torch across the floor. Once they'd made it to her room, she closed the door firmly behind them, walked to her bedside table, and grabbed her phone and its charger. In the middle of the room, Jonathan packed their research into the box while Grace gathered cushions from the bed. Camille grabbed the laptop and placed it in the box, then grabbed her share of the cushions. Then the trio hurried back downstairs, keeping their eyes trained on the floor in front of them.

When they entered the kitchen, Camille paused at the sight of Lachlan and Jayne sitting on the stools at the island, Jayne's head resting on his shoulder. Without a word, Camille dumped the cushions in the corner before going to the bench on the other side of the island. She kept her back toward Lachlan as she plugged in her phone.

"While you two are just sitting there doing nothing…" Jonathan joked and heaved the box up onto the island.

"You know, Jayne, I could really use a distraction— and your expertise," Lachlan said, gently shrugging so Jayne would list her head. Then he reached into the box and pulled out the laptop. "Will you help me upload this new footage to the blog?" "Do you really feel like listening to music right now?"

"Not really. But I also don't want to sit around waiting to hear any more creepy scratching sounds, either."

"Fair call." Jonathan sat at the island, gesturing for Grace to join him, but she shook her head. Her crossed arms mirrored Camille's tense stance.

"Okay. If we're going to stay, the only way I can stay sane is if we try to work out what the hell's going on instead of just waiting for the next scary episode," Grace said.

Camille nodded, half listening to the thunder rolling away. "Agreed."

"Things are obviously escalating," Lachlan said, not taking his eyes from the laptop screen as Jayne typed furiously away. "I mean, they haven't been this bad before now, right? Or have you been down-playing how mental this place actually is?"

"No, this is definitely the worst," Camille replied. "I don't know if it's the storm, or having you guys here, or both. Or maybe it has nothing to do with either of those. Maybe this is all because we might be getting close to some kind of truth that someone... or something ... doesn't want us to know about."

"Maybe." Jonathan sighed. "I mean, things have gotten worse since you found about Caroline and the adoption."

"Yeah, but that was a dream." Camille started pacing.

"The letter wasn't. Someone must have left it for you," Lachlan said.

"So, which one is it, then? Someone wants me to find out about this place. Or they don't?"

Lachlan shrugged, still focused on the laptop.

"What if it's both?" Grace asked, pacing now too.

Camille paused. "How do you mean?"

"Well, what if it's more than one... person? Or whatever. Like, one's trying to help you uncover the truth for whatever reason, and someone else is trying to prevent it."

Camille frowned and resumed her pacing. She stopped in front of the window in the kitchen's back door and sighed. "I'm not sure I like the idea of there being more than one… thing trying to get through to me. But it does kind of make sense."

A flash of lightning lit up the grounds, and Camille unfolded her arms, pressing her hands against the glass instead. "Hey, guys. Come here."

"What?" Lachlan asked, sliding off the stool. Camille waived them over, focusing only on the grounds through the window.

Grace reached her first and peered out into the darkness. "Is that…"

Camille nodded. "The McAllister's."

"What are they doing walking around in this?" Jayne exclaimed. "Are they crazy? They don't even have an umbrella or anything."

"Curiouser and curiouser…" Camille whispered.

"Where do you think they're going?" Lachlan peered over Camille's shoulder as Jayne and Jonathan joined them.

"Looks like they're headed for the woods." Camille rubbed her forehead and the small headache kicking in. But she kept watching with her friends until the McAllister's made it to the forest and disappeared beyond the trees.

"Can this night get any weirder?" Jonathan asked.

"Don't jinx—"

Lightning flashed, and the music stopped playing, leaving them all in a sudden, eerie silence.

"Please tell me that was just your phone running out of battery…" Jayne whispered.

Camille glanced at her phone still connected to its charger, then turned back toward her friends. No one said a word. Then voices spilled from her phone and shattered the silence. Camille hurried toward the bench and yanked her phone from the charger. The music app was gone, and the video Lachlan had captured earlier on his phone now played on hers. She held the phone up to show them.

"What?" Lachlan crossed the room toward her for a closer look. "How is that even possible? It's not done uploading to the site yet."

"I have no idea, but nothing surprises me now." She tried to turn it off, to turn it down, but the video kept playing. Camille dropped her phone onto the bench and put a hand to her pounding forehead again. Her other head went absently to her stomach as she tried to calm the flurry of nervous fear gripping her.

A child's muffled laughter came from the phone. Everyone jerked their heads toward it.

"That's not from the video," Grace said softly.

"She's back…" Jonathan whispered.

"I don't think she ever left," Camille muttered. She felt like she was going to be sick as she slowly picked up the phone, turning it over so they could all see. The laughter continued, and the camera moved as if someone held it while running. All they could see was a wooden floor, but nothing to confirm which room. Camille pushed past her friends and ran out of the kitchen, Lachlan hot on her heels.

"Wait!" Jayne called. "Wasn't the point of staying in the kitchen to avoid any more run-ins with the house?" When Grace and Jonathan left after Camille and Lachlan, Jayne called rolled her eyes and reluctantly followed.

Camille took the stairs two at a time, the child's laughter playfully taunting her as she and her friends reached the top landing and ran to her bedroom. They burst inside, skidding to a stop when they found the room empty. The thump of feet pounding across the attic floor above them made the laughing child sound like she weighed a tonne. Then the footsteps changed direction, ran toward the far wall, and stopped above the wardrobe. Camille's heart pounded as heavily as those thumping feet above her; she wondered if her friends could hear it too.

Then something pounded furiously inside the wardrobe, as though someone had been locked inside and was now desperate to get out. Jayne yelped. Camille jumped when Lachlan grabbed her arm. "What the hell is that?" he whispered.

Her paralysing fear made it impossible to answer him.

Lachlan took a deep breath, released her, and swiftly approached the wardrobe with his phone ready for recording. Camille wanted to tell him to stop, to stay back, but with each bang against the old wood, her terror grew. He yanked open one side wardrobe door with his free hand to reveal absolutely nothing there, and the wardrobe fell silent. Once he'd slowly pried open the second door, Lachlan turned back around to shrug at the rest of them, looking both disappointed and entirely relieved.

"I can't take much more of this." Jayne whimpered. Grace put a comforting arm around her and shot Camille a questioning glance.

Camille swallowed. "I don't know what to say…"

"You don't have to say anything," Lachlan told her. "We know this isn't your fault. You're not the one doing this. Honestly, I think we all did this together when we started digging into the house."

"Well, that's easy, then," Jayne said, tightly hugging herself. "Let's just promise not to dig any deeper. Then everything can go back to normal, and I won't have to go to therapy for the rest of my life."

"I don't think I can do that," Lachlan said, and Camille turned to him in surprise. "Given everything that's happened tonight, I think we've come way too far to give up now."

"Look, man, I get that this is personal for you," Jonathan said. "Of course you want to find out what happened to your uncle. But dude, seriously, you can't really want to see this shit get worse."

"Of course I don't want to see things get worse. But I do want answers. Something's obviously working really hard to make sure we don't get them."

"Exactly," Jayne added. "Which is why we should quit while we're ahead. Maybe then Camille's parents will miraculously wake up, and we can get out of here."

"Camille?" Grace asked gently. "What do you think?"

Camille looked at each of them in turn, focusing on Lachlan; he seemed to be pleading with her to back him up. "I want answers. But I think we need to rethink how we go about getting them."

"What we're doing obviously isn't getting us anywhere," Jayne muttered.

Camille had to force away the image of her reflection in the broken mirror before continuing. "Exactly. I don't want to wait until it does. Obviously, trying to do all this in the middle of the night during a massive thunderstorm isn't working out for us."

"So, what should we do, then?" Jonathan asked.

Camille stared out at the storm beyond her window. "I think we pack up our research for now. I'm starting to think it's really not safe to be looking through any of it here. I know it sounds crazy, but just hear me out. I have a…" She clenched her eyes shut for a moment, trying to match the words with the sensation. "I have a feeling the house is watching us. Like it'll know that we're looking into it if we try to put the pieces together here."

"Yeah, that does sound crazy," Lachlan muttered. "But I have the exact same feeling."

"So maybe if we make a bit of a show of putting everything away," Jayne added, "you think it'll stop?"

Camille nodded. "Exactly."

"Well you don't have to tell me twice." Jayne uncrossed her arms, moved toward the door, then seemed to have second thoughts about entering the hallway on her own.

"Looks like we're heading back to the kitchen," Jonathan said. "I, for one, vote not to come back to Camille's room again for the rest of the night." He grabbed Grace's hand and stepped around Jayne, leading the way back into the hall.

Once they'd all returned to the kitchen, Lachlan closed the laptop and put it back in the box with the research. He lifted the box off the bench and turned toward Camille. "Where do you want it?"

"Uh…" She scanned the kitchen for the best place and pointed at the dumb waiter across the room. "In there."

"Oh, cool," Grace exclaimed. "I've never seen one of these for real before."

Camille slid the door up to reveal a surprisingly large cavity behind it. With a grunt, Jonathan heaved the box up onto the ledge and closed the door. "There. Out of sight, out of mind, right?"

"I wouldn't go that far," Grace retorted. "But out of sight's a start. Now let's see if it makes any difference."

A digital chime sounded, and they all looked around for the source. Camille pulled her phone from her pocket, and the chime only grew louder.

"Is that an alarm?"

"Yeah, sounds like it. But I didn't set it."

"What time is it?" Lachlan asked.

"Three in the morning." Camille turned off the alarm and set her phone on the bench.

"Well that's not half creepy." Jonathan scoffed, climbing onto a stool and pulling Grace against him.

Camille walked to the back door again and with a sigh peered through the glass. The storm had all but passed, but the sky still lit up periodically with the lightning in the distance.

"Maybe we should try to get some sleep," Jayne said, her suggestion falling on deaf ears when Camille caught movement outside again. "Hey, come look at this." Jayne groaned, but they all gathered around one more time. Out of the woods came the McAllister's again, side by side, moving purposefully back toward the house.

"What do you think they were doing in there?" Grace asked.

"I have no idea…" Camille admitted.

"I bet we could find out," Lachlan suggested.

"I thought we weren't doing any more snooping in the house?" Jayne snapped.

Lachlan raised his hands in defence. "Technically, it's not in the house, is it? And no one said you have to come." Jayne looked quickly away from him, blinking at the floor.

Camille was really starting to feel sorry for the girl, but that wasn't the most important issue right now. "We don't have to worry about that tonight. It looks like the storm's finally over too. On its way out."

"And nothing weird has happened since we packed everything up," Jonathan said. "I mean, except for the alarm you didn't set."

"Maybe the house, or whatever's behind all this creepiness, has actually had enough with us for one night," Grace suggested with a tight, hopeful smile.

"Maybe." Camille still watched the McAllister's.

"Well, if that's what's happening, I'm relieved," Jonathan said. "If we put the two mattresses side by side, that should be big enough for the three of you girls to sleep. Jonathan and I can make do with the cushions."

Camille stared out her window as her friends dragged the mattresses together. The McAllister's were almost at the house now. Miss McAllister stopped and looked straight up at the kitchen door. Camille jumped back, hoping she hadn't been seen. She headed toward the mattresses, figuring she just wouldn't mention it to the others. Then she lay on the edge, not wanting to take up too much room; she didn't plan to actually sleep.

But as soon as her head hit the pillow, a wave of exhaustion crashed over her, and her body longed for rest. She turned her head to look at Lachlan lying atop a configuration of pillows, and he was already staring back at her. Then she closed her eyes and fell instantly to sleep.

CHAPTER SIXTEEN

CAMILLE WOKE UP with a start and scanned the room, feeling a little disorientated. Everyone was still fast asleep, and the faint light coming through the back-door window told her it was still really early; she obviously hadn't slept for very long. Despite that, she felt strangely rested — more than she had in days — as if she'd just a full eight hours.

Moving carefully, she slipped off the mattresses and manoeuvred toward the hallway, careful not to trip over her friends. Everything felt surreal and unfamiliar, and she decided she wanted to use her own bathroom rather than either of the two on the main floor. She scurried up the stairs but paused in front of her bathroom, recalling the broken glass there. For a moment, she debated whether to go and grab some shoes from her room, but she didn't really want to go in there on her own.

When she opened the bathroom door, she froze. The room was spotless, not a shard of glass to be seen. Even more confusing was the sight of the vanity mirror still intact and in its place above the vanity. Camille walked toward it, her mouth hanging open in disbelief. She had to touch it to make sure it was real, then stared at her stunned reflection. Her need to use the toilet vanished, and she dashed out into the hall to where they'd found the terrifying message scratched into the wall. That too was gone.

Camille shook her head, backing away from the incomprehensible sight. A yelp escaped her when she knocked into something, and she whirled around to find Miss McAllister standing there. "What the hell are you doing?" Camille hissed. Miss McAllister said nothing. "Well?" Camille prompted. For the first time, she really didn't care how haughty she sounded. The old woman glanced slowly at the blank wall, then returned her gaze to Camille. "Was it you? You got rid of the... evidence?" Camille sighed. "It doesn't matter. We recorded it all anyway."

Miss McAllister's eyes narrowed. "You're a foolish girl, Mistress. Things could have worked out so differently, but you just wouldn't listen. You've set into motion a terrible chain of events, and I'm afraid they cannot be broken now that it's begun. I tried to warn you. I told you to leave well enough alone." The woman turned on her heel and walked soundlessly away, leaving Camille staring after her.

"HEY. DID YOU even sleep?" Grace asked, sitting up as Camille walked back into the kitchen.

"Some." Camille offered a small smile. Jayne popped up in bed too, looking around with a frown before she saw the boys on floor and quickly tried to smooth down her bed-hair.

Grace climbed off the mattress and stretched.

Camille walked past her friends to the door and peered out the window. The sky was still grey and heavy with clouds, but they moved quickly now, and the rain had stopped. The wind stirring the thick branches of the forest beckoned her.

"You're thinking about going in there, aren't you?" Grace asked. It was completely without judgment—just a simple fact.

Camille nodded. Jayne flopped back onto the bed with a groan.

"What's going on?" Jonathan propped himself up and ran a hand through his messy mop of hair. Then he reached over and thumped Lachlan on the back. "Wake up, dude. Hey, did last night even happen, or was it all just one seriously messed-up dream?"

"Definitely feels like a bad dream," Grace muttered, then stifled a yawn. "Everything looks so normal this morning."

"So," Jonathan said, attempting to untangle himself from his blanket, "what's a guy gotta do to get some breakfast around here? I'm starving."

"Jon!" Grace snapped.

Camille laughed. "Yeah, I'm sure we can find something." She took one last look out the window before walking to the fridge.

"Good morning," Allysha said from the doorway, looking them over. "Dare I ask why you're all camped out in my kitchen?"

"Let's just call it a social experiment." Jonathan grinned.

Allysha shook her head in amusement. "How did you all sleep?"

Camille's friends glanced at her in hesitation. "Uh, yeah. Okay," Camille replied. "I mean, the storm was pretty full-on, but once that was over, it wasn't so bad."

"Storm? I don't remember hearing much of it. Then again, your father and I fell asleep in the sitting room! I think all this renovating has taken more out of us than we thought. Must've been around three a.m. when we finally went up to bed."

"I'm surprised you're up so early, then," replied Camille. She lay some fruit on the bench and started cutting it up.

"Oddly enough, I feel like I slept for a whole day. Very well-rested. Maybe we need to fall asleep on that old lounge more often." Allysha smiled at them before walking to the stove and turning it on. Camille and her friends chuckled awkwardly and eyed each other. Camille shrugged and gestured for them to sit at the four stools on the other side of the bench.

"Uh, would you like a hand with anything?" Grace asked as she took her seat.

"No, thanks. I'm feeling quite ravenous after such a good sleep. This'll be a great Sunday breakfast. Bacon and eggs, and I'll even throw in some pancakes. Camille, when you're finished with that fruit, can you please organise some coffee? We'll take everything into the dining room."

"Where's Dad?" Camille asked, sneaking half a strawberry into her mouth.

"He was feeling pretty energetic when we got up this morning. So he's already outside taking stock of what he needs to get from the hardware store today. I'll put a plate aside for him."

Camille was grateful for the silence as they sat around one end of the dining table, hungrily devouring their breakfast. She still tried to wrap her mind around everything that had happened the night before; the image of herself in the broken mirror still sent a chill down her spine when she thought of it.

"Phillipe and I have to head into town a little later on," Allysha said. "Does anyone need a lift home? Save your parents the trip out here?"

"That's okay," Lachlan said. "Thanks, Mrs LeRoux. I drove up here, so I'm happy to drive everyone home."

"Please, call me Allysha. Don't feel like you have to rush off. We still have all day! Do you have plans for this morning?"

"Uh, yeah, actually." Camille glanced at her friends. "We thought we might take a little walk through the woods at the back of the property." Jayne was the only one avoiding her stare.

"I don't really like that idea very much," Allysha said. "Though I appreciate the curiosity. I suppose you are in a group... Just promise me you will stay together and not venture too far in. I don't want to have to send out a search party." She smiled, and they all chuckled politely.

"COME ON, GUYS," Jayne whined, bringing up the rear of their group as they moved across the property gardens toward the woods. "You can't really tell me you all think this is a good idea."

"Aren't you in the least bit curious?" Grace asked.

"Curious, yes. Crazy, no."

Camille looked up at Lachlan to see him watching her, and they exchanged a small smile.

"Well, you could have stayed back at the manor," Jonathan teased with a wink.

"Ha. You're always so funny, Jonathan." Even still, Jayne picked up the pace.

"I know. It's a gift." He grabbed Grace's hand.

The smile stayed on Camille's face, as she appreciated the normalcy of the banter. The morning air felt crisp and refreshing on her face, and she inhaled deeply. The grounds smelled amazing after the night's storm, and she felt as though she could smell every flower, every leaf, and every blade of grass. Then a pang of longing struck her as she remembered the smell of the eucalyptus from the gum trees after the rain back home. Since they'd moved, this was the first time in days she'd felt homesick, though by now, she felt like she'd known her new friends all her life.

As they walked through the last arrangement of shrubbery, she saw Mr McAllister standing in one of the garden beds, a shovel in one hand. He stared at her, his expression unreadable from where she walked, but it was all Camille could do not to shiver. Even as she looked away, she could still feel his eyes on her and her friends as they drew nearer to the woods.

Once they reached the tree line, they stopped.

"So, what do you think?" Camille said. "Just walk in a straight line for a bit, and if we don't find anything, we can just turn around and come back."

Lachlan chuckled. "Or I have a compass app on my phone, so we can have a bit of a wander and not get lost."

"Yeah, that's also an excellent plan." She smiled and stepped aside. "You should lead the way, then."

Lachlan didn't need a second invitation; he grabbed his phone from his pocket and stepped across the tree line, pulling up the ap. Camille followed, with Jayne close behind her, who clearly didn't want to let Lachlan out of her sight, and Grace and Jonathan brought up the rear. They walked on in silence for a while, and Camille felt hypnotised by the crunch of dead leaves underfoot.

"Listen." Lachlan paused.

"What is it?" Camille asked.

"Nothing." He turned and looked at them.

"I don't get it," Jonathan said.

"There should be birds in here, at the very least. Especially this time of day." Camille looked up at the canopy of trees in realisation.

"What does that mean?" Jayne asked. "Or do I not want to know?"

"I don't know that it means anything," Lachlan replied. "It just seems odd." He turned and headed farther into the woods.

The others followed, and all the peace and joy Camille had felt moments before dissipated, leaving her uneasy and anxious. She knew Lachlan was right, and it served to remind them of why they were actually here in the first place—to find out what the McAllister's had gotten up to the night before. Then she felt dizzy, and the strange sensation appeared again; she felt both there and absent at the same time—almost like a memory or being somewhere else. She had trouble defining it and chalked that up to her sudden nerves about their expedition.

"How much farther are we going to walk?" Jayne asked with a sigh.

Lachlan shrugged. "Until we find something, I guess." His voice was edged with annoyance, and Jayne refrained from questing further, choosing to look down at her feet instead.

"Hey, stop!" Jonathan called out.

"What?" Camille whirled around.

"What's that over there?" He pointed toward their left.

"I don't see anything," Lachlan said. Camille stepped up beside him, trying to see.

"On the ground. Between those two trees there that look like they're leaning into each other."

Finally, Camille saw it—something red nestled amongst fallen leaves. "Let's check it out!" She took off through the trees, Lachlan only a step behind her.

"Be careful!" Grace called, but the others all followed.

Camille reached the trees first and passed through them to the other side for a better look. Gasping, she clasped her hands to her mouth and quickly turned away. A second later, she heard Lachlan swear.

"What? What is it?" Jonathan hurried toward them.

"I have a feeling I don't to want to know." Jayne stopped a metre out from the trees.

Grace touched her friend's arm, then passed Jayne to satisfy her curiosity. "Oh, wow..." She took a step back and glanced at Jayne. "You were right to stay back."

"Why? What's that red thing?"

"Looks like we have ourselves a body..." Jonathan declared.

"It's been here for ages, by the looks of it," Lachlan added.

Camille took a deep breath, forcing herself to turn around. The body was really just a skeleton in clothes, propped up against a tree. Its legs were stretched out in front of it, and its arms hung by its sides. The red they had seen was the windbreaker over what looked to be a flannel shirt and jeans. One of the feet still wore a sneaker, the other bare. She knelt to get a closer look.

"Don't get too close," Grace warned.

"Why?" Jonathan frowned at his girlfriend. "It's a skeleton. What's it going to do?"

"After what we've seen recently, I don't think we can be too careful," Lachlan said.

Camille nodded; he had a point. Then she leaned closer, squinting at the odd shape on the skeleton's forehead. "You've got to be kidding me..."

"What?" Lachlan stepped forward.

"There's a... symbol engraved in this guy's forehead." Nausea overwhelmed Camille, and she forced herself to her feet, trying to banish the image from her mind.

"Woah, what?" Jonathan leaned in with Lachlan for a closer look.

"Oh, that is messed up..." Now Grace looked as pale and shaky as Camille felt.

"Do you think it was done before or after he was dead?" Jonathan asked.

"I hope for his sake it was done after," Camille replied.

Lachlan crouched down so his head was almost at the same level as the skeleton. "Looks like it was cut fairly deeply too. Almost like it's gone straight through the thickness of the skull." He turned his head and squinted, as though trying to picture what this person would have seen when he died. "Unbelievable."

"You can say that again," Jayne stated.

"No. I mean, from down here, whoever this person was, the last thing they would have seen was the exact same symbol. Looking through this clearing and straight through. There's a full view of the LeRoux weathervane."

"No way..." Camille crouched on the other side of the body, careful not to touch the skeleton. "Wow. The same symbol. What's the point of that?"

Lachlan shook his head, then gently patted down the skeleton.

"What on earth are you doing?" Jonathan asked. Lachlan didn't answer as he moved down to the jeans and, brushing away the leaves coating the skeleton's lap, felt for the pockets. From the closest pocket, he pulled out a wallet.

"You're not going to rob the poor guy, are you?" Grace asked, mortified.

"Hardly. I want to know who he is." Lachlan opened the wallet and froze, staring at the driver's license.

"Lachlan?" Camille stood and walked toward him. The others closed in as well, and when she looked down at the open wallet and the unsmiling photo of the driver's licence, she froze too. Her expression told the others all they needed to know.

"Lachlan, I'm so sorry, man." Jonathan stepped forward.

The wallet fell from Lachlan's hands. He stood, turned, and stormed deeper into the woods.

"I'll go after him," Camille said, ignoring Jayne's glare.

"Wait. You're not just going to leave us standing here with the body, are you?" Jayne asked.

Camille was more concerned about the possibility of Lachlan getting lost. He moved quickly, and she could barely see him ahead as he weaved through the trees. "Lachlan," she called. He didn't slow down or turn around. "Lachlan, please!"

This time, he stopped, but only before pacing between he trees, his hands clasped behind his head.

"I am so sorry you had to see your uncle like that. I truly am. But we can't go running off into the woods, either."

He lowered his hands, pressed one of them over his eyes, and turned away from her, his shoulders trembling. Camille slowly walked toward him and gently touched his back, not knowing what to say but wanting him to know she was there for him. They stood like that for a moment before he turned and pulled her toward him into an embrace. His lips gently touched hers. Camille felt everything melt away as she gave herself up to the kiss.

When he released her, she felt like they had both stood there for ages; at the same time, the moment had passed all too quickly. Her heart skipped as he looked into her eyes.

"Are you okay?" she whispered, not knowing what else to say without sounding ridiculous. He nodded and pulled her against him again for another hug. She wrapped her arms around him and squeezed, resting her head against his chest.

"I just need a minute before we go back to the others. But I'm glad you're here."

"So am I." She meant it.

"We're going to have to tell your parents what we found."

"I know. Will you call your parents?"

Lachlan sighed. "I'm not looking forward to it, but it's better coming from me rather than the police. I just wish there was some way for us to figure out what happened to him. And that symbol on his skull. How messed up is that?"

Camille only nodded, guilt clutching her heart. She knew she wasn't responsible, but at the same time, this was her family's home now, and his uncle had died on their property.

"We'll find out what happened to him. Who did that to him. I promise." She gazed up at him, and he kissed her on the forehead. Camille offered a small smile, aware that it wasn't the appropriate time to show how happy she was despite how the awful circumstances. She rested her head against his chest again, not wanting the moment between them to end. Then she saw something through the trees. "What's that?" She pulled away and headed through the trees. She heard him following her, and after a few metres, they stepped into a tiny clearing.

In the middle stood a single gravestone mostly buried under leaves and branches. She could just make out the top of it and walked closer for a better look.

"Wait..." Lachlan cautioned.

"It's just a tombstone." She looked over her shoulder and gave him a reassuring smile, though the wave of nausea grew within her the closer she approached.

"Look. The symbol's there too." Lachlan pointed to the top of the gravestone.

Camille nodded, struggling against the urge to be sick. She stepped closer and gripped the top of the tombstone as the cloying dizziness took over again.

"Are you okay?" Lachlan reached out to her in concern.

Camille couldn't answer as she pulled herself around the tombstone and fell to her knees, vomiting violently across the dead leaves. Her chest and stomach heaved, fighting back the panic threatening to take hold of her. She felt like she couldn't breathe. Releasing the tombstone, she braced her hands against the forest floor, trying to take slow, deep breaths. Finally, the nausea faded.

"Camille, are you okay?" Lachlan frowned at her in concern. "What can I do?"

She discreetly wiped her mouth with the sleeve of her jacket and stood. "Nothing. I'll be okay. I don't know where that came from."

"We can come back for a closer look another time."

"Yeah." She sighed. "We should probably get back to the others. They'll be wondering where we are."

He lifted his phone and took a quick photo of the grave before taking her hand and leading her through the trees. She was grateful for his sense of direction as much as the warmth spreading from his hand up into her chest, making her heart flutter. The nausea was still present but seemed to lessen a little with each step closer to the manor.

As they stepped away from the tombstone and through the trees toward the others ahead, Camille tried to release Lachlan's hand. She didn't want to upset Jayne, but he held on tightly. As their friends looked up to see them, Camille lowered her gaze so she wouldn't have to see the look on Jayne's face.

"What took you guys so long?" Jonathan asked, seemingly oblivious to the handholding. "We were about to send out a search party."

"We found a tombstone in the woods." Lachlan finally released Camille's hand so she could show the image on her phone.

"Whose?" Jonathan asked.

"That's what we need to find out," Camille replied.

"That's it! I can't take any more of this!" Jayne burst into tears and stormed off through the trees toward the manor.

Grace leaned toward Camille and whispered, "Don't feel bad. Lachlan's liked you since the moment he met you. She just needs some time."

Before Camille could say anything, Grace hurried through the trees, calling out for Jayne to stop.

"We should go." Camille led the way after them.

As they stepped across the tree line and back onto the manor grounds, she was surprised to see Grace and Jayne already halfway across the gardens. Grace was a few steps behind Jayne, clearly still trying to get her to stop or at the very least slow down. Camille couldn't help feeling guilty for Jayne's outburst.

Then she saw her parents step out from behind a tree, hand in hand as they enjoyed a Sunday-morning walk. "Oh, crap," Camille muttered. Her parents looked up at Jayne and Grace's approach.

"Hi, girls," Allysha called, and Camille broke into a jog, the boys on either side of her.

Her mother shielded her eyes with a hand to search the ground, and once she found her daughter and the boys, she lowered her hand and approached Jayne. Grace put a hand on her friend's shoulder, but Jayne shook it off.

"What's the matter?" Allysha asked. Phillipe lingered a few steps behind her, awkwardly shuffling from one foot to other, clearly not wanting to get involved in any teenage girl drama.

"We found a body!" Jayne blurted, then burst into tears again.

Camille swore under her breath as she and the boys closed in the last few meters.

"What? What do you mean? Camille!"

"She's right, Mum," Camille said. "There's a body in the woods. Well, a skeleton. It's been there awhile. We're pretty sure it's Lachlan's uncle."

Allysha stared at them, her mouth agape.

"Now hold on a minute," Phillipe said. "What? Why would Lachlan's uncle's body be in the woods, and how do you know who it is?"

"There was a wallet. We checked the driver's license," Lachlan replied.

"And why on Earth would your uncle have been in the woods?" Phillipe asked again.

"It's kind of a long story," Camille added.

"Well I think you'd all better get inside and start talking before I call the police." Allysha wrapped an arm around Jayne and led the girl back to the house with her husband at her side. He kept looking over his shoulder at Camille and her other friends before glancing beyond them toward the trees.

"What are you going to tell them?" Grace hissed.

Camille looked at the ground as she walked. "I'm not sure. Obviously that we found him, but I don't think we need to tell them much else. I mean, we can tell them what we know about Lachlan's uncle's arrangement with Great Uncle Charles, but I don't see why we have to tell them the whole story."

"What about the symbol on him?" Jonathan asked in a hushed whisper.

"We'll play dumb. Like we were so freaked out by the body that we didn't notice it."

"Do you think they'll buy that?" Lachlan asked.

"Honestly, yes. At least for now. I think they're too shocked to question us that much."

"They're not the only ones," Grace added as they reached the manor and followed Camille's parents into the kitchen.

Miss McAllister looked up as they entered, eyeing each one of them suspiciously before staring at Camille. Camille stared back in defiance while her friends took up seats at the counter. Miss McAllister's gaze narrowed before she turned and strode out of the kitchen.

"Miss McAllister?" Allysha called after her. "I could use a hand." The old woman had either not heard her or had chosen to ignore her.

Camille joined her friends at the counter. Her mother muttered under her breath and bustled about to put the kettle on and pull out clean cups.

Lachlan leaned toward Camille and whispered, "Are you feeling any better?"

She smiled, enjoying the sensation of him being so close to her. "I am. Thanks. Must have just been something I ate." Still, he didn't look convinced. He grabbed her hand beneath the counter, and she felt herself blush again but didn't push him way.

"Right." Phillipe leaned on the bench and looked at each of them in turn. "Start talking."

"There isn't much to say, Dad," Camille started. "We went for a walk in the woods, and we found the body... the skeleton... on the ground. Well, kind of on the ground. It was sitting up against a tree."

"And you say the licence showed it was your uncle." Lachlan nodded.

"I am so sorry you found that," Allysha said, still consoling a teary-eyed Jayne. "It must have been terrible." The concerned look she shot her husband didn't escape Camille's notice.

Phillipe sighed and fished his mobile from his back pocket. "I'll call the police."

"Do you want to call your parents and let them know?" Camille asked Lachlan quietly.

He opened his mouth, then shook his head. "I don't know. Maybe I should wait. You know, just in case. Maybe someone else had his wallet. I don't want to upset them if it's not really him."

Camille just nodded and squeezed his hand, not wanting to push the issue. She felt the intensity of Jayne's stare without having to look up. The heat rose from her chest and into her cheeks, partly in guilt for hurting Jayne's feelings in wanting to be there for Lachlan, but also from the way her heart pounded at the feeling of her hand in his.

"I think I want to go home now," Jayne said quietly, looking only at Allysha.

"Of course. I'll drive you into town. Your parents should hear what's happened from me. Does anyone else want a ride?"

"I've got my car, so I can drive Lachlan and Grace," Jonathan said. "But thanks."

"Make sure your parents call us if they have any concerns," Phillipe said. "Or even if they're just angry that their children found a body in the woods."

"Phillipe…" Allysha said softly.

He walked toward her and kissed his wife's cheek. "I'll go wait out the front for the police." He didn't look at anyone else as he left the room, but Camille saw in the way his shoulders hunched forward that he was upset by the news. She knew how much he wanted to make a life for them at the manor—how much he wanted them to enjoy his family's home.

"Allysha," Lachlan said, "do you mind if I hang around? I'd like to know what happens with my—with the body."

Allysha nodded. "Of course." She looked at her daughter. "I shouldn't be too long." Then, when Lachlan looked down at his hands, she mouthed at Camille, 'Door open.'

Camille rolled her eyes but nodded.

Jayne didn't say goodbye to any of them as she followed Allysha out the door.

"Well, she's clearly not happy," Jonathan half-joked.

"You know," Grace added, "she's not great with scary stuff when it's fake, let alone when it's real."

"True… but I think it was seeing these two lovebirds come strolling out of the woods that tipped her over the edge." He laughed when Grace whacked him. "What? That's what happened."

Camille sighed. "I'm so sorry. I—"

"Don't apologise, Camille." Lachlan shook his head. "We're not doing anything wrong. I can't help it that I don't feel that way about Jayne. She's a good friend, and I don't want to lose her as a friend, but I'm not going to avoid being happy with someone else just to spare her feelings."

"While I probably wouldn't have put it quite like that," Grace added, "Lachlan's right. It was going to happen sooner or later. It's probably a good thing. Maybe now she can move on."

"Speaking of moving on." Jonathan pushed himself off the stool. "It's been real, but I think it's time we head out."

Grace got up and walked toward Camille to give her a big hug. "I'm so happy for you," she whispered. "He's a great guy."

Camille couldn't stop the smile from spreading across her face when Grace released her.

"Camille, congratulations on destroying my preconceived notions of what happens at a girl's sleepover. It was one hell of a night." Jonathan bowed.

"Get out of here, you idiot." Lachlan playfully swatted his mate.

"Call me later?" Grace said. "Or earlier, if you have any update or find out anything else."

Camille nodded and waved at her other friends leaving the kitchen.

"Then there were two." Lachlan turned on the stool to face her and grabbed her other hand to now hold them both. Camille swallowed thickly, suddenly feeling very nervous and unsure of herself. "Are you feeling better?" he asked.

"Yeah. It's weird. I feel fine now, like nothing happened. I'm actually... I'm so embarrassed I threw up in front of you."

Lachlan chuckled, and the sound made her heart flutter. "Do you want to take the research back upstairs?

Now that its daylight, it feels safer. A distraction until we find out more about what's happening with... in the woods?"

"Yeah, that sounds like a good idea, actually. At least we have a good view from there too without anyone noticing."

CHAPTER SEVENTEEN

N OW THAT IT was just the two of them, Camille felt shy about them being in her room and found herself avoiding looking Lachlan in the eye. She distracted herself with yanking the box of albums out from under her bed.

"Here, let me get that for you," he offered. She shifted to the side and scooped up the pile of research from under the bed as well. "Where do you want it?"

Camille looked down at her bed before quickly glancing at the window seat. "How about over there?"

He placed the box in the middle of the window seat and sat at one end, glancing out at the woods. Camille sat at the opposite end, watching him while pretending to also stare out the window. She didn't have to ask to know he was thinking about his uncle. Shuddering, she realised that every time she'd been gazing out into the woods, there had been a dead man staring back at her.

"Are you okay?" Lachlan asked, and she gave him a quick smile.

"Yeah, of course. Just tired, I guess." Without paying much attention to what she was doing, she pulled an album from the box and tried focusing her attentions on the images. They were of the manor and seemed to be more of the staff than of the LeRoux family. When the

LeRoux's did appear, it was with the staff. Camille admired the close bond they seemed to have had with their employees. She turned the page and noticed a missing photo, running her fingers around the browned outline of where the photo had once been. How long had it been missing? And who would have taken it? She turned the page and found the same on the other side. Perplexed, she flipped through the rest of album, but all the remaining images were still in place.

"What's up?" Lachlan asked, looking up from his reading to observe her frantic flipping.

"I'm not sure. Two photos are missing."

"Hmm…" He stared out the window. When he didn't elaborate further, Camille looked at him before following his gaze outside. Below, her father strode across the grounds, accompanied by two police officers as they headed toward the woods. "Creepy much?" Lachlan pointed at the right side of the garden, where the McAllister's stood mostly obscured by shrubbery as they watched the party walk past.

"I wish I knew what they were up to," Camille whispered. They tried to return to their research, but Camille could feel that Lachlan's attention was down in the woods. She carefully stole looks at him, wishing there was something she could do; she couldn't bear the thought of finding one of her own loved ones out there, alone and abandoned in the woods. Before she could say anything, Lachlan's mobile rang.

"It's Mum." He slid off the window seat and answered it.

Camille tried not to listen to the conversation, but it was hard not to when they were in the same room. Looking out the window again, she watched her mother lead three more men toward the woods, where one of the police officers waited for them at the tree line.

Lachlan sat back down on the edge of the window seat, and Camille jumped in surprise.

"Sorry. What's going on?"

"Looks like more people showed up. They aren't police, though. Not sure who they are."

Lachlan sighed. "Mum and Dad already got the call that the police think it's my uncle. They want me to come home."

"Why don't they just come here?" She felt selfish for even suggesting it, as the offer had more to do with her not wanting him to leave.

"I already brought that up, but the police apparently told them not to come to the manor. That they'll come see my parents once they have more information. I think Dad will have to go make some kind of formal ID, but I don't know."

"Okay." With a small smile, Camille grasped his hand. Lachlan scooted closer, cupped her cheek, and leaned in to kiss her. For a moment, she forgot all about the woods, the manor, and all its mysteries.

With a frustrated groan, Lachlan finally pulled away. "I'll see you at school tomorrow?"

"Are you going to want to go to school tomorrow after all this?" she asked, gesturing toward the woods.

He nodded. "I need to stay busy. Plus, I want to see you."

"Well, in that case, I'll be there."

He kissed her again before forcing himself to stand. "I'll text you later?" he asked, still holding her hand. Camille nodded and squeezed his fingers. He returned the pressure before finally releasing her and walked out of the room.

Pulling her knees to her chest, she sighed. She didn't think she'd ever felt so many emotions at once. Fatigue threatening to pull her under, she yawned and turned to see two officers stringing yellow crime-scene tape across the tree line.

A LOUD BANG startled her awake. The album had fallen from her lap and onto the wooden floor. Camille yawned, unsure of how long she'd been asleep. She looked out the window, but all she could see was the yellow tape flapping in the wind, the trees behind it whipping their branches as if in protest. She wondered if the body was still there, watching her, with its mysterious symbol engraved on the skull—or if had already been taken away.

She got up off the window seat, and stretched, then bent to pick up the album. A blue piece of paper stuck up above the other pages. Slowly, she turned to the back of the album to find a concealed pocket she hadn't noticed before. She gently tugged the paper out of the pocket, set down the album, and unfolded her new find. Her mouth dropped open as she stared at what appeared to be blueprints of the manor. She quickly located her floor and traced the path from the staircase to her room. Frowning, she pulled the prints closer for a better look. A pit sank in her stomach. According to the drawings, there was a narrow room adjacent to the wall of her own — where the wardrobe stood.

Camille couldn't believe what she was seeing as she pawed over the papers, looking for any hint or instruction on how to access that other room. The drawing simply showed the two rooms with the wardrobe crossing into each, the second running the length of her room before it was left open-ended. Camille had no idea what that meant, but she thought over every time she'd thought she'd heard a sound coming from that wardrobe, plus the scratching on the walls. Chewing on her bottom lip, she lowered the drawing and stared at the wardrobe. Suddenly, somehow, it felt alive.

She picked up her phone and checked the time; Lachlan should have long been home by now. Camille quickly called him, holding the phone to her ear and eyeing the wardrobe from the safety of the window seat.

Lachlan picked up on the third ring. "Miss me already?" he joked, and though Camille wanted to smile at the sound of his voice, she couldn't ignore how sad he sounded.

"I'm sorry. I didn't even think before I called. It's probably not a good time — "

"Of course it is. It's nice to hear your voice, to be honest. Mum and Dad are still in the loungeroom with the police, and I'm just pacing around in my room, waiting to be called down. So, I'm actually keen for the distraction."

"Well, in that case, I think I found something."

"Yeah, that sounds like a pretty good distraction."

Camille filled him in on her findings and received only silence in reply. "Hello?" She pulled the phone away from her ear and checked the screen, thinking they must have been disconnected, but he was still on the line. "Lachlan?"

"Yeah, I'm here. I was just thinking. What if it isn't a secret room but more like a tunnel? That could explain why it's open-ended in the drawing."

"I don't know which thought I like least..." Camille replied quietly.

"I want to come back up to the manor, but my parents... my Dad... Well, you know. I need to hang around here for a bit."

"Of course. Don't even worry about it. I just needed to tell someone."

"I'm glad I was the one you wanted to share it with," he replied, his voice softening. "Just promise me something."

"Sure."

"Promise me you won't look into it by yourself. Wait until someone else is with you. Preferably me. After everything that happened last night, we have no idea what you'll walk into."

"Something's still bothering me about all this."

"You mean aside from the fact that you found a secret tunnel leading from your bedroom wardrobe?" he asked dryly.

Camille smiled. "Yeah, aside from that. Everything I've seen or experienced since moving into the manor makes me think this is some kind of ghost."

"Right."

"So why would a ghost need a tunnel?"

Lachlan let the question sink in a little longer before giving her any response. "Please be careful."

CHAPTER EIGHTEEN

CAMILLE SAT ON the window seat, alternating her attention between the beckoning wardrobe and the fresh wave of people below in the manor grounds. Her mother stood in front of the crime-scene tape, helping to direct authorities as they arrived periodically. Mr McAllister stood in one of the garden beds, a pair of shears held open in front of a branch that he hadn't actually cut in the ten minutes he'd been there. Camille strained to see directly beneath her window, where Miss McAllister stood at the base of the stairs leading from the back veranda to the grounds, her back rigid and her hands clasped tightly in front of her. As though feeling Camille's gaze, she turned and looked up. Camille instinctively pulled back from the window, unsure why she felt the necessity to hide. So, she glanced at the wardrobe instead.

The longer she gazed at it, the more she felt her resolve crumbling beneath her curiosity. She took the blueprint to her bed and spread it out atop her bedcovers.

Due to the sheer size of the manor, the section of the blueprint that made up her bedroom was tiny. She leaned closer, trying to find any clue as to accessing the hidden tunnel from her side of the wardrobe. Nothing stood out. With a sigh, Camille paced her room, her hands clasped on her forehead. Her gaze fell on the album, and she rushed toward the window seat to pick it up. Finding the back pocket again, she carefully slipped her fingers inside and tried to feel around without tearing it. There it was—the edges of another piece of paper at the bottom. It took some careful tugging, but she finally slipped it out held it up to the window. The seemingly random lines there made her frown, but she had to keep looking.

Walking to the wardrobe, she held the slip of paper up in front of her, hoping to make sense of it. When that didn't work, she folded the wardrobe doors open and tried again. Camille's hope increased as the lines seemed to coincide with the shelves and racks. Feeling like she was onto something, she took a step closer, trying to link the two together. While her father had tried pushing and tapping on the rear of the wardrobe, the drawing in her hand seemed to indicate that, while the tunnel was behind the back of the wardrobe, one of the shelves acted as the means to open it.

Camille ran her hands over the shelves lining the left side. A scuffmark marred the shelf third from the bottom, but as she leaned down, she could see it was actually multiple marks, as if that shelf had been scraped repeatedly. Running her finger over them, she tried to determine how they were caused. Camille pressed against the side of the shelf, but nothing happened. Still, she was sure this was her way in. Stepping back out of the wardrobe, she studied the front of the shelf for any other clues, pushed some of her clothes aside, and slid her arm along the inside of the shelf. When she pushed it toward the outside, something let out an audible click. The shelf had moved only a centimetre or so—hardly noticeable if she hadn't been aware of it. Right before she stood, wondering if she'd merely broken it, the siding slowly withdrew into the wardrobe. Camille stared at it in awe, and with another click, the back of the wardrobe slid aside. She'd expected the thing to creak or groan with lack of use; instead, it was completely silent.

Camille scurried out of the wardrobe, unsure what to expect.

She stared at the gaping black hole in the back of the wardrobe, waiting for something to happen and feeling silly when nothing did. Lachlan's voice echoed in her head, telling her not to go in there alone. Still, she knew she wasn't patient enough to wait for him to return to the manor. This was the perfect opportunity to explore while her parents and the McAllister's were preoccupied by what was happening in the woods. She certainly didn't want Miss McAllister lurking around to find her out.

With her decision made, Camille snatched her phone off the window seat, shoved it in her jacket pocket, and armed herself with one of the torches her mum had provided during the storm. She took a moment to stare at the wardrobe and took a deep breath. Then she stepped quickly toward it before she could talk herself out of this.

Stepping into the wardrobe, she turned on the flashlight and reluctantly opened the camera on her phone to record whatever she encountered. She felt she owed Lachlan that much for not waiting for him. Camille directed the beam into the opening and was relieved to see the light bounce off the wall only a couple metres away. Taking a deep breath, she lifted her phone and stepped inside. On her right, she found the end of the tunnel. That left only one way to go.

It took all her focus to put one foot in front of the other, her bravado evaporating with each step. The darkness felt old and thick, like she was blanketed in a velvety ink. Even the torchlight struggled to penetrate it. It felt unnatural somehow, as though the darkness was an entity in itself, pushing back with every step she took. The ground felt smooth, perhaps angling downward slightly, yet she couldn't be completely certain. She felt her bearings slipping away. Just like in the woods, the nausea returned, cinching her stomach in a barbed grasp. Camille swallowed thickly, willing it to pass. Instead, it only worsened the farther she descended. More than once, she had to stop and brace herself against the wall.

Camille was about to give up and turn around, thinking she'd be sick at any moment—but then the torchlight caught something up ahead. Her heart skipped a beat as she stumbled forward, then she found an old wooden trunk placed against the wall. She almost forgot her sickly unease as she shone the light over the lid, making sure her phone captured everything. Looking down at the intricate carvings decorating the lid, she realised she had seen it before—in her dream about the attic.

Her breathing felt shallow as she stared at the faded surface, unsure whether she was really seeing it or if it was just another dream. It looked older now, aged, with a crack running up the side before disappearing under the lid. There was also a chip in the bottom right corner. Camille forced herself to walk beside it. Placing the butt of the torch in her mouth, she used her free hand to release the twin latches of the lid. It was a struggle to heave open the heavy top with one hand, and the wood groaned in resistance. When she was sure the thing would stay open, she took the torch out of her mouth and focused it on the contents of the trunk. From where she set her phone against the inside of the lid, it could record everything.

The top layer appeared to be blankets knitted in dull shades and neatly folded. Camille rested the torch on the side of the trunk and carefully lifted the blankets before placing them on the floor beside her. The next layer was a fine tissue paper that came apart in her hands as she tried to lift it. Beneath the paper, atop folded clothes, was the silver hairbrush and the mirror she recalled from her dream.

Camille doubled over as another wave of nausea overcame her. She forced herself to breathe slowly, exhaling through her mouth while willing it to pass. It lessened enough that she thought she could lift her head, and with a shaking hand, she grabbed the hairbrush and mirror and pulled them out of the trunk. Then she reached back inside to pull out the first item of clothing. She didn't need to let it unfold; she'd recognise a leather jacket anywhere. Camille was happy to see it appeared to be in good condition. She set it atop the blankets on the ground beside her.

The next item was a grey t-shirt, nothing special, until she turned it around to see the front. There was a large white star in the centre of the shirt, partially obscured by a splatter. Camille lowered the shirt into the trunk and picked up the torch for a better look. The stain was dark, but Camille was certain it was dry blood. She grabbed the phone to document the finding. There was something about the shirt, but before she could study it more, she suffered another wave of nausea even more powerful than the last. Bile rose into her mouth. She forced herself to swallow it, and her eyes watered.

Placing the camera and torch back in place, she dumped the shirt alongside the jacket without a second glance. As she grabbed the next item of clothing, she knew immediately that it was a pair of jeans. Camille unfolded them, laying them out across the length of the trunk. They were dirty with what looked like dry mud, especially around the knees, which had also started to tear on the left leg.

Camille lowered her head, forcing herself to take deep breaths. She was so overcome with nausea that all she wanted to do was curl up and rest her head on the cool ground. Instead, she forced herself to push on. She dropped the jeans and grabbed a pair of boots. She heard a slight tinkle and turned them on their side to see two small charms hanging from the zipper — a tiny kangaroo and an emu. She dropped the boots back into the trunk as though they were on fire.

A sudden chill gripped her, and she tentatively wiped at the sweat beading across her forehead. Looking at her recording phone, she opened and closed her mouth, unsure of her ability to speak. Pawing over the shirt and jacket, she tried to refute her theory, but there was no mistaking it. The clothes were hers.

This time, the nausea won. Camille lurched sideways and vomited across the tunnel floor. When she finished, she sat up and wiped her mouth with her sleeve. Staring at the offending clothes, she felt a chill run up her spine. Without a second thought, she shoved them back into the trunk, then grabbed her phone and torch. The trunk's lid fell with a loud bang that reverberated up and down the tunnel.

Camille headed back up the tunnel at a run, stumbling as she exited the wardrobe. The torch and her phone flew from her hands and skidded across the floor. She got to her feet and rummaged through her own clothes in the wardrobe. When she found what she wanted, she hurried to her bed and laid the outfit across the covers — her favourite pair of jeans that had slightly worn through on the left knee, her favourite leather jacket, her grey t-shirt with the white star, and her favourite pair of boots with the charms on the zipper. But these clothes were clean and devoid of any stains. In fact, the shirt was new; she'd bought it before the move and hadn't even worn it yet.

Camille paced around the room, trying to make sense of it. Her mouth felt dry, and she couldn't swallow as butterflies flew viciously around her stomach. She did, with some gratitude, realise that the nausea had for the most part left her. Then she looked back toward the wardrobe.

She rushed back to it and quickly pressed against the third shelf from the bottom before standing back. The rear wall of the wardrobe returned. After closing the doors, she stooped to retrieve the torch and her phone to stop the recovering. Her thumb hovered over the screen, and she wondered who she needed to call first, Grace or Lachlan.

Instead, her phone rang. She nearly dropped it in surprise. Grace's name appeared on the screen and Camille quickly answered the call. "Hey. I was just about to call you."

"Well, that was good timing! I was just calling to see how everything's going." Grace's voice was full of concern.

Camille glanced up at the wardrobe for a moment before replying. "It's been an interesting afternoon…"

"I bet. It's not every day you find the body of your boyfriend's missing uncle in your own private forest— I'm sorry. That came out wrong. I hope that didn't sound completely insensitive."

"It's fine," Camille replied dismissively. "It's about something else, actually. I found something…" She proceeded to fill Grace in on her discovery of the blueprints and the secret passage.

"Holy shit! An actual secret passage? That's amazing! Please tell me you didn't go in there on your own. Wait, of course you did…"

Camille smiled at the fact that Grace already knew her so well.

"Well, come on, then. Don't leave me hanging. What did you find in there?"

"That's where it got really weird…"

"Because it hadn't been weird at all before then," Grace joked.

"Okay, weirder. I found the trunk. You know, the one from my dream in the attic?"

"No way… are you serious? What was it doing in the middle of a tunnel? What was inside it?"

"I have no idea why it was in the tunnel, but when I opened it, I found some clothes. My clothes. Only they can't be my clothes, because my clothes are on my bed."

"Hang on, wait. What? You've lost me…"

"I found clothes in the trunk that match mine exactly, only the ones in the trunk were dirty. I think the shirt was even bloody."

"Woah." Grace paused. "Are you sure?"

"Pretty sure. I don't understand how — I mean, they're exactly the same as my clothes, right down to tiny details, like the charms on my boots. But my clothes aren't missing. It doesn't make any sense."

"No, it doesn't…"

"I'll send you the video if you don't believe me."

"Of course I believe you! I'm sure you can appreciate it's a little hard to take in, though."

"Tell me about it. I thought I'd film it for the blog, but now I'm not so sure that's a good idea."

"I don't think so. I mean, I think we should maybe keep the discovery to ourselves until we can work out what's going on. If that's even possible."

"Yeah, exactly." Camille walked to the window seat and, placing one knee on the cushion, leaned forward to see her parents walking across the grounds toward the house. The McAllister's were nowhere in sight.

"Have you told the others yet?" Grace asked.

"No. You called right while I was trying to decide what to do."

"I can call them for you if you want. What are you going to do?"

Camille pulled away from the window with a sudden idea. "I think I'm going to track down Miss McAllister and get some answers. I know they have way more of an idea about what's going on here than they're letting on."

"Okay, sounds good. Text me when you're done, and the four of us can Facetime so you can fill us in."

"Right. I'll talk to you soon." Camille ended the call. Taking one last look at the clothes on her bed, she quickly walked out of the room and closed the door behind her.

CHAPTER NINETEEN

AMILLE HURRIED ALONG the landing, checking the time on her phone as she tried to think where in the manor Miss McAllister would be lurking. She heard voices at the bottom of the staircase, and she followed them around to the sitting room. Her parents stood on opposite sides of the lounge, facing each other while nursing hot cups of tea. They almost looked like a mirror image.

"Hi, sweetheart," her mother said, her voice heavy with fatigue as Camille entered the room.

"Hey. Did Jayne get home okay?"

Her mother smiled wryly at her. "Yes, though she was most upset. I can't say I blame her. It wasn't a pretty sight, seeing that body out there. I don't think her mother was too impressed with the state I bought her home in, either."

"That's not your fault, Mum. I think only a small part of the reason why Jayne was so upset had to do with the woods."

"Oh?" her father asked.

Camille felt herself turn red as a flush of heat rushed from her neck up into her face. "Uh, yeah. Jayne's liked Lachlan for a long time, and, uh… he kind of likes me…"

She caught the smile on her father's face, though he tried to hide it by taking another sip of tea.

"Ahh, well that certainly explains why she was so much more upset than the rest of you," Allysha replied kindly.

"So, what's going on out there, anyway?" Camille asked, wanting to change the subject.

"Quite a bit, actually." Phillipe placed his teacup on the coffee table. "There's a whole team of criminal and forensic specialists milling around out there. The detective said it was most unusual, which we could see for ourselves, but there's lots of photo-taking and 'evidence'-collecting. They were pretty unhappy that Lachlan disturbed the body when he searched for the wallet."

"Yeah, I guess we weren't really thinking about that," Camille admitted.

"It doesn't matter now," Phillipe continued. "They were removing the body and taking it back to the morgue for further investigation when we left them. I imagine poor Lachlan's father will be asked to head down there at some point."

"Yes, it must be so awful for them," Allysha added. "Especially for Lachlan to have found him."

"What do they think happened to him?" Camille asked, thinking of the symbol they'd found etched in the man's skull.

"No idea. They wouldn't say much to us. I asked if it was a case of exposure. You know, getting lost in the woods. But the detective said they were confident that wasn't the case. I'm sure we'll find out eventually."

"Do they know how long he's been out there?" Camille asked.

"They'll work that out too. Probably years, if I had to guess. It would have to be." Phillipe shrugged.

"So, they would have to question the McAllister's, then? Since they've lived here the whole time?"

Phillipe nodded. "I suppose they will. I don't think they have yet."

"Speaking of, have you seen either of them since you came in?" Camille asked, trying to be subtle.

Her mother nodded. "Miss McAllister brought us in the lovely tea."

"And I'm pretty sure I saw Mr McAllister head out to tend the front gardens," Phillipe added. "Though I have a feeling that was just his excuse to watch all the comings and goings."

"How so?" Camille asked, trying to hide the surprise in her voice. Maybe her parents knew more about the McAllister's than she thought.

"Oh, just that he seems to be very protective of the grounds and doesn't seem in the least bit happy to have people walking all over them. Not that they're in great condition, mind you. But I suppose it's still his pride and joy."

"Right." Camille nodded. "Okay. Well, I might go grab myself an apple from the kitchen." She turned and headed toward the door.

"Don't ruin your appetite," her mother called behind her. "I think we'll have an early dinner tonight."

Camille was already passing the staircase. When she stormed into the kitchen, she found Miss McAllister wiping down the kitchen bench. She looked up as Camille entered, and they stared at each other, each waiting for the other to talk.

"Can I get you something, miss?" Miss McAllister asked, the tone of her voice clearly indicating it was the last thing she was interested in doing.

"You can tell me what you and your brother were doing walking into the woods last night."

Miss McAllister didn't even pause. "I beg your pardon, miss, but you must be mistaken. It stormed last night. Hardly the weather to be walking anywhere, let alone the woods."

"I know what I saw."

"Are you sure about that?" This time, Miss McAllister paused her wiping and looked straight at Camille. "One can never be certain of what they see in this place."

Camille said nothing but narrowed her eyes. It didn't surprise her that the McAllister's knew more than they let on. She just had to work out how to get them to talk. "I know about the tunnel."

Miss McAllister turned her back as she rinsed the cloth in the sink. Camille waited, but it was as though the woman hoped her turned back would make Camille give up and leave.

"The old woman I keep seeing," Camille said, changing her tactic. "I hear her. At least, I think it's her. In the walls and in the attic. Sometimes, I see her right before I fall asleep, when I'm still partly awake—"

"It would seem, then, that you are simply dreaming. The imagination can run away with you in a place this size."

"No. I know the difference between being awake and being asleep. She's here. But what I want to know is how here is she?"

Miss McAllister hung the cloth over the edge of the sink and finally turned around. "There are no answers to the questions you have."

"Of course there are. There are always answers. You just don't want to tell me what they are."

The woman folded her arms. "Now you want to listen to me?" she hissed. "I've been trying to make you listen since you and your family moved in."

Camille blinked at the sudden venom in the woman's tone. "What are you talking about?"

"I told you to stop digging. To leave things alone. Not only did you ignore me, but you also involved your little friends."

"What do you care so much about what we find here?"

"I don't. But you should." Miss McAllister's eyes widened before she turned her back once more and proceeded to wipe down the already clean sink.

"What's that supposed to mean?" Camille asked, her voice almost a whisper beneath a new wave of dread.

"You should have left well enough alone. It doesn't matter now. It's too late."

"For what?"

Miss McAllister ignored her, and Camille tapped her fingers on the counter in frustration. She eyed the woman's back and ran through the interactions they'd had since the day her family arrived at the manor. Could it really be that in some strange way, Miss McAllister had been looking out for her? From what, though? And why would she do that if it 'didn't matter'? "The woman I've seen. Is she real? Or is she a ghost?" The question hung in the air before it dwindled away, unanswered. Admitting defeat, Camille turned away to head out of the kitchen.

"She is neither," Ms McAllister said. "And both. As is the manor."

Camille frowned, mulling over the words as she turned back toward the woman. "That doesn't make sense. How can she be both? How can a house be both?"

"It's of no consequence whether it makes sense to you. The end result will be the same. It always is."

"Your riddles aren't helping me at all." Camille slapped a hand down on the counter. "I know there's something going on here. I went into the tunnel. The one that leads from my room. I found the trunk and the clothes inside it. My clothes. So, you need to tell me how that's even possible."

Miss McAllister refused to look Camille in the eye as she walked around the counter and left the kitchen. Camille just stared after her in disbelief, standing there with even more questions now and still no answers.

CHAPTER TWENTY

CAMILLE GROANED IN her sleep. It felt like someone was trying to pull her out of her dream, but she fought to hold onto it despite not knowing exactly what the dream was. Opening her eyes, she groaned again. The air felt heavy and stuffy, like it hung over her in a thick cloud. Reaching out, she tapped the bedside table until she found the lamp and turned on the switch.

The old woman's face illuminated right in front of her, just inches away. Camille screamed, but no sound come out. She scrambled backward over the bed until she bumped against the headboard and had nowhere else to go. The woman held her gaze with the eyes Camille had seen a dozen times—though instead of the mischievous glint, there was something darker, almost malicious.

Camille's heart pounded painfully against her chest as she struggled to breathe. The old woman's presence seemed to suck the very air from the room. She wanted to speak, but no sound whatsoever came from her mouth, even when she felt like a gaping goldfish. Forcing herself to calm the hysteria threatening to overcome her, she instead broke the stare and gazed at the rest of the woman's body.

The old woman bent at the waist to lower herself toward where Camille had been sleeping. She looked real enough—there was certainly nothing ethereal about her. When she reached out to touch the woman, she quickly yanked her hand back at from the firm arm beneath the white cotton sleeve. The old woman leaned in closer, and Camille tried to push herself farther against the headboard. She had the distinct impression that the woman was going to kiss her, and she turned her head, squeezing her eyes shut. Instead, the old woman's ice-cold hand brushed against her cheek in a dry caress. Then that hand wrapped around Camille's throat, though her grasp wasn't tight enough to hurt. The woman leaned closer still. "You will help me."

Camille tried to free herself from the grasp, but her eyelids grew heavy, and she felt herself slipping back into slumber.

A WOMAN'S VOICE made Camille stir from her sleep again. There was a familiarity to it that she couldn't place. The voice grew louder and closer the more awake Camille felt, and when she finally opened her eyes, she found herself standing and surrounded by trees.

There was a young girl in front of her. She held the hand of an older woman who was a couple steps ahead of her. The woman talked excitedly as she navigated their path through the trees. The young girl turned and looked over her shoulder, as if she sensed Camille there.

Camille knew immediately that that little girl was Mena. When the woman turned her head to be sure of the girl beside her, Camille also recognised Caroline.

A wave of dizziness made her close her eyes. She willed herself to wake from what she knew had to be a dream. Instead, when she opened her eyes again, she was looking through Mena's eyes now instead of her own. It was disorientating; she felt like a passenger — an intruder in someone else's body. Camille wanted nothing more than to wake up, but with each step Mena took, Camille's vivid connection with the girl intensified. She knew, somehow, that this was a memory, that it was being revealed to her for a reason. She also knew she wouldn't be released until she knew why.

Camille tried to focus on Caroline's voice. There was no mistaking the woman's excitement. She rarely waited for Mena — or Alice, as she now called the girl — to respond as she moved on to the next question or random fact about the manor. It sounded like Caroline had already convinced herself of the child's being an orphan and was already planning their future at the manor together. Camille could feel Mena's curiosity, her eagerness to return to the manor, and she was somewhat surprised to find Mena's thoughts came as clearly to her as if they were her own.

It wasn't that she expected to see her family; Mena knew that many years had passed since she'd stepped into that cave, even though it had felt like only a few seconds. They stopped when they broke free of the woods and entered the manicured grounds. Camille gasped at the beauty of the gardens before her, only slightly aware of Mena taking it all in too. The manor up ahead was still as grand as the day of her father's party, and yet, Mena noticed that the shiny newness of her home was gone. She wondered just how many years had passed.

Caroline got down on her knees and took both of Mena's hands in hers. "Alice, this might sound crazy, but I feel like you have been brought to me. That you're the answer to my prayers. Naturally, we will have to seek out your parents, but if they truly are gone like you said, then I want you to know that I'd like to adopt you as my own. It doesn't have to be right away. We can take all the time you need to get to know me, my husband, and our daughter Sybil, though she is a grown woman herself. Is that something you think you might like?" Caroline looked intently at the little girl, who stared back with a wide-eyed innocence only Camille knew wasn't real. A sunny smile spread across Caroline's face when Mena nodded.

The woman embraced her, and Mena fought her instinct to pull away. It surprised Camille how repulsed the young girl was by the touch of another. Even more surprising was how well Mena hid it. Camille had to keep reminding herself that this was only a child, though something about her made her seem older, wiser, and certainly intelligent beyond her years.

Caroline guided them up the back stairs and ushered them through the kitchen, through the servant's corridor, and into a generously sized servants' quarter. She chattered away as she led Mena into the bathroom and turned on the taps. Sitting on the edge of the bathtub, she faced the girl, and Camille got her first good look at the woman. Caroline's pale blue eyes radiated both kindness and sadness, yet the lines spreading from the corners of her eyes showed how much she loved to laugh. She was probably in her mid-forties and quite slim — at least from what could be seen with the full skirt and long sleeves of her uniform. Her hair was a mousey brown and pulled back in a neat bun. It reminded Camille of the old woman she'd been seeing around the manor.

"Would you like me to help you undress? We will need to get you cleaned up before I take you to see the mistress."

"I can do it," Mena replied as her little fingers fumbled with the buttons running down the front of her dress. Caroline discretely gave the child some privacy and reached back to run her hand through the bathwater. When she was satisfied with the temperature, she helped Mena into the tub. Camille felt the delicious warmth of the water enveloping her, felt the relief of the caked-on dirt and filth starting to slip away from Mena's skin. She almost groaned when Caroline poured a jug of water over her head, gently massaging the dirt from Mena's hair. The woman's voice was almost hypnotic as she talked of Mistress LeRoux and her kindness, of how she would take Mena to meet her as soon as she was ready. Caroline alternated between talking to the child and talking to herself, and Camille found it increasingly harder to pay attention the more Mena relaxed. Finally, their eyes slipped shut.

'I know you are here with me.'

Camille opened her eyes, startled. She wasn't sure if she'd spoken the words or if they were Mena's, but she realised she'd somehow dozed off. Now, they were out of the bath, being wrapped in a towel. Caroline led Mena back to her room, still talking, and sat the girl on the bed. Then she went to the trunk at the foot of the bed and opened it. Camille recognised the carvings on the lid as the same trunk inside the tunnel. She watched Caroline rummage around for a few moments before withdrawing a clothbound parcel. The woman laid it on the bed and gently opened it. Within was a number of little girl's dresses.

"These were my daughter's. Sybil. Though she hasn't been little for a good many years now. I was saving them for… well, that doesn't matter now. I think they should be a perfect fit for you." She held one up to inspect it — a navy pinafore with a white, long-sleeved shirt underneath it. Mena let the woman dress her, sitting quietly as Caroline ran the hairbrush through the child's wet hair. Camille felt the conflict rising inside the girl — the irritation of another's touch but also the enjoyment rising from Caroline's fingers expertly weaving Mena's hair into a flawless braid.

Mena was exactly where — and when — she wanted to be.

CHAPTER TWENY-ONE

CAMILLE OPENED HER eyes and was instantly hit with a wave of dizziness. She waited for it to pass, but it only lessened slightly. Relenting, she blinked rapidly to clear her blurry vision and looked around in the darkness, hoping to see her bedroom furniture. Yet, once again, she wasn't in her room. She wasn't in the attic, either.

Reaching out with both hands, she took a tentative step forward and felt cold, hard surface of the stone wall at her fingertips. Camille turned around and found the same behind her. As the remnants of the dream cleared, she realised she was in the tunnel — only she had no way of knowing how far down it she'd travelled. Sliding her foot along the ground, she felt for the angling floor and realized it sloped down in front of her. So, she turned around to head back toward her room, but the dream lingering in her mind convinced her that she'd woken in the tunnel for a reason. She stood there, unsure what to do and wishing she had her phone on her. But she knew that if she returned for her phone, there was a good chance she wouldn't re-enter the tunnel. At least, not alone. Between the unease and the waves of nausea, Camille recognised the urgency of her decision. If she didn't go now, she would never find the answers she wanted. Squinting through the darkness in the tunnel, she thought she saw the faintest glowing light. It was enough to stoke her curiosity, and she tentatively stepped through the wardrobe. After only a few steps, that same sudden nausea washed over her, this time so strong, she doubled over. She tried to wait it out, but again, it only subsided a little. Lifting her head, she tried to focus on the glowing light as she forced herself forward. Each step was a struggle; she couldn't think clearly, and the tunnel somehow seemed to lengthen the farther she tried to go. The slight decline finally levelled out, encouraging Camille to keep going despite the fact that it seemed she'd made no progress at all. Yet that possibility only made Camille all the more determined to find out why.

With her next step, the nausea flared up again and brought her to her knees. She vomited, the acrid smell stinging her nose and bringing tears to her eyes. Unable to get to her feet, Camille forced herself to push forward on her hands and knees as she heaved and wretched.

The farther she went, the sicker and weaker she felt. Still, she didn't want to give up, knowing it would take just as long to head back up the tunnel toward her room, with or without her answers. Knowing the tunnel couldn't possibly go on forever, she crawled along with her eyes closed. When the smooth surface of the tunnel floor gave way to something more rough and jagged, Camille opened her eyes, pushed herself back onto her knees, and stared around in awe.

The dark tunnel had given way to what looked like a salt cave. She touched the hard, peach-coloured rock and felt its energy vibrating through her hands. Feeling more alert now as her nausea fell away, she scanned the walls and ceiling, trying to find the source of the light. It seemed the cave itself was generating its own light.

Camille leaned her head against the wall, allowing herself a moment to regain her strength and clarity. There was no way she was going back now; she had to see what was beyond the cave, to see what else the tunnel had to show her. Watching her footing over the uneven floor, she carefully made her way through the narrowing cavern. She had to duck under the larger stalactites and squinted. The farther she walked through the narrowing tunnel, the more the light dimmed.

When the cave walls seemed to close in around her, she forced herself to take slow, deep breaths against the impending claustrophobia. She had come too far to panic now. As she found herself once again in darkness, Camille held her hands out in front of her, using them for guidance. Within a few more steps, her hands came upon a smooth surface in front of her. Running her fingers over it, she prayed it wasn't a dead end and that her journey had been for nothing. Still, there seemed to be no way forward.

Tired and overwhelmed, Camille slid down the wall with a strangled sob. She couldn't bear the thought of having to go all the way back; all she wanted was to close her eyes and sleep, but the images of Lachlan's uncle propped up against the tree forced her to open her eyes again. Willing herself to calm down, to try thinking rationally, she felt something digging into her back leaned away from the wall. After running her fingers along the surface behind her, at the notch jutting from the wall before giving way to a small groove. Not caring that it might not have been for her, or that she might regret revealing its purpose, she slipped her fingers into the groove and pushed.

Nothing happened. She tried pushing to the right, and her hand shook as she changed her grasp and pushed to the left. Finally, the notch shifted, and the wall in front of her slid aside. There was nothing beyond it but more darkness, yet Camille climbed to her feet and stepped forward anyway.

When her outstretched hands brushed against something soft in the darkness, she yelped and jerked her hands back against her chest. She tried to calm her breathing and her racing heart again, listening intently for any sounds to prove she wasn't alone. But she was. After a few more seconds, she tentatively reached out again and touched the item before her. It didn't move or withdraw, and she grabbed a better hold to determine what it was. A growing panic crept over her as she realised these were clothes in her hands. She ran her fingers down the length of what felt like a jacket sleeve, and her panic eased when there was no hand protruding from the end of it. Then she felt for the collar and the coat hanger beneath it.

A smile spread across Camille's face as she realised how silly it was to let the darkness get the better of her. She stepped forward through the clothes until she felt the hard, wooden door to the wardrobe in front of her. No light seeped through from the other side, but Camille pressed her ear against the door to listen again.

Confident that there was no one there, she slowly opened the door and stepped out. Tears stung her eyes, surprising her with how relieved she was to be free of the tunnel again. Making the most of it, she stretched out her limbs, grateful to freely move around again.

She was here for a reason, though, and she studied the new room. It was a bedroom, small but neat. There was a double bed on an old-fashioned brass frame, neatly made up with crisp white pillows and an intricate quilt of mottled greens reminding her of the woods. Beside the bed on the left was a brass nightstand — glass-topped with a candle in a stand, the wax perfectly in place in varying stages of drip before pooling in a dried puddle at the base. Camille went to the table and touched the wax, finding it cool and hard. Beside the nightstand was a chair that also looked old, its dark-green, velvet upholstery worn in places. One of the round buttons sewn into the seat was loose, its frayed thread visible. She ran her fingers along the edge of the armrest as she walked to the window a bit farther down from the wardrobe. It was a modest window, only about a metre wide and half a metre high, and Camille had to stand on her tiptoes to see out of it. There was nothing to see except a clearing lined by a wall of trees so thick, reaching so high, that she could hardly tell if the sky was darkening or if the trees just cast too large a shadow.

Camille frowned. She knew the woods were part of the estate, but she'd found no mention of another property on the grounds. She doubted her parents knew of its existence; if the police had found it while investigating the body of Lachlan's uncle, they would have told her. She wondered if this was where the McAllister's had come during the storm, but that didn't quite make sense. Why would they come all the way out here when they had their own residence in the manor?

She tiptoed across the room and stood at the open door, listening for anyone else's presence before she ventured out to explore further. She'd expected so see a hallway, but instead, the rest of the living area opened up before her. It wasn't a large space—more like a cosy cottage. Feeling exposed, she quickly scanned the room but confirmed that she was alone.

Slowly, she walked around the room, taking in as many details as she could. To the far right was a small kitchen, the benches and sink spotless, devoid of any crockery or appliances. Farther along the wall was the front door with a small peek-hole but no other windows. The other side of the room held two more windows like the one in the bedroom. To her left was a closed door, which Camille assumed to be the bathroom. She walked carefully toward it, wary of making the wooden floor creak beneath her. When she neared the bathroom, she didn't hear any movement or running water there, either. So, she really was alone.

Turning her attention to the centre of the room, she walked toward the small couch and a side chair that matched the one in the bedroom. A crocheted blanket draped over the back of the couch, made from wool and also in numerous shades of green. A single cushion nestled against the armrest. The couch faced a fireplace, and Camille wondered why she had never seen smoke rising through the trees in all the time she'd spent gazing out at the woods. After studying it more closely, she realised it was electric and made to look like a traditional fireplace. It seemed out of place in the cottage—modern and the only electrical item Camille could see. A matching side table sat beside a small wooden coffee table, both boasting half-used candles.

A very old-looking book with its cover worn and the spine cracked was the only other thing on the coffee table. Camille picked it up, trying to make out the faded writing of the title: Through the Looking Glass. She carefully placed it back on the table and realised there were no light fittings in the cottage, and she didn't see any power points in the walls.

She walked toward the kitchen, running her fingers along the cool white benchtop. The small stovetop seemed to be gas, and a metal kettle rested atop one of the hotplates. Camille carefully touched the kettle and found it cold as well. She frowned, turning around, and stared at the room. Despite the immaculate cleanliness, it was clearly lived in. But by whom?

Her gaze fell upon a single photo frame half-obscured by a candelabra on the mantel. Crossing the room once more, she removed the frame for a better look, noting the lack of dust. Then she saw the photo, dropped the frame, and stepped back. The photo's shattering glass seemed excessively loud in the silent cottage, but Camille hardly noticed. Her breath came in short, host bursts as she stared at the photo, struggling to comprehend the image while feeling as though the ground were opening up beneath her to swallow her whole. It couldn't be real. She knew that. It just wasn't possible.

On shaky legs, Camille knelt and barely registered the sharp pricks of broken glass piercing through her jeans and her skin. She plucked the photo from the broken frame and lifted it up for a better look, telling herself over and over that she was mistaken. The photo was old, sepia-toned, not unlike those she'd found in the attic. On the left stood the old woman she'd seen at the manor. Though the woman looked slightly younger, perhaps in her forties, her hair was still white and fastened in a severe bun. The collar of her dress sat high, topped with a flourish of white ruffle. Her hands were clasped before her above the skirts of her black dress billowing down to the floor and revealing only the tips of her pointy-toed boots. Despite her solemn expression, there was a twinkle in her eye Camille knew was Mena's. The truth dawned on her, and her mouth fell open. Mena was the woman in her forties now—the same old woman Camille had seen roaming the estate grounds.

How? She'd have to be over a hundred years old. That's not even possible?

What troubled her further was the woman standing beside Mena. In a dress almost identical though with a more modest collar stood an elderly woman. Her hair was also white, and while it was also fastened in a bun, it was softer than her companion's, loose tendrils of hair framing her face. A black shawl draped across her shoulders, with a hole in the shoulder that she'd tried to hide. If Camille hadn't known where to look for it, she would never have noticed it, but she knew it was the same black shawl stashed in her wardrobe at the manor. Her heart thundered against her chest as she forced herself to look at the face of this second woman staring back at her.

It was her own.

Her hands were trembling now. There was no mistaking it. She was there, in the photo, with Mena. Despite the difference in age, those were definitely her eyes staring back at her. When she turned the photo over, she found the words Alice and Catherine, 1910 written in elegant cursive. Letting the photo drop to the floor again, she forced herself to her feet and half ran, half stumbled toward the door. She didn't even think about the tunnel that had brought her here as she yanked open the door and dashed into the woods, guided only by her fear and the desire to get as far away from the cottage — and the photo — as she could.

The trees grasped and tugged at her, catching on her clothes and her hair. She stumbled and lurched through the last of the trees and into the manor gardens, sprawling across the ground. A group of people had gathered at the entry point for the investigation farther along the tree line, but her vision blurred with tears and she couldn't make out their faces. Picking herself up, she ignored their calls, sobbing and gasping and running at full speed toward the manor.

As she took the stairs two at a time, her mother walked out of the kitchen, holding a tray of snacks. Camille barrelled into her, sending the tray crashing to the floor as she collapsed at her mother's feet.

"Camille! What's wrong?" Allysha helped her daughter to her feet again, and Camille clung to her, sobbing. "Camille?" Allysha's concern only heightened as she repeatedly tried to coax from her daughter what had happened.

When Camille finally caught her breath, she stepped back, still gripping her mother. "I think I'm losing my mind."

Allysha's mouth fell open, and she scanned her daughter's face in confusion. "Why would you say that?"

"The manor... this place... I don't know. I think it's haunted. Or I'm haunted. I've seen things, Mum. Things that... aren't possible. None of it makes sense. I feel like something's after me."

Allysha said nothing as she embraced her daughter, rubbing her child's back. It comforted them both, and when the woman finally spoke again, the slight edge in her voice surprised Camille. "I think finding Lachlan's uncle in the woods took a greater toll on you than we thought. That, and I think all the research you've been doing on the manor... Don't bother denying it. I'm not silly. I think all that has your imagination running wild. I know it's been a massive change for you, picking up your life and moving halfway around the world. Your father and I should have done a better job at making sure you were settling in instead of getting so caught up in our renovations. We just thought, since you made friends so quickly, that you were adjusting well..."

"That's not it, Mum. There's more to it—"

"No. I don't think there is. I think enough is enough. No more research and ghost stories. You need a good night's sleep." Allysha grabbed her daughter's hand and led her into the house.

A new heaviness weighed on Camille when she realised her mother didn't believe her. She let Allysha guide her upstairs to her room, then she climbed willingly up on her bed and rubbed her eyes. They now felt dry and sore after crying.

Allysha turned toward the door, and her mouth popped open when she saw Miss McAllister lurking in the doorway. "Oh, I was just going to come to you. I'd like you to please make some tea and bring it up."

"Tea isn't going to help matters much—"

"Excuse me?" Allysha snapped.

Camille almost felt bad for Miss McAllister and the fierce glare she received from Allysha. But she looked away, feeling awful for stressing her mother out even more after an already stressful day. She wished she'd never said anything. Now that she was out of the woods and across the grounds, it was easier to convince herself she might have been mistaken.

"I'll bring it straight up, ma'am," Miss McAllister replied, her lips pursed tightly as she left.

Allysha turned to her daughter, her anger slowly dissipating into a worried frown. "Now I want you to get some rest. I promise everything will seem better after you catch up on a little sleep. I'll wait with you until your tea arrives, or even until you're asleep, if you like."

The thought instantly comforted Camille. "That would be nice, Mum." While the prospect of a hot cup of tea was wonderful, her simmering emotions left her exhausted. The minute she closed her eyes, she fell asleep.

CHAPTER TWENTY-TWO

THE SOUND OF hushed whispers tugged away at her slumber, and Camille felt sluggish and foggy as she strained to both listen and hold onto the deep sleep she'd been thoroughly enjoying.

"Surely you cannot tell me you haven't noticed..." came the slightly high-pitched voice of a woman.

"You're being ridiculous, Sybil. What you speak of is not possible." The voice of the second woman sounded familiar, and, putting two and two together, Camille realised it was Caroline talking to her daughter.

"Don't you think I know that, Mother? Of course it's ridiculous. It's downright absurd! Yet here we are. They're unnatural. The pair of them."

"Nonsense. You've never been fond of either of them. You never warmed up to Catherine when she joined the staff, and you certainly disliked the fact that we adopted Alice. You were far too accustomed to being an only child, though I would have expected better from a grown woman."

"That has nothing to do with it. There's just so much about them that doesn't add up. They are all but inseparable, as if they've known each other for years..."

"They have known each other for years."

"You know what I mean, Mother." Sybil sighed, unable to hide her frustration. "They always look so secretive, like they know something I don't. Catherine has never spoken a word in all the time we've known her, not to mention the fact she's in her eighties and doesn't yet look a day over fifty. How is that possible? And as for Alice, with her white hair, always lurking around, appearing out of nowhere. She's utterly unnerving. It's not right for a girl that age to behave the way she does."

"That's enough, Sybil!" Caroline interjected, her voice raising. "My goodness. Who raised you to be such an uncharitable soul? It certainly wasn't your father and me."

"I just don't understand how the mistress can welcome people into her staff when she knows absolutely nothing about them. Has everyone forgotten what happened to the poor LeRoux girl? It's dangerous!"

"That's quite enough!" Caroline shouted. "What happened with the LeRoux child was a long time ago. When has Catherine—or even Alice, for that matter—ever given you cause to question their loyalty to the manor or to the LeRoux family? They both work hard and deserve the same amount of respect that you would expect for yourself. The fact that they may be a little different is all the more reason to welcome them, not to conjure reasons for ostracising them. Honestly, Sybil, I don't know what has gotten into you..."

As Camille heard the brisk clip of shoes striding angrily off along the wooden floor, she found herself sinking back into a deep, feverish sleep.

"CAMILLE? SWEETHEART?" CAMILLE groaned as she tried to wriggle out from beneath the hands gently shaking her by the shoulders. "Oh, you're drenched in sweat. You must have a fever." Allysha pulled back the covers.

"I'm fine..." Camille tried to assure her mother without opening her eyes, but her tongue felt think and her mouth dry. "How long was I asleep?"

"You slept straight through from late yesterday afternoon. And you're staying home from school today—"

"Mum!"

"No arguments. Why don't you go have a shower, and I'll put fresh sheets on the bed for you?"

Camille opened her eyes and saw the look in her mother's—a combination of concern and guilt. She sighed and forced herself up onto her elbows, trying to hide how much it made her head spin and her stomach heave.

"Do you need a hand?" Allysha stepped forward, but Camille shook her head.

"I told you I'm fine, Mum. I can get to the bathroom myself."

Allysha stepped aside, looking unconvinced as Camille slid herself off the bed and hobbled toward the bedroom door. She didn't want to admit it to her mother, but she really did feel awful. Her legs were shaky, and she felt completely drained. Once in the hallway and beyond the watchful stare of her mother, Camille braced herself against the wall, hoping she would feel better after a shower.

The hot spray of the water provided relief, but her muscles and even her skin ached where the shower hit her. She wondered if she'd caught the flu running through the woods in the cold. The night's escapade rushed back to her, and the photo of herself as an old woman pushed through first and foremost. Camille gasped as a wave of anxiety swept over her, and she ducked her head under the water, wanting to wash it all away as a bad dream. Yet she knew it wasn't.

Feeling slightly less feeble after the shower, she walked back to her room slowly albeit unaided and was grateful to see her mother had changed the sheets for her. The thought of going back to sleep and ignoring the day appealed to her more and more. Part of her wanted to forget what she'd found, while the other part of her wanted time to process it.

Camille had just climbed into bed again and pulled the covers over herself when her phone vibrated on the bedside table. Picking it up, she was surprised by the number of missed calls and messages from both Lachlan and Grace; she even had one from Jayne. She felt guilty for making them worry but didn't feel up to talking or updating them, either. She knew them both well enough to know they wouldn't believe her if she said she was fine, and they'd want to know exactly what happened. Instead, she sent them each a simple text. 'I'm fine, just a bit under the weather and slept straight through from yesterday. Mum's making me stay home from school, but I'll message you later.'

Switching her phone from vibrate to silent, she placed it back on the bedside table as her mother entered the room, carrying a tray.

"You didn't have to do that, Mum." Camille gave her mother a weak smile of gratitude as she hoisted herself upright against the pillows.

"Well you rarely get sick, and honestly, I was a bit hard on you yesterday," Allysha admitted as she rested the tray across Camille's lap.

"Oh, my god. Is that vegemite?" Camille pointed excitedly at the toast.

"It sure is." Allysha took a seat on the edge of the bed.

"Yum! Where did you find it?" Camille picked up the hot toast and took the biggest bite she could manage.

"I didn't. Your Aunty Jen sent it over from back home."

"I'll text her later and tell her she's my favourite aunty." Camille smiled again.

Allysha patted her leg. "There's tea and orange juice there too. I want everything gone by the time I get back."

"Where are you going?" Camille asked.

"I have to pop into town for a few things, but I promise I'll be back as soon as I can. Your father's working on the study, and Mr McAllister is in the rear gardens, though I think it's more that he wants to keep an eye on the investigation in the woods..."

"What more is there to look at? Didn't they remove the body yesterday?"

Allysha nodded. "Yes, but I guess they're looking for evidence. I have no idea, to be honest. I just know they told your father yesterday they'd be back again today. I think he feels somehow responsible, which is ridiculous, but you know how stubborn your father gets."

Camille could only nod as she picked up the orange juice to wash down the toast. She hadn't realised how hungry she was, though she hadn't eaten anything since breakfast the day before. Breakfast with her friends felt like an eternity ago.

"I already see some colour returning to your face." Allysha stated as she peered closely at her daughter.

"Must be the vegemite."

"Regardless, you are to stay in bed today. I think there's been a little too much excitement on top of adjusting to the colder weather. I don't want you to make yourself sicker by not resting, thank you." Camille nodded. "And I will ask Miss McAllister to check in on you while I'm gone."

Camille groaned. "Please don't…"

"It will make me feel better knowing someone's here if you need anything." Allysha patted her daughter's lap again before standing and placing a kiss on Camille's head. "Get some rest, and I'll try not to be too long."

Camille watched her mother leave the room. Finishing the last of her toast, she pushed the tray over to the other side of the bed and sank down into her pillows. Just before she fell asleep, the floorboards creaked, and she opened her eyes to find Miss McAllister hovering in the doorway.

"I've come for the tray," she said, walking into the room without invitation. With a sigh, Camille sat up and reached for the tray to pass it to her. As Miss McAllister took a hold of it, she stared intently at Camille. "You shouldn't wander through the woods on your own."

"It wasn't exactly by choice. And how did you know, anyway? Are you spying on me?" Camille's eyes narrowed.

"Your mother told me you came running out of the woods, hysterical," Miss McAllister stated, completely without emotion. "I underestimated how much this place wants you…"

"What are you talking about?" Camille demanded.

The older woman looked her squarely in the eyes. "The manor has a will of its own. It always has and always will. If you'd listened to me, you may have been able to stop it from happening again, but now we'll never know." She turned and walked away.

"Stop what from happening?" Camille called after her, but Miss McAllister left the room; only the sound of the empty teacup rattling on the saucer followed her. Camille stared at the empty doorway, her unease intensifying, and she questioned if it had been such a smart idea to eat her breakfast so quickly. Unsure if it was Miss McAllister's creepy warning or her own illness, Camille felt the heat rising back into her face. Dizziness swept over her again, and she lay against the pillows. Within a matter of seconds, she was asleep again.

What do you want from me? Tell me. Show me. Why am I here?

Camille tossed and turned, not quite awake and not quite asleep as the fever kicked in. Throwing off the blankets, she rolled onto her stomach, but that only seemed to make her feel worse. It took a few attempts to roll onto her back again as her arms shook.

Why am I here? She couldn't tell if she had asked the question out aloud or if it was only in her head. Either way, it seemed the house had heard her; a dragging, scratching sound came from above her. A surge of energy coursed through her as she sat up and stared at the ceiling, wondering if she'd just imagined it. The sound came again, and Camille pushed herself out of the bed. Still tangled in the sheets, she fell to the floor and didn't even register the pain of her knees hitting the wood. The she scrambled to her feet and rushed out of her room toward the attic. She swayed from one side of the hallway to the other, her head spinning, and she focused on trying to walk straight. Her pounding head and blurred vision distorted everything.

Camille paused at the staircase and leaned over the balustrade, listening for Miss McAllister lurking around. She was so dizzy that she lost her footing when she leaned too far over and only just managed to right herself. But her balance deceived her, and she tumbled backward onto the floor instead. Not trusting herself to move, she lay there for a moment, hoping the commotion hadn't alerted Miss McAllister to the fact that she was out of bed. When no one came, Camille shakily got to her feet and continued unsteadily across the landing.

At the bottom of the attic staircase, she opened the door and looked over her shoulder one last time. Then she pulled the cord for the stairwell light and crawled more than walked up the stairs; their numbers felt twice as many as she remembered. More than once, she wanted to lower her head onto her arms and rest, but the thought of staying on the staircase any longer than she had to was enough to spur her on.

When she finally crawled onto the attic floor, she looked up to see the ghostly forms of draped sheets lurking ominously around the room. She rested a moment, her legs folded beneath her, and stared at the drapes. She told herself it was only her mind playing tricks on her. Then she thought she saw the edge of a sheet move, as though disturbed by a passing breeze. Camille blinked rapidly through her blurred vision. That only stoked the dizziness, and the attic spun. The dusty sheets looked like they were moving, swaying to and froe, taunting her. Camille closed her eyes, and both the dizziness and her headache intensified. She clutched her temples, and just as she thought she'd pass out, a young girl's giggle echoed through the attic.

Camille froze. She hardly breathed as she waited for another giggle. Instead came the sound of tiny feet running across the floor toward the right side of the attic.

"Come on, Catherine! Over here!"

Catherine. Catherine.

A wave of recognition swept over Camille as the child called her name. The fog of her mind lifted. She tried to reply but found her mouth unable to form the words. Her only answer was silent. I'm here…

The footsteps continued past her, weaving through the ghostly figures covering the furniture.

"Hurry! Before Mother comes and finds us!"

Camille tried to stand but didn't have the strength. Instead, she crawled on her hands and knees, trying to find the source of the voice. A flash of white curls bounced around a little head as the girlish giggle weaved around her. Camille did her best to keep up, half wondering if this was all a dream.

"Over here!" the child called, and Camille finally broke free to the other side of the attic and found little Mena LeRoux — or Alice — trying to move a small shelf away from the wall. Camille crawled toward her and did her best to help, though in her current state, she wasn't much stronger than the child beside her.

"It's behind here. I followed my Daddy up here once, a long time ago. My first Daddy." Mena shot Camille a knowing, mischievous smile. "I know you know my secret, Catherine. But that's okay, because you can't speak, so no one else will ever hear it." Mena squeezed through the small gap they'd made between the shelf and the wall and placed her hands on either side of panelling.

Intrigued, Camille watched Mena give a gentle push. Something clicked, and the panel popped inward about a centimetre. Camille crept closer, her curiosity taking over, but she was too big to fit all the way in the small gap. Mena gently shifted the panel sideways, where it slid effortlessly into the wall to reveal a secret hiding place.

Be careful... Camille couldn't stop the warning from forming in her mind, frustrated again by her inability to speak aloud.

Mena slipped her tiny arms into the hole and withdrew a wooden box. It looked huge in her hands, and she gently lowered it to the ground before sliding it across the floor toward Camille. "You should open it."

Camille looked down at the box before her, her vision now perfectly clear. Engravings of strange symbols covered the lid, most of which she had never seen before — except the one in the middle, the symbol that seemed intrinsically tied to the manor. The minute she touched that symbol, she immediately felt an energy run through her hands and up her arms like a small electrical current. Her hands tingled slightly, yet she didn't let go. Despite the odd sensation, she felt her strength slowly returning to her with each passing second.

"Are you going to hurry up and open it?" Mena asked, scooting impatiently across the floor for a closer look.

Camille gently lifted the lid and carefully turned it over, placing it on the floor beside them as she inspected the contents. She withdrew a small dagger first, no longer than her forearm. It was silver, the hilt covered in what looked like tiny crystals and what she now thought of as the LeRoux symbol engraved in silver at the top. She placed the dagger beside the lid and reached back inside the box. There was also a small silver chalice, again with the symbol engraved on it, and what looked like a wooden wand with a large, clear quartz attached to one end. A smaller piece of what might have been amethyst was attached to the other end. Remaining in the box were four jars of herbs or seeds, but she wasn't game to open them for further investigation.

"Look." Mena pointed at the upturned lid.

Camille bent over it, looking at the inscription she'd not noticed. Picking it up, she held it close, trying to read the script carved into the wood. Of course, when she tried to utter the words aloud, no sound came from her mouth. But reading the words had a hypnotic effect on her; she felt as though she were being carried along to some unknown destination. Feeling dizzy, she closed her eyes and thought she heard a woman singing. The minute that thought occurred, the woman's voice disappeared, lost to the darkness, taunting her. Her body tingled, the sensation of moving intensified, and at the same time, she was certain she could still feel the hardness of the wooden floor beneath her. It was entirely confusing to feel both present in the attic and floating away from the attic, light and untethered, unable to see anything but darkness.

When the feeling of drifting away ceased, Camille heard a soft, whispering voice. She strained to hear what it said and turned her head from side to side, desperately wanting to know even as it faded away. Instead, she picked up other sounds and smells, and she knew she wasn't in the attic. The scent of damp leaves rejuvenated by recent rain was only too strong. Listening intently, she heard the drops of water rolling off one leaf and onto the next. She thought she felt a cold droplet fall onto her shoulder and shivered. A bird called, the song a pretty one both foreign and familiar. She forgot about the bird the second she heard that whispered voice again, so quiet and just out of range, as if the words themselves were too precious for her to hear.

The darkness cleared from Camille's vision. Her mouth fell open. She stood amongst the trees, hidden from view. A couple metres ahead, the trees gave way to a large clearing with the cottage at its centre. Camille crept forward for a better look, careful to remain hidden, unsure of what or who was responsible for the whispering. She reached the tree line and looked up; the branches stretched toward the full moon hanging directly above her like a giant, ethereal spotlight. She thought she could see faces peering through the trees on the other side of the clearing, but the more she tried to focus, the more elusive they became, leaving her to doubt herself.

A wind rushed not through the trees but down from the sky, sweeping up the leaves and circling around the cottage. Then an eerie silence fell over the clearing as the wind died down, and Camille slowly broke through the trees and out into the open space. As she stepped through a ring of stones, she could have sworn they hadn't been there before. She studied the cottage and wondered if it was the same one to which the tunnel had led her; when she'd run back to the manor, she hadn't given the outside of that cottage a second glance.

By the time she made it halfway across the clearing, the front door opened. Camille froze, completely exposed. She didn't even have time to consider running back into the woods before a woman stepped out of the house. She wore a simple dress of white cotton that fell to her ankles, brushing against the grass below her feet. Camille tried to take a step backward, but she found herself unable to move. Gasping for breath, she tried to move her other foot, her arms, anything, all to no avail. The woman turned to face her, and Camille was startled to find Mena staring at her. She was older, late teens or early twenties, but there was no mistaking those eyes. They twinkled mischievously at Camille just before Mena's head turned a full one hundred and eighty degrees on her shoulders to reveal another face on the back of her head.

Camille's own face stared back at her, and she screamed. The last thing she saw was the woman reaching out for her as she fell to the ground.

CHAPTER TWENTY-THREE

CAMILLE OPENED HER eyes and rubbed her aching head. She was more angry than surprised to find herself alone and lying on the floor of the attic. Scrambling to her feet, she looked around for the box, but it was gone. Rubbing her forehead with her eyes squeezed shut, she wondered if there was something wrong with her—that she'd imagined the whole thing. It seemed the only explanation that made any sense. Yet when she opened her eyes, she noticed the shelf against the wall, the end closest to her not quite flush. She hurried toward it and this time had no trouble pulling it away from the wall.

She knelt down before the wall and tried to remember the panel she'd seen Mena locate. When she thought she had the right one, she placed her hands on either side and gently pushed. A smile tugged at the corners of her mouth as she heard the click, and the panel slid backward. This panel she slid to the side and peered into the space beyond, certain she was proving her own sanity. The cavity was there, but it was empty. There was no sign of the box, or anything else.

With a sigh Camille sat back on the floor, leaning against the shelf with her head in her hands. Hot tears stung her eyes as frustration threatened to overcome her. Fiercely wiping them away with the back of her hand, she reminded herself that her friends had also witnessed the insanity of the manor, so it couldn't be her imagination. She wasn't seeing things. Still, she couldn't continue without some answers as to why she was being targeted, why she was having strange dreams and waking up to find herself somewhere other than her bed.

Lifting her head, she found the memories of her dream in the woods coming back to her. She definitely didn't think it a coincidence that she'd had this dream after discovering the cottage at the end of the tunnel. Getting to her feet, Camille felt a new resolve and determination. While she wasn't exactly keen to return to the cottage, she now believed that the answers to everything happening to her at the manor had to be there. It was the only place left to look.

Camille left the shelf where it stood and hurried out of the attic, taking the stairs two at a time, ignoring the claustrophobia and vertigo clawing at her as she descended. She all but ran down the hall and down the stairs to the ground floor. She briefly had a look around for her parents or the McAllister's before sneaking into the kitchen to rummage through drawers and cupboards. Once she found a torch, she then walked past the kitchen bench and grabbed a knife from the knife block, just in case. She kept it discreetly at her side as she made her way back up the stairs and to her bedroom.

Closing the door quietly behind her, Camille went straight to the wardrobe, hesitating as she grabbed a hold of the handle. She couldn't recall much about her journey through the tunnel, but she did recall feeling sick to her stomach. Trying to relocate the cottage through the woods was too risky without knowing where she was going; the last thing she needed was to get herself lost. Though now that she stood in front of the wardrobe, part of her really didn't want to revisit. As she stood there, arguing with herself, her curiosity and need for answers won out. So, she opened the doors.

Her clothes were still shoved to either side of the rack, and the opening to the tunnel remained open, gaping at her like a demonic mouth waiting to devour her. With a deep breath, she turned on the torch and walked inside.

Camille fought back the first waves of nausea as she started the descent into the tunnel. She willed herself to stay focused and alert, but despite her best intentions, the farther she went, the worse she felt. Only this time, Camille felt sluggish; every movement took concentration and effort, as though something were physically trying to stop her. She closed her eyes briefly, breathing through the next wave of nausea. The light from her torch momentarily flickered, but she saw the faint glow of the salt walls farther down. Using the wall as support, she put one foot in front of the other when all she really wanted to do was curl up on the cold floor.

Whispers fluttered through the air, and Camille waved the voices away. The woman's whispers were too soft to make out the words. Camille opened her eyes and was shocked to find that she'd stopped walking and fallen asleep—or passed out—against the wall. The thought of someone finding her remains lost in the tunnel terrified her, and she blinked furiously, forcing alertness. Then she pushed herself off the wall and stumbled forward.

Within a few metres, she found herself surrounded by the glowing hue of the salt. Camille stumbled as the dizziness threatened to overcome her, and her heart skipped a beat with the fear that she would pass out again. She reached out in attempt to steady herself and was instantly blinded by a flash of light.

ALLYSHA OPENED CAMILLE'S door as quietly as she could, not wanting to wake her daughter if she was asleep. Stepping into the room, she frowned at the empty bed. She left and hurried down to the kitchen, where she'd just left Miss McAllister to unpack the groceries. "Have you seen Camille?" she asked.

Miss McAllister didn't look up as she stacked fruit into the bowl in front of her. "No, ma'am, I haven't. Though I have spent most of the morning in the laundry."

"I'd asked you to keep an eye on her while I was out," Allysha replied.

"Babysitting is not one of my duties, nor has it ever been. Not that your daughter would listen to me if it were."

Allysha stared at her, eyebrows raised and her mouth open, unsure how to respond in her anger. Instead, she turned on her heel and stormed through the house, going from room to room and looking for her daughter until she came to the room that was halfway to becoming a study. Her husband looked up from his work, smiled, and turned the volume down on his phone. The voices of Louis Armstrong and Ella Fitzgerald reduced to a mellow murmur.

"Hi, sweetheart. How was town? What do you think so far?" He stepped back from the wooden trellis where his sketches for the room were spread out.

Allysha disregarded his questions and grabbed her husband by the arm. "Have you seen Camille since I left?"

He looked at his wife in concern. "No, I haven't. I assumed she was still in bed upstairs. You've only been gone an hour or so."

"She's not there. She wasn't in the bathroom, either. Miss McAllister says she hasn't seen her, and I haven't found her in any of the rooms I've looked in." Allysha heard the rising panic in her own voice and tried to tell herself she was being ridiculous, yet she couldn't shake the feeling that something was wrong.

Phillipe turned from the table, grabbed his wife's shoulders, and looked into her eyes. "The manor is a big place. Maybe she just couldn't sleep, or she got bored and decided to explore a little. Has she mentioned anywhere that she's taken an interest in? You might look there."

Allysha chewed her bottom lip and tried to ignore the inner voice screaming at her to hurry. She didn't know if it was a mother's instinct, or a sixth sense, or just the manor, but she knew she wouldn't find her daughter unless she could think rationally. "The attic. She was interested in some of the old things stored up there."

"There you go. That's probably where she is. I'll come with you. You'll see. She'll be fine." Phillipe grabbed his wife's hand and led her out of the room, weaving through the manor without a word until they reached the attic door. It stood ajar, and Allysha ducked in front of her husband to yank it fully open. Then she rushed as quickly as she could up the steep staircase.

"Camille?" she called, stepping up onto the attic floor. She exchanged a worried look with Phillipe as he stepped up beside her.

"I'll check over that side," he said, and they split up, walking through the sheeted objects around the room.

Allysha grew more and more frantic as she looked behind one thing after another. She knew her daughter wasn't there; Camille would have answered them if she were. The girl's mother didn't know what else to do or where else to look.

"This is weird," Phillipe called out.

Allysha weaved her way to the other side of the attic and found her husband kneeling beside a shelf that had been pulled away from the wall. "What is it?"

"I'm not sure. I just thought it was strange this shelf was standing here like this, but when I got down to have a look, there's an open section in the wall."

"Is there anything in it?" Allysha peered over her husband's shoulder.

"No, doesn't appear to be. That's not to say that there wasn't."

"Do you think Camille found this and took whatever was inside?"

Phillipe signed as he used the shelf to get back to his feet. "Who knows? But I can say she isn't up here. And I'm starting to feel as worried about her as you are."

"So, what now? Where else could she be?" Allysha leaned into her husband's chest.

He was silent for a moment, stroking her back and thinking. "What about her phone? Was that still in her room?"

Allysha pulled back and looked up at him. "I didn't even check."

"Well there we go. She's a teenager. She'd never leave the house without her phone. If it's gone, then we call her and find out where the hell she is. If it's there, then I suggest we call her friends and see if they know what's going on."

Allysha grabbed her husband's hand and led him from the attic and back into Camille's room. She didn't know whether she felt relieved or dismayed when she saw Camille's phone on the bedside table, plugged into the charger. Unplugging it, she activated the screen, grateful her daughter had ignored her advice on password protection.

"Six missed calls," she stated.

"Who from?" Phillipe asked as he stopped next to his wife and stared at the screen.

"Looks like two are from Grace and four are from Lachlan."

"That seems a little persistent to me. Like maybe they're worried."

"That's not very reassuring…" Allysha whispered.

"Start with Lachlan. He's called the most. Maybe he can tell us something."

His wife hit the speaker-phone button with a shaking hand. Lachlan answered on the first ring.

"Camille? Are you okay? I've been worried —"

"Lachlan, it's Allysha. We think Camille's gone somewhere, but she hasn't taken her phone. She's not well, and we're worried about her."

"Uh, Allysha…" The boy didn't say anything else.

"Please, Lachlan," Phillipe added. "If you know anything that will help us find her…"

Lachlan cleared his throat.

CHAPTER TWENTY-FOUR

THE FLASH OF light passed as quickly as it took Camille to remove her hand from the salt. Looking back the way she'd come, she found herself about halfway across the salt cave, yet she couldn't remember walking this far. The nausea was now interchangeable with the dizziness, and she hardly knew if she stood upright or hunched over. Despite her efforts to stay away from the walls, she stumbled and instinctively shot her hand out to steady herself.

Another flash of light overcame her, and when it passed, an eerie sense of déjà vu overcame her. She was back in the attic.

"Catherine, come find me!" A giggle rose through the air, followed by the sound of small footsteps across the wooden floor. A flash of movement caught her attention, and she peered around a stack of suitcases as Mena darted out from behind them, her mischievous laughter following her.

Camille smiled, distracted by an antique, full-length mirror half draped in an old sheet. She approached it and reached out to grab the sheet, but it fell away before she could touch it. She saw a much older woman staring back at her and somehow knew the reflection was her own; she also knew she was far older than she appeared, and yet neither of these things bothered her. She didn't feel scared or overwhelmed but safe. Content.

"Catherine! Come on... You have to find me. It's the game," Mena called.

Camille stomped her feet across the floor, making as much noise as possible so Mena would know where she was. It was times like these she missed her ability to speak. She shoved the thought aside; she had so much to be grateful for, and the past was the past.

She found Mena crouched beside a shelf, and the girl giggled as a voice sounded up the stairs. "Alice? Catherine? I know you're up here!"

They didn't answer, instead preferring to make Sybil come all the way into the attic, knowing how much she hated it up there. Sybil got to the top of the stairs and glared at them. "Alice, you're supposed to be helping Mother in the kitchen. And Catherine, you're supposed to be helping me change the linens. Now hurry up."

The pair exchanged a mischievous look, trying to hide their amusement as they walked toward the stairs.

"Really, Catherine. You're as bad as the child..."

"A TUNNEL?" ALLYSHA echoed in disbelief.

"That's what she said. She'd found some drawing in an album that showed an entrance... or exit... through the back of her wardrobe," Lachlan clarified.

"Are you sure?"

"I haven't seen it yet. She found it yesterday after we'd already left, but that was what she said."

"Did you know anything about this?" Allysha looked at Phillipe, and he shook his head.

"No, of course not. I would have told you. There's nothing on any of the blueprints I've seen about an odd tunnel through a wardrobe. It's not exactly something I would overlook."

"We'll take a look. Thanks, Lachlan."

"Wait. Can you please let me know when you find her? Just let me know she's okay, even if it's just a message?"

"Of course we will," Allysha reassured him. "Talk to you later." Rather than place Camille's phone back on the bedside table, Allysha put it in the back pocket of her jeans, then turned and looked down at the bed.

"What is it?" Phillipe asked. She lifted the edge of the thrown-back blanket and revealed the blueprint Lachlan had described. Phillipe quickly straightened it out, running his fingers expertly over the drawings as he mapped his way to Camille's room. "He was right," he said, pointing out the few tiny lines that indicated a structure beyond the wardrobe.

"Why is it drawn like that? It doesn't show where it leads." Allysha looked from the drawing to the wardrobe and back again.

"It could be that it wasn't complete when this sketch was done, or that the person who drew this didn't actually know where it led. Just that it was there."

"Remember she said she saw someone in there? And we told her she was imagining things."

"That's not what we said…"

"It's pretty much what we implied. What if she did see someone? What if they've taken her?" Allysha whimpered, raising her hand to her mouth as she fought to hold back the tears.

"Now, now." Her husband put his arm around her shoulders. "Let's not jump to conclusions. We both know how curious Camille is, and the thought of a secret tunnel would certainly intrigue her. I honestly don't think anyone beyond the LeRoux family would have known about it. It's surely long forgotten, so I don't think it likely anyone came in this way. We'll find her in there. Or even on her way back." He released his wife and walked to the window seat, where Camille's research lay scattered amongst the old albums. "What's all this?"

"Oh, that's probably the assignment they were all working on last night. They have to do some family-tree project," Allysha replied, wanting to get into the tunnel and find her daughter.

"This looks like more than just our family tree..." He picked up the journal and opened the cover. "I think this belonged to Lachlan's uncle." Phillipe looked up and out the window toward the woods, frowning.

"Okay... so Lachlan must have brought it with him. We can hand it over to the police later, if you think it's relevant. But for now, it's not important. Finding Camille is."

With one last glance at the research, Phillipe grabbed his wife's hand. He paused halfway across the room and picked up one of the discarded torches from the night before. Then they approached the wardrobe, and he turned on the torch to shine the light across the black hole gaping at them through Camille's clothes.

"Let's go." Allysha nudged her husband forward, unable to hide the fear in her voice, though she was unsure what terrified her more—not finding their daughter or finding something had happened to her.

CAMILLE GASPED, PUSHING herself away from the wall. She tried to shake the vision from her mind, but it wasn't possible. She was Camille. Her name was Camille, and she was here, now. Pinching herself hard on the arm, she repeated her mantra over and over, reassuring herself that she was not only herself, but she could also talk. This calmed her until she was determined enough to push past the nausea and dizziness and get out of the tunnel as fast as she could. She forced herself forward.

The salt cave closed in around her the closer she got to the end. She did her best to ignore the sudden claustrophobia, but the dizziness intensified. She lost her balance and stumbled against the wall before she could stop herself. "No!" Another flash of white swept over her.

This time, when she opened her eyes, she stood in a doorway, leaning heavily on a dark, wooden cane in her hand, topped with an ornate silver handle. What startled her more was the appearance of her hand. It was gnarled, with bulbous veins protruding from underneath the paper-thin skin. As her heart sped up and her breathing quickened, she gripped the walking stick tightly, fearing she would pass out from the panic.

"Since when do you lurk in doorways?" came a voice beside her. Camille lifted her head to find Mena standing beside her, though she was no longer a little girl. She was now a woman in her fifties, her hair as white as ever and fixed tightly into an immaculate bun. Yet there was no mistaking the mischievous glint in her eyes. Seeing the look on Camille's face, Mena grabbed a hold of her arm. "Don't fret, old friend. New life is something to be celebrated. There is plenty of time for existential deliberation later."

Camille didn't move, unsure if she physically couldn't, or if she was paralysed by her fear of what was happening.

Mena sighed. "You can't help it, can you? You've always found it harder to accept that we're different than everyone else. They all know it. How could they not? Even dear Caroline never spoke of the strange way in which you and I age. Or why. I've never heard any of them question it. At least not within earshot."

Camille turned and looked at Mena, her eyebrow raised.

"Yes, you're right. We both know Sybil was curious, to say the least. Not that she would have believed us if we'd told her. It's a shame she died in childbirth..." Mena didn't sound in the least bit remorseful.

Camille nodded, pretending to know what Mena was talking about as she feigned interest in the goings on of the room before them.

"I mean, look at me. I don't look a day over fifty, though we both know I am well into my seventies. And you, my dear, old, friend. A miraculous one hundred and forty-two years!"

Camille gasped and tried to speak, momentarily forgetting that she couldn't.

"Do not be alarmed," Mena said, giving her arm a gentle squeeze. "You don't look a day over ninety. A young ninety."

Camille couldn't think straight. It didn't make any sense. Yet here she was, on old woman, still in the manor, but it wasn't her manor — at least, not when she lived there. Mena's ramblings faded into background noise as Camille tried to piece together what she'd been shown — tried to work out the how and the why.

A baby's sudden cry startled her, and she peered into the room, only now realising she stood in the doorway of a grand sitting room. The walls were covered in a rich mahogany wallpaper decorated with an intricate pattern of gold lines and arches, giving the appearance of row upon row of splayed peacock feathers. From the high ceiling hung two extravagant chandeliers, though they weren't needed with the sunlight streaming from the large, arched windows spanning across the wall to her left. The wooden floor was as rich in colour as the wallpaper, with large, plush cream rugs spanning over most of it.

Camille looked at a woman rising from the lounge chair. She was tall and slim, her hair immaculately styled in victory rolls — a chestnut brown with hints of grey stemming from her temples. This woman had to be a LeRoux — the lady of the house. Judging by the style of clothing, Camille guessed this was Georgette LeRoux — her great-great grandmother.

Georgette nodded to two women who had entered the room from the other end. A man in a crisp suit stood aside and gestured for the women to approach Mrs LeRoux.

One of them looked to be in her mid-twenties, the other in her teens. Both wore matching maids' outfits, and each held a baby, tightly swaddled — one in a blue blanket and the other in pink.

"Lucy, congratulations on the birth of your twins. Such a joy for you and Thomas," Georgette declared, her hands clasped in front of her as she impatiently awaited the newborns.

The baby girl fussed in the younger woman's arms, as though knowing her mother and brother were nearby.

"Oh, come now, little one…" Georgette cooed as she took the baby from the girl's arms and gestured for them to sit on the lounge. Both the maids looked uncomfortable at the offer and tried to hide it by focusing on the babies. "What names did you decide on?" Georgette asked.

"You're holding Margaret," Lucy replied. "And this is Robert."

"Margaret and Robert McAllister. What grand names." Georgette rocked Margaret back and forth.

Camille's eyes widened, and she felt her breath catch in her throat. Her grip on the walking stick loosened just enough for her to grasp the doorframe beside her with all the strength she could muster. It was all she could do to hold herself upright.

"Now, Lucy, you know we think of you and all the staff as family. So, if you need anything at all, please don't be afraid to ask."

"Thank you, ma'am."

"Do tell me why you're in your uniform. You should be resting. Spending time with your babies."

"There's always so much to be done, ma'am…"

"Nonsense. You need to rest. If it makes you feel better, you can still oversee everything from within your living quarters. If it's more staff we need, then I will speak to Frederic about it this evening."

Lucy smiled and gave her mistress a nod.

"Now Catherine, Alice, don't think I haven't noticed the two of you standing there…" Georgette turned and looked over her shoulder at them with a kindly smile. "Do come in and take a look at these beautiful new additions to the manor."

They stepped forward, Mena's arm still holding onto Camille's, who was entirely grateful for the support. She felt herself shaking, assuring herself it was more from panic than old age. Then she looked down at the babies. So little. She thought of the McAllister twins she knew — had known — though they were much older.

Are they a memory, or a dream? It seems like another lifetime… Camille frowned, unable to remember as she stared into the eyes of the baby Margaret McAllister.

CHAPTER TWENTY-FIVE

ALLYSHA GRIPPED THE back of her husband's shirt as he led them through the tunnel. They moved as quickly as they dared, the light from his torch barely illuminating the way. "Ouch!" Phillipe yelled, almost dropping the torch as his voice resonated off the walls around them.

"What? What happened?" Allysha anxiously tried to peer around him.

"I just stubbed my toe on something." He pointed the torch down to reveal the trunk, its lid still raised. "Seems like a weird place to store a trunk." The torchlight ran over the seemingly uninteresting contents.

"We'll look at it later," Allysha urged, and Phillipe led them around the trunk and onward down the tunnel.

"What's that?" she asked, futilely pointing ahead.

"Looks like a light. A dim one." Phillipe lowered the torch for a moment.

"Raise the torch again," Allysha whispered. "This is making me really nervous."

Her husband complied, and they edged along until they reached the cave.

"Wow… would you look at this…" Allysha gazed at the glowing salt surrounding them.

"This is unreal…"

"Really had no idea this was here?" she asked.

Phillipe shook his head. "It would seem there's a great deal about this place that I don't know."

CAMILLE CRASHED THROUGH the wardrobe, falling to the floor of the cottage bedroom. She lay there for a moment, waiting for her energy to return to her, however slightly. She thought she heard voices coming from the tunnel behind her, and she forced herself to her feet. Staggering across the room, she entered the living area.

For a moment, she stared at the broken glass on the floor in front of the fireplace, the photo of Alice and Catherine—her and Mena—taunting her. She groped at the lounge in front of her and moved around it to collapse on the cushions. All she could do was stare at the photo, at her own face—albeit older—staring back at her.

How? She closed her eyes, rubbing them with her palms. It must be an ancestor… Just someone who looks like me.

That didn't quite make sense, either; her ancestors were the LeRoux's, not the staff who had worked for them. Camille gripped the cushion beneath her as she recalled the gravestone she'd seen in the woods. With renewed energy, she pushed herself up off the couch and ran out the front door into the clearing. Trying to determine which way to go, she thought she saw someone move through the trees. She took off after the figure, struggling to keep the person in sight as she weaved through the trees.

"WHAT IN GOD'S name…" Phillipe exclaimed.

"What is it?"

He stepped forward through the cupboard, leading his wife into the bedroom of the cottage.

"Does someone live here?" Allysha asked.

"Hello?" Phillipe called, moving to the doorway. Peering out, he had full view of the rest of the empty cottage. "Someone must live here. It's sparse and neat and definitely lived in. Look at the melted candles." Confident they were alone, he walked to the small shelf at the back of the couch and ran his fingers along the top. "There's no dust."

"Who would live all the way out here? This is still LeRoux property, isn't it?" Allysha went to the other side of the room.

"To my knowledge, it is. But I was led to believed there have never been any tenants."

"Phillipe, what if whoever lived here was responsible for Lachlan's uncle? We've just exposed our daughter to them…" Her voice came out in a high pitch, and she clutched at her chest, taking short, sharp breaths.

"Hey, come on, now. We can't think that way. We can speculate later. After we find her." Phillipe embraced his wife, waiting for her to show she was ready before he released her.

When she pulled back, Allysha's eyes were wide and teary, but she gave him a small nod before glancing over his shoulder at the window. She walked toward it. "It looks like we're in some kind of clearing. It must be a fair distance from the manor. This just doesn't make any sense. The manor's huge. Why would someone live all the way out here and need a tunnel to get to and from the house?"

"Believe me, I wish I had some answers."

Allysha turned from the window, about to walk out the front door, then spotted the broken glass on the floor. "Phillipe." She nudged her husband and rushed toward the broken glass to pluck the photo from the broken frame. It took her a few seconds to really see the image in her hand. With a shout of surprise, she dropped the photo as though it were on fire and stood fully, both hands clamped over her mouth.

Her husband hurried toward her, quickly taking in the sight of shattered glass before picking up the photograph. He took a quick look at it, then turned it over. "Alice and Catherine..." he read. "I don't get it."

"Look at her face! It's Camille..."

With narrowed eyes, he looked at his wife as though she had lost her mind. But he drew the photo closer for a second look. As he stared at the women's faces, the blood drained from his face. Despite the woman's age, he could've sworn those were his daughters' eyes staring back at him; he'd know those eyes anywhere. He let the photo fall once more to the floor as denial kicked in. "It's not possible. Just a likeness. This place is getting the better of us. Camille clearly isn't here, so we need to keep looking."

"Where is our daughter?" Allysha sobbed, and Phillipe embraced her, wondering the same.

CAMILLE BROKE THROUGH the trees and found herself standing in a second, smaller clearing. In the centre stood the gravestone still covered in debris of rotting leaves and branches from the trees towering over it. She froze at the sight of the old Mena standing behind it, her head bowed. The woman didn't give any indication that she knew she was no longer alone. Camille's heart raced as she braced herself against a tree. Despite coming this far, she was terrified of revealing the truth. It took all her courage to let go of the tree and step into the clearing.

Unsure of herself, Camille paused and noticed that this clearing was also lined with rough pieces of quartz. She wondered why she hadn't noticed them the first time she'd been here. But then thoughts of Lachlan flashed through her head, and she quickly cast them aside.

She approached the gravestone and almost jumped out of her skin when Mena moved with slow, purposeful grace, lowering her arms so her hands hovered on either side of the tombstone, palms facing Camille as though in offering.

Camille frowned, unsure if she should get any closer. As always, her curiosity won out, and she crept forward. Kneeling on the ground, she cast aside the leaves and branches, tearing at the overgrown vines that had wrapped themselves tightly around the stone. They seemed to fight against her, their thorns tearing into her hands. She hacked away at them with the kitchen knife, but even that was a struggle. Finally, she tore the last section away to reveal a single name.

Catherine

There was no date of birth, just the year 1950, the words, 'Beloved Friend', and a quote that seemed familiar, though she couldn't place it.

'I can't go back to yesterday. I was a different person then.'

Her chest ached from the ferocity of her heartbeat as she leaned forward and touched the words. A surge of energy raced up her arm and into her forehead. Camille clutched her head in agony, as if she'd eaten something too cold too quickly and had somehow magnified the pain.

She saw herself standing behind the gravestone and looking down, only when she looked down at the grave in front of her, the ground was freshly turned. She looked up at Mena — Alice — an old woman, a dark veil over her face as she reached under it to wipe away tears with a lace handkerchief. On either side of her stood two identical children about eight years old, and Camille knew she was looking at the McAllister twins.

"Don't cry, children," Mean said quietly. "You will see her again." The children nodded; their eyes filled with sadness.

Camille felt the hysteria finally take over as she released the grave and ended the vision. Scurrying across the grass, she backed away as quickly as she could.

"What do you want from me?" she yelled. She tripped and fell backward to the ground, almost cutting herself with the knife still in her hand. When she opened her eyes, she found the old woman standing above her, the woman she now knew was Mena, with her hand outstretched toward Camille. The girl didn't take Mena's hand. "I don't understand any of this…"

"You will."

"What do you want from me?" she asked again.

"There cannot be darkness without light."

"What?"

"We are two sides of the same coin; you and I. Darkness has always graced me. It's something I've learned to hide with greater success the older I've become. Though the desires are always there, whispering in the background, waiting for a sign of weakness. A sign that they can now speak louder. It's only with the other half of my soul that I can keep the urges at bay. To protect the few people I care for and the legacy of my family."

"You're not making any sense!" Camille yelled, clutching at her temples in frustration and fear.

"It's not something I can explain to you. You must experience it for yourself to truly understand. I've suffered for so long, waiting for another woman to be born into the LeRoux line. Another child with the hair the colour of fiery autumn leaves. The colour my hair once was. Finally, the Goddess deemed me worthy of the revenge I have so long desired."

"Revenge for what?" Camille asked, gaping.

"Revenge for what my father did to me."

"Caleb? What did he do? I don't understand."

"Come with me and you will understand everything."

"Camille!"

She turned as she heard her name called from the woods behind her. "My parents... how did they know about the cottage?"

"It doesn't matter now, but they aren't far. You don't have much time. You can stay here and wait for your parents and continue to live at the manor as though nothing ever happened. Or you can come with me."

"I want answers first. I want to know why—how—we are in the photo together."

"I can't tell you. I can only show you." Mena held out her hand once again.

Camille looked back once more as she heard her parents' shouts again. She wanted to call out to them, to let them know that she was okay, but she knew she couldn't—not when she finally had the chance to get answers. They would be angry when she returned, but she would explain everything to them, make everything right. Reaching up, she clasped Mena's hand, surprised by the old woman's strength as Mena heaved her to her feet. She turned and led Camille across the clearing and into the trees on the other side at a near-inhuman speed.

Camille tried to get her bearings as they weaved through the trees and could barely feel her feet touching the ground. When they finally slowed to a more manageable pace, Mena released her hand and looked at her. "How old do you think I am?"

"Seriously? Is that a trick question?" When Mena didn't answer, Camille swallowed thickly and took a guess. "I don't know. I mean, I know when you were born, and I know you disappeared and returned years later the same age, but other than that, I have no idea."

"Then I will tell you. I am one hundred and fifty years old."

Camille remembered the vision she'd had of the manor and the McAllister babies and that Mena had told her she herself was over a hundred. "How are you... why... that's impossible, though."

"Not at all. But you must come with me. Once we complete the circle, you will see everything for what it is. For what it was meant to be."

Mena stopped, and Camille looked around her to see they now stood in front of a large rock formation rising from within the woods. Water trickled down across the rocks before disappearing somewhere beneath them. She saw a narrow opening between two of the largest rocks and looked at Mena. "You want me to go in there. Are you insane?"

Without a word, Mena brought her hand up to Camille's cheek. The girl gasped, her entire body shuddering with the foreign energy surging through her. Then she found herself looking through someone else's eyes—a child's eyes—walking toward the same rock formation.

"Is it... am I... you?" Camille asked through the haze. Mena didn't answer, yet Camille innately knew she was right. She saw her hands on the pantleg of a man before her; she released him and hurried toward the rocks, having spotted the opening. She was thinking of what animals might be hiding in there as she got down on her hands and knees and crawled inside. She felt the hard shove from behind, followed by shock and surprise and the realisation that she was falling into nothingness. "Daddy!" she screamed, but there was no answer.

As she fell, tears pricked her eyes. She loved her Daddy. Why would he do this to her? Why didn't he want her anymore? Camille could no longer see through Mena's eyes; she could only see the inside of her own eyelids as she struggled to open them. But she was so overcome by pain; her body convulsed with the intensity of heartbreak and rage to which Mena had clung all these years. She felt it seeping into her own body, winding its way into her mind and her heart like a poisonous vine.

Camille felt herself being led to the cave, and she didn't protest. She no longer felt in control of herself, and at the same time, she felt a connection to Mena unlike anything she'd ever experienced, as though Mena's emotions, her past, were Camille's—that they really were one and the same, two halves connecting. Through the anger, she felt something else welling within her. It made her tremble with power, and she thought of the goddess she'd seen and the devotion the men had offered her.

Finally opening her eyes, she saw they were at the entrance to the cave. "It looks too small for us," she whispered.

"Don't let it deceive you. It's meant to keep people away. We will fit." Mena stepped aside.

Camille stepped forward into the darkness; she thought her heart was breaking, though she did not understand why. Mena's voice sounded far away despite her presence close behind Camille. "My revenge is the end of my journey, but you will see me again."

Camille didn't understand, but as she stepped into the cave, she felt the anger intensify, clearing her mind of all other thought.

"Are you ready?" Mena asked. Camille didn't know what for, but she knew she was where she was meant to be. Before she could think about it, Mena nudged them forward, and they were falling into nothing. The fall seemed to last for both seconds and an eternity. She found a strange comfort in Mena's embrace despite the way her stomach lurched at their rapid descent. But the farther they fell, the more of Mena's emotions — her entire history — poured into Camille.

Then Mena started to slip away from her. "No!" Camille cried. She flailed in the darkness, trying to grab a hold of the woman, but her hands closed around nothing.

'Thank you.'

It was Mena's voice one last time. Then Camille hit the ground with a thud.

Groaning, she slowly sat up and saw only darkness. She waited for her eyes to adjust, but the darkness was all-encompassing. Tentatively reaching out around her, she felt rock not far above her head. In front of her, though, there was nothing but air. The tension from her clenched jaw moved up into her forehead, deepening her scowl. All she could think of, all she could feel, was a lifetime of anger, and her body shook beneath its ferocity.

Finally, she caught a sliver of light from over her left shoulder, and she scurried onto her knees. One hand grasped tightly around the knife she'd somehow managed to grip this whole time. The sliver of light grew the closer she crawled until it revealed a way out of the cave. When she crawled through it, the sudden daylight was blinding. Camille shielded her eyes with a hand and waited for her vision to adjust again.

The faint sound of music wafted toward her — old-fashioned violins playing a pretty, festive tune. Without understanding why, the sound angered her even more. She felt betrayed by it somehow — by the fact that people were enjoying themselves when all she wanted was to scream.

Blinking a couple times as she lowered her arm, her vision adjusted, and she saw a gentleman in a black suit walking away from her through the woods.

Caleb.

Camille gripped the knife even tighter, her breathing now rapid and shallow as the anger engulfed her. With an image of a young Mena fixed firmly in her mind, she charged toward the man.

Caleb stopped, unsure of the sound behind him, but before he had the chance to turn around, she raised the knife high in the air with both hands and plunged it down into his back. He fell first to his knees, swaying slightly. Camille stood there and watched him, her hands braced on her knees as she panted and sneered. A gurgle rose from the man's throat, and a small pool of blood formed beside his knee. He tried to reach over his shoulder and grab the knife, but it was impossible. The motion made him moan in pain, and he swayed back just a little before falling flat on his face. The thud of his body hitting the ground pulled her out of her — Mena's — rage, and Camille stared at the body.

Then the reality of what she had done hit her. She opened her mouth and screamed, but no sound came out. Camille clutched at her throat; her eyes wide as everything she'd been shown finally made sense. With a silent sob, she turned and ran as fast as she could through the woods.

CHAPTER TWENTY-SIX

WHEN CAMILLE STOPPED running, she had no idea how far she'd gone, and she didn't care. Exhaustion caught up with her, and she sank to the ground at the foot of a tree. Pulling her knees to her chest, she buried her face in her hands, screamed, and could only imagine the sound of it echoing through the trees, sending startled birds from their nests.

Somewhere close by, a few branches snapped. She looked up, her eyes as wide as a cornered animal's. She cowered, wishing she could disappear as a woman stepped from the trees in front of her. The woman looked up, saw her, and stifled a yelp. Camille could only imagine how she must look—especially when the woman before her was dressed in a black, old-fashioned maid's dress, the hem dirty from traipsing through the woods. Her white cap was askew, and a leaf protrude from her bun.

"My goodness, child. You startled me..." The woman lowered her hand from her mouth as she looked Camille up and down.

"What on earth has happened to you? Is that blood?" She rushed toward Camille. "Oh, you poor thing. Were you attacked too? How did you manage to escape?" She grasped Camille's shoulders and looked into the girl's eyes.

Camille tried to speak, but no sound came out. She tried again, but there was nothing; after everything she could have said, it seemed as if her mind had shut her off from that ability as well, just to keep her safe. Tears wells in her eyes, and her heart pounded against her chest as the reality of what had happened hit her.

The maid clicked her tongue in sympathy. "You must come with me. The woods aren't safe. The master was found murdered, and the young mistress is missing. I hate to think what kind of monster could be responsible for this travesty. And on such a jubilant day. You're lucky I found you when I did. The whole town is out in these woods, trying to find Miss Mena." The woman held her hands out and helped Camille to her feet. "You can come back to the house with me. I will keep you safe there until you can tell me who you are and we can get you home safely. There are so many new staff members at the manor now that it's finished. No one will notice another new face…." She paused and turned to Camille. "Please excuse me. The traumatic events of this afternoon seem to have robbed me of my manners. I'm Anne. Anne McNally."

Camille opened her mouth and closed it again, her eyes brimming with tears as she pointed to her throat.

"Oh, you poor lass. A mute! No wonder no one heard you scream. Oh, what you must have endured! Can you write?"

Camille hesitated before shaking her head. There was no point. Who would believe her? She'd already seen the way her life would play out; she'd already had visions of the past, which were now her memories of the future. All she could do was wait for Mena.

Anne patted her hand. "For now, I will call you Catherine."

EPILOGUE

THE TOWN OF *Woodville is reeling with the news from LeRoux Manor. On Sunday, authorities revealed a body had been found in the Woodville Forest by a group of local teenagers: Grace Harker, Jayne West, Lachlan River, Jonathan Glasser, and Camille LeRoux. The teens had spent the night at the manor, where Miss LeRoux and her parents moved in earlier this month. Her father, Phillipe LeRoux, inherited the family estate after the passing of his uncle, Charles LeRoux, in September of last year.*

Authorities have reason to believe the body belongs to that of Professor Robert Rivers, who went missing back in 1999, though no official comment on the victim's identity or the nature of his death has been provided to the press. However, there is some speculation as to what he could have been doing in the woods, which have been private property of the LeRoux estate since the early 1800s.

Less than twenty-four hours later, Phillipe and Allysha LeRoux reported their daughter, Camille, missing after she was thought to have returned to the woods on her own. Concern for the young woman's safety are heightened by the fact she was thought to be unwell at the time. Despite an extensive search of both the manor and the woods, as of yet, there has been no sign of her.

There is a sense of history repeating itself for the LeRoux family, as six-year-old Mena LeRoux also vanished without a trace in 1817, while the body of her father and town founder, Caleb LeRoux, was found in the woods.

The family have declined to speak to us other than to request privacy during this difficult time.

If you have any information, please contact the Woodville Police…

Lachlan reached toward his phone in the middle of the dinner table. And shut it off.

Jonathan, sitting opposite him, leaned back against the booth and sighed.

"We shouldn't have left her there. After everything we saw that night, how could we just leave her there?" Lachlan rested his head against clenched fists.

"I think we were all scared," Grace said softly, "between what we saw and then finding your uncle… But you're right. We shouldn't have left her there. Not when her parents didn't know what was happening."

Amy skated up to their table at and unloaded a tray of shakes and a basket of fries. "On the house, guys," she said with a sad smile and skated off again before they had the chance to say anything. Jonathan absently grabbed a chip, then dropped it back into the basket.

"Where do you think she went?" Jayne asked, gazing at her hands clasped in her lap.

"All I know is she found a map showing a tunnel at the back of her wardrobe. But when I mentioned it to her parents, they told me they had moved the wardrobe and there was no tunnel. So, I have no idea. I just hope… I hope…" Lachlan's voice broke.

"She'll be okay. They'll find her." Grace reached across the table to grab his arm.

Lachlan shook her hand away and looked up at his friends. "You don't believe that any more than I do."

"IT WAS RIGHT here, wasn't it?" Allysha asked, her voice unsteady from crying. "We didn't imagine it?"

Phillipe cleared his throat as he looked around the now empty clearing, "We couldn't have imagined it. The cottage was here. We were here."

"Then where is it, Phil? I mean, we walked through the tunnel, just like we did before, so how can it just not be here now? Cottages don't just vanish into thin air!"

"We should never have come here. This is all my fault. We should have just stayed in Australia, and none of this would have happened." Phillipe covered his eyes with his hand as the last of his resolve gave away.

Allysha turned to her husband and pulled his hand away "This is not your fault. We made the decision to come here together. I just want to know what happened to our daughter."

He placed a kiss on this wife's head, then something in the grass caught his eye.

"What?"

He walked around her for a closer look, then bent down and picked up the photo they'd found in the cottage. "Do you still think this is here?" Phillipe asked softly.

"Look at her eyes," she replied sadly. "I would know them anywhere."

"I don't understand what the hell's happening."

Allysha didn't reply as she gazed at the photo.

"Do you think we'll ever see her again?"

A sob overcome her as she tried to form the words. "I hope so."

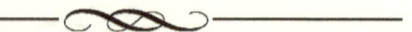

MARGARET MCALLISTER STARED out the window. The night was dark, with only the smallest sliver of a moon in the sky. Yet she could still see the trees at the edge of the grounds. The manor was silent around her, but it also felt lighter—as though a heavy blanket of secrets had been yanked from atop it. She couldn't recall it ever feeling this way before. It was almost ... peaceful.

Margaret didn't jump when the hand grasped her shoulder. She patted it gently and turned to look at her brother. He looked past her briefly, out toward the trees, before glancing back at her. With a slight nod, she followed her brother back into the shadows of the manor.

THE END

About the Author

Liz Butcher resides in Brisbane, Australia, with her husband, daughter, and two cats, Pandora and Zeus. While writing is her passion, her numerous interests include history, astronomy, the paranormal, mythology, reading, art, knitting and music — all of which fuel her imagination. She also loves being out in nature, especially amongst the trees or near the water.

Liz's previous works include numerous short stories published in various anthologies and her own short story collection, *After Dark*. Her first novel, *Fates' Fury,* released in 2019.

Facebook: https://www.facebook.com/lizbutcherauthor/ Website: http://lizbutcherauthor.wixsite.com/lizbutcher Twitter: @lunaloveliz

Did you enjoy the book? I would love to hear your thoughts, so feel free to leave a review or drop a comment on my website.